G U T S
a comedy of manners

GUTS
a comedy of manners

David Langford and John Grant

Cosmos Books, an imprint of **Wildside Press**
New Jersey . New York . California . Ohio

GUTS

Published by:

Cosmos Books, an imprint of Wildside Press
P.O. Box 45, Gillette, NJ 07933-0045
www.wildsidepress.com

For more information, contact Wildside Press.

ISBN: 1-58715-336-X (trade paperback edition)
ISBN: 1-58715-448-X (hardcover edition)

CONTENTS

ACKNOWLEDGEMENTS

Ramsey Campbell, Simon Ian Childer, Graham Masterton and Guy N. Smith each gave us several encouraging words (culled from who knows what obscene dictionary of the nameless Old Ones) for which the authors are truly grateful. Mark Rodgers of *Oink!* magazine kindly arranged permission for the quotation from Banx's moving "Disembodied Organ Blues". Neil Gaiman and Kim Newman were generously not asked permission for the steals from their seminal collection *Ghastly Beyond Belief*. Pamela D. Scoville benignly tolerated having to watch the final stages of text preparation. Hazel Langford, Catherine Barnett and Jane Barnett made the authors' lives and consciences a great deal easier by adamantly refusing to read the first draft, or any other.

DEDICATION

for Martin Hoare
who was inspirational

The languid stomach curses even the pure
Delicious fat, and all the race of oil:
For more the oily aliments relax
Its feeble tone; and with the eager lymph
(Fond to incorporate with all it meets)
Coyly they mix, and shun with slippery wiles
The woo'd embrace. The irresoluble oil,
So gentle late and blandishing, in floods
Of rancid bile o'erflows: what tumults hence,
What horrors rise, were nauseous to relate.
Choose leaner viands, ye whose jovial make
Too fast the gummy nutriment imbibes.
    Dr John Armstrong, *The Art of Preserving Health*, 1744

PROLOGUE

Forced to make love to beautiful women! This is adult science
fiction at its best.
> Blurb for *Pagan Passions* by Randall Garrett and Larry
> M. Harris

Her heart lurched.

The room was dark with a darkness spawned in the deepest chasms of
hell – darker. The air was as thick as the tapioca she should have refused
at the drive-in diner. The temperature was as hot as the inside of a microwave oven. The smell was as bad as a ten-year old egg. The fear was as per-
vasive as her own libido.

She wasn't just terrified: she was frightened, too.

It wasn't the stillness – she'd encountered stillness before. It was
something more than that. It was . . . it was . . . she knew not what. It was a
mixture of everything she had always loathed – greasy commuters –
slinky spiders in the bath – slug-juice under the fingernails – rats gnaw-
ing your toes in bed – L. Ron Hubbard novels – suppurating boils –
slime-infested drinking water – succubi (or was it incubi? – she could
never remember) – nightmares . . . It all summed up to crawling, slithering dread.

Somewhere, an owl hooted.

She'd booked into the motel three hours earlier, glad to have shaken
off Hunk, with his ever-groping hands. She'd felt somehow . . . sullied . . .
by his attentions, and had been unable to face the thought of going
home, where Ma with her drunkenly crooked grin and Pa with his cari-
catured smirk of total failure would have been waiting to ask her if she'd
let Hunk's hands stray beyond her insteps (*for God's sakes!!*). So she'd
booked into this sleazy dump in order to avoid explanations. Now she
was convinced that this had been a mistake.

Why?

Well, why not?

It was the darkness again. It assailed her on every side. Three in the
morning in a lousy flea-bitten motel and she was terrified. There was no

sound, yet she *knew* there was something – perhaps some*body* – there in the room with her. The smell of it – him – was ubiquitous. She was sitting bolt upright in the narrow bed, the dingy sheets clasped to her gratuitously naked bosom. Although she couldn't see herself in the blackness, she knew that she was petite, curvaceous, blonde, rosy-cheeked, lovable, well contoured, exquisite, youthful and normally smiling.

But she wasn't smiling now.

Her face was a rictus grin of stark fright. She tried to peer into the silent darkness of the room, but failed – as she'd known she would fail. Not a single photon of light illumined the room. The key, she knew, was firmly turned in the lock. Even if she screamed, she knew that no one would be able to break down the door in time to rescue her from this nameless monstrosity. But she was too drained of life-force even to consider screaming.

Then there was a sound!

It came from the corner, over there by the slot machine for the Magic Fingers vibrabed unit.

And it was a slow, sucking, slithering, slimy noise – like a snail being pulled off a window. It was a noise which shattered what few senses she had left. It was a noise from the deepest chasms of hell itself (rather like the darkness, in fact). It was a noise which coruscated the full length of her spinal cord and then turned, ready to go back the other way. It was a noise that curdled her very brain. It was a noisome noise.

"Who are you?" she said into the nothingness.

"Hi babe," said a voice.

"What do you want?"

"*You.*" The word was almost spat.

"Why me?"

"Because you're kinda cute. And I admire your mind."

"Who are you? – *What* are you?"

"Why, it's Hunk. Who did you think it was?"

She'd never have thought that she could be pleased to find Hunk Brady lurking in her motel room, naked and vulnerable as she was. But for a moment she'd thought back there that she was in for a death worse than fate. It struck her that this was what usually happened to innocent young virgins in the opening pages of the horror novels which formed her fave reading, and that she'd had a lucky escape. She felt kind of . . . *empty* . . . with relief.

It was probably for this reason that she did something she'd never done before. "Come into bed here with me, Hunk," she said, "and love me good. I've never been loved in bed with a man before, but I do know I do need to be loved good this night."

"Here I come, babe," said the voice. "Wow! You're not gonna be sorry."

The blank air was filled with the noise of tearing cloth, snapping bootlaces, pinging buttons and the shrill sound of a hastily applied underarm deodorant.

Which was curious, because the . . . the *thing* in the room with her had no underarms. But she didn't know that yet.

And, by the time it had finished with her, she was in no condition to know anything, ever again.

She'd never been strangled by a slithery hollow tube before, and in her dying moments she was glad about that.

Once was quite enough . . .

CHAPTER ONE

SPASM

> It took courage to write this book, and it will take courage to read it.
>
> Erich von Däniken, *Chariots of the Gods?* (trans. 1969)

one

It was a day.

The sun was shining and the sky was blue. Had any further proof been needed, there were no stars visible, even though the heavens were cloudless.

Yes, it was a day, all right.

It was certainly not, for example, a dark and stormy night.

More than that David Whitlow did not know. To be precise, he did not know exactly which day it was. Not just whether it was a Monday or a Saturday or any other day of the week, but even the year in which this day fell. He stood on the burning sands and looked all around him with the vacant yet endlessly curious eyes of a child. The rays of sunlight beat down harshly on the sere desert, parching the sands as if they were on the inside of a vast volcano. All that disturbed the great expanse of torrid emptiness were scattered cacti, roasting brownly in the baking heat.

He could remember nothing. He didn't know how he'd got here and he didn't know where he'd been going. He didn't know his name or his age or his sex – or even that there were such things as sexes. His eyes saw the strident brightness of the sky, the whirling dots of distantly flying birds, the callosities on his two feet (*0.6096 of a metre*, whispered a punctilious voice inside him) planted firmly on the sands. But they understood nothing. Yet in a strange sort of a way he was aware that there was, somewhere within him, a reservoir of memories just waiting for him to discover the right means of releasing the floodgates or breaching the dam to let them come pouring back into his conscious mind. He was aware of very little else, however.

Moving clumsily, like a toddler taking its first steps, he walked slowly over to the minimal, miserly shade offered by the nearest cactus. He sat down in the shadow and leaned his back wearily against the plant.

Pain, he thought, *that's an intriguing sensation. And now I have a word for it, too: "Yarrough!"*

Standing once more, he looked with a mixture of resentment and gratitude at the surly brown vegetable. It had taught him his very first datum: things can hurt you. His mind began to extrapolate from this, beginning to move into gear as if some time – long, long ago – it had been a highly trained instrument. *Item*: things can hurt you. *Item*: they can hurt you even when you haven't done anything naughty. *Conclusion*: the Universe is not necessarily a very friendly place. *Query*: is it actively hostile? *Response*: insufficient data for a definitive reply, but retain as a working hypothesis.

He was staggered by the swiftness and efficiency of his mental processes. A word to describe them struggled to make its way into his consciousness: int . . . intel . . . inte . . . *integration!* That was it! He was possessed of *integration*. Metaphorically he ran his tongue around this new word, testing it for texture and flavour and discovering that he rather liked it. That was two words he had now: *yarrough* and *integration*. And the exciting part about it all was that they each meant something different. Only an idiot would say *integration* when a three-inch (76.2mm) cactus-spine went forcefully into his back; well, or someone speaking a foreign language.

One of the birds fluttered down out of the sky and settled on the cactus, looking at him speculatively. He smiled at his new-found friend, and once again instinct took over. He held out his hand to it, rubbing his thumb against his fingers, and said gently: "Kitty, kitty. Here, kitty kitty."

The bird made no response.

All at once he became aware of his nakedness. At first it was only a matter of interest rather than embarrassment to him. He studied his hands and his arms, his legs and his feet, his chest and his taut stomach. He had a sudden idea, and began to count. This was a brand-new idea – *numbers* – and he couldn't at once see its practical usefulness, but it certainly had possibilities for hours of intellectual entertainment should he ever become bored. He worked slowly along the toes of his left foot, and the names of the numbers came unbidden into his conscious mind: *one . . . two . . . three . . . four . . . five.* For a moment he wondered what to do next, and then, making a giant conceptual leap, he turned his attentions to his right foot and carried on: *. . . six . . . seven . . . eight . . . nine . . . TEN!* This was exciting: he'd got into double figures! *Next – next – well, let me see, I could try my hands.*

Some time later, he reached the number twenty-one and realized he could go no further. But there was something about that final number that seemed familiar, almost as if – almost as if it had been programmed into him by some farsighted scientist who had realized that, inevitably, even had all his memories been lost from his consciousness, he would instinctively teach himself to count, and that having started to do so he would be brought inexorably to the number twenty-one. He turned his attention back to it, and allowed his mind to explore all its nooks and crannies. The number grew larger and larger in his inner vision, until it began to blot out large areas of the merciless sky. And, just as it seemed he would be crushed under its weight, something happened . . . something like a dam cracking.

My God! That's it! That's the key! The number twenty-one! . . . My name is David Whitlow and I'm thirty-three years of age and I . . .

And all at once his mind was filled with complete, crystal-clear memories of all the literally gut-wrenching horrors of the past few months . . .

Somewhere, an owl hooted.

two

"Empedocles!" exclaimed David Whitlow, pushing an unruly lock of hair back from his forehead.

"David," said his nubile assistant, "I trust you're not speaking dirty *again*."

Whitlow was sitting amid the clutter of his laboratory, his elbows on the desk, looking at his youthful assistant, Miranda Eschar. "Don't get me wrong, sugar. I was talking about my discovery and saying I wasn't the first to come to this conclusion: the great Greek philosopher Empedocles intuitively arrived at it thousands of years earlier. See here, it says in this excellent reference book (*A Directory of Discarded Ideas* by John Grant, in point of fact) that 'Empedocles (*c*490-430BC) is reported to have thought that the earliest creatures were not wholly formed, but consisted of unconnected limbs. The idea of a hand flapping along the primaeval beach looking for an arm to join onto has a certain macabre appeal.' Well, that wise old sage didn't have it *quite* right, but he came pretty close."

"Wow," breathed Miranda. Her eyes glowed.

"It's taken me years of patient research to discover exactly how it is that all previous versions of the theory of evolution have been subtly wrong, but – hot dingus! – I've done it. This could be – this *is* – the biggest thing since Darwin."

"Gosh," whispered Miranda.

He looked at her with a frank, lascivious appreciation which he was careful to disguise whenever her father, Professor Hank G. Eschar, was around. She was 5ft 3in (1.6002m) in height, and there wasn't an inch (25.4mm) that wasn't beautiful. She had copper-red hair that flowed down like a waterfall over strong yet petite shoulders; a pale skin (perhaps a reminder of her Celtic forebears) with infectiously witty freckles; an adorable little button-nose; and green eyes, which flashed mysteriously whenever she was angry - which was never with him.

She was also an articulate conversationalist and an internationally acclaimed exponent of the rumba.

"Gosh," she repeated.

"Yes," he said, "it's all written there in the fossil history, if only you're prepared to read it. Some time in the long-lost Precambrian there were two qualitatively *different* kinds of organism. Some had distinct tendencies towards, shall we say, backbonishness; others were invertebrates - but with a vengeance! They had no rigid structures whatsoever. They certainly had advanced 'way beyond the stage of being protozoa (i.e., single-celled organisms) but somehow they'd never developed the need for a fixed form. You could call them 'polymorphs' if you liked." That unruly lock of hair was trying to fall down over his forehead again, and he brushed it back impatiently.

"Golly," husked Miranda.

"So we can envisage that primeval beach some time later, perhaps in the Devonian, with various organisms making their slow and weary way across it. Some of them moving like worms, by performing simple rhythms of contraction and expansion; others - the ones with backbones - crawling laboriously. And then - bingo!"

"Anyone for a coffee?" came a chummily mechanical voice. In through the door rolled Basil-Duane, the cutely lovable little domestic robot which the Professor had built lo these many years ago. For some time after his construction, the Professor had wavered between calling him Duane 'Droid or settling for Basil 'Bot - it was hard to work out which was the cuter - but he'd eventually opted for Basil-Duane: there was no need constantly to remind the cheery little feller of his artificial origins. And cheery he was - over 99% of his software capacities were taken up with user-friendly systems, a feature which tended to limit his usefulness to that of household drudge. But the whole family - and David was now considered "part of the family" - loved Basil-Duane just the way he was, and saw no reason to change him.

"Oh, hi there, B-D," said Miranda pleasantly. "David was just telling me about his new theory of evolution."

"Evolution? Don't believe him, Miranda. There ain't no such thing. I done heard it from the preacher man just this last Sabbath Day that talk of evolution is ungodly and will bring damnation in its wake."

"I'll take my coffee with cream and four sugars," said David, adroitly changing the subject.

"Oh, really, David," moued Miranda. "You know that isn't good for you. Think of your heart!"

"I lost my heart to you long ago, honey," smirked David, grinning even more broadly as a blush suffused her features. "Just let me have the coffee the way I like it."

"If you's wanting your coffee with cream and sugar you just have it with cream and sugar," said the 'droid. "A man should pay never-no-mind to the fussings of his womenfolk, that's what I allus says. That's the way that God ordained it when he made Adam fust and then put Eve in the garden to do his bidding, glory be."

Miranda bridled a little at this, but she knew there was no point in arguing with Basil-Duane. He really was a card. "I'd just like a cup of jasmine tea with a dash of lemon juice," she murmured.

The 'bot left the laboratory whistling merrily (thanks to his built-in kettle) to go and find some mugs.

"Isn't old B-D the limit?" giggled Miranda, and then settled back to listen to these marvels which David was announcing.

"Of course, the vertebrates in those days didn't look much like the ones we have today," said the young genius with a reassuring smile. "A typical example might be *Ichthyostega*, which had a kind of fish-like tail and fins which had been evolutionarily modified into functional limbs. It was wobbling around, in and out of swamps, in the late Devonian and the Mississippian (or lower Carboniferous, as the British call it). In fact, it was while studying *Ichthyostega* and its close relatives that I first began to get suspicious about the orthodox theories of evolution. You see, plenty of fossils have been found of the bones of *Ichthyostega*, but not a single one of them has any soft organs - digestive system and so on - associated with it. Pretty indicative, I'd have thought."

"Goodness!" said Miranda, looking impressed. "It's funny no one ever thought of this before."

"Yeah, well, as I say," stammered David with a modest gesture, "it's like I always used to keep telling people back in college. Half of the palaeontologists in the world are as fossilized as the things they study. It's difficult for them even to conceive that matters might be a little different from what orthodoxy proclaims. It takes a radical new approach to things before any progress can be made. They laughed at Charles Darwin, they laughed at Alfred Russel Wallace, they laughed at Oscar Kiss Maerth - but look who had the last laugh!"

"Too true," Miranda assented. "Carry on."

Whitlow stood up and walked to the window. Outside, the sun was shining and the birds were singing in the trees. Over his shoulder she could see a pair of grey squirrels scampering lazily across the well tended lawn. But she knew that he was blind to all of these, that his eyes were focused on the distant vistas of infinity. She had to lean forward to catch what he was saying.

"Yes, yes, that must have been the way of it. Which came first, the rectum or the stomach, or maybe even the colon? Who can tell? My guess is that it was the stomach . . . the others might have had difficulty surviving long enough to be viable over the long millions of years of evolutionary time. How could they have reproduced, for one thing? But an independent stomach – no problem! Perhaps the others weren't much like the way they are nowadays . . . perhaps they were quite different animals which the stomachs took to themselves and adapted. Who will ever know? Perhaps, now that I've discovered this much, researchers in the field will find plenty of specimens to fill in all these gaps in the fossil record? I sure hope so."

"I've brought you guys and gals your hot drinks!" boomed Basil-Duane, crashing in through the laboratory door. "Coffee for the gentleman and jasmine tea for the lady." He thunked the empty mugs down on the laboratory bench, climbed up with some difficulty onto a chair, and manipulated his spigot to fill the mugs up with the correct beverages. Then he stood there, his lights flashing and fizzing happily in response to their voluble demonstrations of delight.

"Always glad to help you youngsters in any way I can," he said at length. "Like I was telling the Perfesser only the other day, God put us all here to help each other, and that goes for a humble little 'bot as much as it does for the Perresident of the United States. So I'm happy to do all my domestic chores because I know that in so doing I'm obeying the Lord's will, bless us all." With a cry of "Hallelujah!" he left them on their own once more.

"He certainly is inimitable," said David with a grin, once the little 'droid was safely out of earshot. "Life just wouldn't be the same around here if anything ever happened to him."

A sad look came to Miranda's eyes. "Let's hope nothing ever does," she said mistily.

"Still," said David, ". . . to return to the point."

"Yes," she urged.

"All of my researches point to the one, indisputable fact that the various soft organs of what we now call the human body evolved separately and then became conjoined. This is diametrically at odds with the orthodox picture of things, but never mind. We can envisage a time, perhaps during the earliest Permian – the geological period whose temporal bounds we can take as being roughly 280 to 225 million years ago – when complete digestive systems of one form or another were oozing graphically over the land, avoiding predators by the simple means of being quite too revolting to consider eating. Meanwhile, the early ancestors of the mammals – the so-called mammal-like reptiles, such as the pelycosaurs and the therapsids – were likewise roaming the world's landmasses, totally unaware of any necessity for them to ingest food in order to generate energy for their survival. We can only speculate, of course, but it seems certain that they relied for their bodily energy on sunlight – in much the same way as plants do even today. Whatever system they used – perhaps, as with the plants, it was photosynthesis – it must have been a rugged and versatile one, because of course around that time there was one of the world's many ice ages."

"Oh?" Miranda pricked up her ears.

"Yes, for tens of millions of years the weather was lousy." David Whitlow beamed broadly at her. "It must have been hell." He shook his head briefly, confused by his own metaphor, then charged on regardless. "Still, the synapsids (as the mammal-like reptiles are often called) survived through it all quite happily. And then, of course, there came the great Age of the Dinosaurs. Those mighty beasts stomped all over the world's surface. And, just as with the mammal-like reptiles, we have no convincing evidence that they had any digestive organs at all! Could these behemoths likewise have derived their energy from some process akin to photosynthesis?"

Miranda looked blank.

"And why not?" said David Whitlow, idly stirring his coffee with a forefinger. "In fact, do we have *any proof whatsoever* that the dinosaurs were animals rather than plants? Oh, sure, their descendants, the modern reptiles, are animals all right (at least, I think so), but we cannot close our eyes to the possibility that the dinosaurs themselves were vegetable – perhaps related to trees, although rather more mobile. Indeed, we can tell from the evidence of what most people call their fossilized bones but what I for obvious reasons prefer to refer to as their fossilized branches that they were very mobile indeed – those powerful hindleg-branches would have been able to take them rampaging across the countryside with the speed and ferocity of an express train. Still, the day of the dinosaurs was not to last forever – and their rather abrupt extinction poses an enigma about which scientists are still arguing."

He drained his coffee with some confidence.

"True, true, we have fairly good evidence that a large meteorite or a small comet struck the Earth some sixty-five million years ago, sending up billions upon billions of tons (tonnes) of detritus into the atmosphere, creating a 'winter' that must have lasted for centuries. And it is the currently popular hypothesis that it was thanks to the adverse effects of this 'winter', such as the unremitting cold, that the dinosaurs died out. Now, this is rather less than convincing if you assume that the dinosaurs were animals. Sure, life might have been tough for them, but they'd have struggled by. Moreover, the synapsids (which indisputably *were* animals) survived without too much difficulty. Apart from anything else, the dinosaurs were so vast and so swift-moving that they'd have been able to run around to keep themselves warm. *Not so if they depended for their energy supplies upon photosynthesis, a process which itself depends on the reception of adequate quantities of sunlight!!*"

He paused for dramatic effect, while Miranda continued to regard him lovingly yet critically. "But surely the synapsids would have been equally vulnerable if, as you say, they too depended upon something like photosynthesis for their life-processes?" she said at length.

"*No!*" He pounded the bench with his fist to emphasize his words. "By that time the mammal-like reptiles had entered into their historic symbiotic relationship with the squishy creatures. Perhaps they even did so consciously as a means of countering the effects of the meteoritic/cometary 'winter' – who knows? At all events, we can be fairly confident that this is what happened – no other hypothesis so conveniently fits all the facts. And, once the partnership had been formed, it was never to be broken – indeed, it became such an established thing that nowadays it is impossible to tell that all of the higher animals are in truth made up out of two interdependent organisms."

He coughed shyly. "Well, almost impossible," he added.

"What do you mean?" asked Miranda. She felt a sudden urge to kiss him, but quenched it immediately: kissing was for married people, and, despite her fervently virginal hopes, he had yet to ask her the vital question. "What do you *mean?*" she repeated.

"Well, it strikes me that those squishy organisms must have been possessed of at least rudimentary intelligence – in fact, they may have been very intelligent indeed, but have left no material traces of their culture (if any) for the very simple reason that, having no hands, opposable thumbs and so on, they were not tool-users. And, if they were intelligent then, there seems no reason to doubt that they are still intelligent today – that somewhere within the organism which we now call the digestive system there might be a seat of the intellect, analogous to our own brain although necessarily functioning somewhat differently. You realize what this means?"

"Gosh," said Miranda, "I've heard people use expressions like 'gut-understanding', but I've never thought that . . ."

"Precisely," snapped Whitlow, kneading his forehead with excitedly sweaty knuckles. "Our intestines are almost certainly sentient! And in that case, we can – indeed, it's our duty to – attempt to *establish communications with that truly alien intelligence that lies within each one of us!* Isn't it *exciting?*"

"Wow!" said Miranda. "Yes it is! Only, um, how do we set about doing this?"

"Telepathy would be ideal," said Whitlow promptly. "If only," he sighed in afterthought, "telepathy were possible . . ."

At that moment the internal telephone on Whitlow's bench squawked. Either it was malfunctioning – a fairly frequent event since the various items of electronic wizardry in the household tended to create interference effects among themselves – or the Professor wished to speak with one of them. Assuming the latter, Whitlow picked up the receiver.

"Hi there, Prof," he said experimentally.

"David-baby, I've done it!" came the excited voice. "I've discovered the secret of telepathy. I've just invented a machine that can be used to read a person's mind!"

"This is, er, something of a *deus ex machina*," agreed Whitlow, but the Professor was babbling on without paying any attention.

"It's all a question of mapping the brain's output of alpha-waves," he said excitedly. "People have done this sort of thing before, of course, for biofeedback reasons and so on, but no one before me has come out with an instrument that can translate the alpha-waves into printed words. This is the breakthrough which I've made with my new widget. I can do it, I can do it! All I need now is to find a suitable volunteer!"

"I was just about to say something of the very sort to Miranda here," said Whitlow, boggled by the size of the coincidence. "We need to find a youthful volunteer who will be prepared to let us contact, by use of your amazing device, the seat of intellect in his or her digestive system! What better than that we try out both your gadget and my mind-staggering theory with the same experiment?"

"Which theory is this?" said the Professor warily. In the last week Whitlow had proved that the Universe was a giant brain, that time was in reversal, that nothing could travel faster than light, and that human blood circulation was purely a result of the global Coriolis Effect. Understandably, Professor Eschar was becoming a little sceptical of Whitlow's hypotheses. For example, things quite probably *could* travel faster than light.

He seemed mollified, however, once David had filled him in about the various points which he had presented to Miranda. "What you say certainly seems to make a lot of sense, youngster," he said finally; David could picture him teasing one of his long strands of silvery-white hair. "The only trouble is, where can we find ourselves a volunteer?"

"You wanna volunteer?" cried Basil-Duane, bursting in through the laboratory door. "I'm always glad to present myself for your service in any experiment, young master, just so long as your enquiries aren't blas ... blas ... blast it, I knew the word yesterday before I downloaded that cussword-deletion programme sent out by the Worldwide Church of God to all of the Lord's 'bots."

"I'm sorry, B-D," said Miranda with a cheerful yet sympathetic smile, "but you just aren't qualified to be the subject of the experiment we're planning. We need a human being."

"Well, the Lord have mercy on us all, but I never thought the day would come when *you*, Missy Miranda, would be discriminating against a poor 'droid just because it didn't have a human physiology," said Basil-Duane accusingly. "You were perfectly content to do all those colonic-irrigation experiments on me, even though I don't have a colon!"

"That was different," muttered Miranda embarrassedly. It had been either the robot's interior or her own . . .

"May Jehovah have mercy on you," said the cuddlable 'bot tartly, and he left the room.

"What a wacky little individual he is!" exclaimed David and Miranda simultaneously.

"What's going on?" complained the Professor down the 'phone. "Have *you* got any ideas about how we can get some sucker . . . that is, some disinterested seeker after the cosmic truth . . . to undergo the kind of experiment we envisage?"

"We could put an advertisement in the newspapers," said Whitlow hesitantly.

"I've got a better idea!" cried Miranda. "You know my old schoolfriend Malacia Furuncle – the girl with the Charles Bronson moustache? She's always saying that she'd like to do something to give me great pleasure, for reasons I cannot imagine. I'm sure that if I put it to her right she'd come across. She's only about twenty-five so she'd be an ideal experimental subject – too young to die. Shall I ask her?"

"That'd be cute," said Whitlow. "Do you know her address or telephone number . . .?"

three

Things are looking a little grim on the neo-Nazi front, reflected Kurt Salpinx as he came out from the doorway of Paris's notorious *Folie à Trois* nightclub. *Now that we've had to admit Jews and Blacks to our numbers in order to beef up our membership, there seems to be hardly anyone else left to blame for the continuing world crisis.* He buttoned up his duffelcoat against the cruel Parisian wind and turned himself towards the Champs Elysées. *I suppose we could try to claim that it was all the fault of the Irish, but there hardly seems any point: they're blamed for so many other ills of mankind that no one would notice. But we've got to have some ethnic group to blame*, someone *to try to exterminate – otherwise people just won't take us seriously any longer. I wrote an enquiring letter to the Saudi Arabian Embassy asking if they'd like to be It, but they bloody well never replied. Perhaps we ought to go back to looking outside the human species altogether? Those goddam cats have been looking a bit bolshevik to me recently: I wonder if it could be them? If not, just what the hell could it be?*

He came to a *pissoir* and stopped to relieve himself. *What a pass it's come to when even the Chosen Race has to urinate*, he thought. *I think that our bodily systems are probably deliberately trying to undermine our confidence by dragging us down to their own level.*

Say, that could be it! . . .

four

Malacia Furuncle was in the jacuzzi rereading *Fear of Flying*. She'd been trying to decide which particular part of men it was that she hated the most. Their navels, with that disgusting knot of matted hair, were peculiarly revolting, but couldn't the same be said – and for exactly the same reasons – about their armpits? Then there were the repulsively stubbly cheeks which they insisted on maintaining at both ends. She thought about the male generative organ for a fleeting, shuddering moment, but banished it from her mind. She was just moving on to consider the male's flat-chestedness when the telephone rang.

"Hello there," she said.

"Is that Malacia?" said a pristine voice.

"Malacia Furuncle at your service," said the oddly chromosomed female with a gruff chuckle.

"It's Miranda Eschar here," said the voice. "You know, the girl in whom you took such an especial interest at school and later at the evening classes in public speaking that we both attended."

Malacia remembered the child now: flame-red hair and a teasingly open mouth. For long enough she'd been tempted to seduce her, but had then discovered that she was conversationally tedious and that her rumba-dancing was much over-rated. Still, she had a curiosity to know a little more about Miranda's coltishly sensual-seeming body.

"Yeah, sure I remember you," grunted the older woman. "How come you're 'phoning me up?"

"Well, look, I must have told you about David Whitlow, the – uh – rather amazing young scientist with whom I work," said Miranda. *Oh shit*, thought Malacia, *she's a latent heterosexual after all*. Miranda was rattling on, ignorant of Malacia's resentful thoughts. "Er, he's just come to an astonishing conclusion about the real nature of evolution," she said, and limpingly went through the whole story. ". . . and the end of it all is that he wants to find a suitable experimental volunteer whose digestive system he can communicate with," she concluded, "and I suddenly remembered that you were perennially short of money, as well as an inveterate seeker after scientific truth, and wondered if you might be interested in the job."

"It sounds kind of lethally dangerous . . ."

"A thousand dollars."

". . . but exceptionally rewarding in an intellectual sense," Malacia added hastily. "If you think that I might be of assistance to you . . ."

"Gosh, yes, Malacia, David and I both think that you'd be ideal! So does the Professor, for that matter. Actually, so does Basil-Duane, but that's probably just a statistical effect; never mind about it."

"What exactly is it that you want me to do?" Malacia was still sensually soaping herself as she stood, wet but warm, at the bedside telephone. She flexed her thigh-muscles tensely and saw that she was in good condition to win the mud-wrestling championships this coming Thursday.

"Well," said Miranda, "perhaps it'd be better if David himself explained. I could send Basil-Duane over to fetch you if you liked . . ."

"No," said Malacia firmly, "for Goddess's sake not good old B-D. I'll come on over to your place under my own steam. Expect me in a half-hour or so . . ."

She put down the 'phone and made her dripping way back to the jacuzzi for a final rinse. All of a sudden she was twisted up by a stomach-wrenching premonition: she was taken over by the overwhelming suspicion that the experiment in which she was so readily prepared to take part would open the very doors of Hell itself, so that horrors without name or number would be unleashed upon the unsuspecting world, clammily clawing their way across the very face of humanity . . .

But she forgot all this when it came to her, as she eased herself down into the jacuzzi's turbulent waters, that the part of the male organism which she *really* disliked the most was its lack of subcutaneous adipose tissue. Her mind turned to Miranda – and her well disposed repositories of subcutaneous adipose tissue. *Perhaps things will all turn out for the good,* she thought; and then she was conquered by the exquisite sensuality of the moving waters . . .

CHAPTER TWO

PERISTALSIS

... and as soon as I had eaten it, my belly was bitter.
    Revelation 10:10

The belly has no ears.
    Proverb quoted in *Brewer's Dictionary of Phrase and Fable*

The eel had swallowed his penis almost up to the root.
    Graham Masterton, *Night Warriors*, 1987

one

Kurt Salpinx was declaiming furiously, his delivery marred only by the intermittent tic which kept flinging his clenched fist ceilingwards and making him lose his place. Flecks of spittle arced lazily through the air, as though the room were the interior of a shaken snowstorm paperweight mysteriously afflicted with halitosis. Steaming sweat drenched his tight brown uniform, and torn-out hair lay about him in heaps. His entire small body vibrated with spasmodic, charismatic energy ...

"Would M'sieu also require an *apéritif?*" shrugged the imperturbable waiter.

"*Nein!* Milk. Bring me a glass of milk."

"You put a lot of energy into ordering dinner," said Salpinx's swarthy companion as the *garçon* glided away.

"I never rest, Melanoma. Never. Only lesser breeds take time *aus* from the Cause for trivia like food: remember *das!*"

L. Ron Melanoma, press officer of the neo-Nazi movement, raised an eyebrow. The characteristic gesture, like his name, confirmed that he was Sicilian, a high-ranking member of *Cosa Nostra*, and an acolyte of the Bavarian Illuminati. "Is this a time for speech-making?" he asked.

"Yes! The restaurant table at which we sit is about to see the most important dress rehearsal the Movement has ever known. I want to let fly with all *mein* irresistible charisma, just as though an ecstatic mob of 100,000 screaming converts were hanging on my words. And I want *you* to say what you think of *der* new party line." Suiting his action to the words, Salpinx chewed on a piece of soap and critically inspected the result in a pocket mirror.

Melanoma knew better than to suggest that the public dining-room of *L'Aisselle d'Or* wasn't the best place for loud and frothing rhetoric. He and the management knew that Salpinx's eccentricities would be tolerated: all sorts of concessions were made to a movement which had such irresistibly amusing ways with midnight japes, blazing crosses, unregistered firearms, and castor oil.

"*Brothers!*" shrieked Salpinx experimentally, tuning the vanadium steel of his implanted prosthetic vocal chords to a murderous 130-decibel scream. "For years, have I not warned you against the UFO-controlled conspirators who seek to drag down our society into the foaming gutters of chaos? Against the godless communist anarchist religious fanatics, capitalist jackals *und* secular humanists whose only goal in life is the utter destruction of the calm and ordered fabric of civilization as *wir* know it, not to mention increased income tax? Have I not spoken again and again – a lone whisper of gentle sanity, a still small voice crying out in the wilderness – of the peril faced by us all but especially by our *fünf*-year-old baby daughters who will all be gang-raped by sadistic lickspittle pacifists in the pay of Albania should my warning fall on deaf ears . . .

"There'll be about ten minutes of that routine stuff," Salpinx foamed in a confidential aside to his press officer. "Then I really let 'em *haben* it between the eyes, like this:

"*The time has come to speak without my previous restraint!* I in parables have spoken – now at last I name the enemy openly! I name *the enemy within!*"

The blast of the final words caught the waiter squarely as he bent to place the meal (a child-size portion of clear *consommé*) before Salpinx. Such was the rigid discipline of *L'Aisselle d'Or* that not the slightest flicker of the servant's impassive mask betrayed the rupturing of both his eardrums. Had Salpinx known, he would have chalked it up as another small martyrdom for the Cause – but without regret. As his favourite saying went, *you can't break eggs without breaking eggs.*

"What is the enemy? *Der* enemy is within us! We have met the enemy and he is us! What loathsome parasitic growth demands that we feed it, and for repayment bloats and ruins the clean lines of human beauty? I speak of an ancient universal foe, or *Schnitzel*, without whose baleful presence it is *absolutely provable* (by the irrefutable classical syllogism known to Aryan logicians as *post hoc ergo propter hoc*) that there would be no digestive upsets! No stomach cancer! No pyloric spasms! No acidosis! No embarrassing eructations! *Nein—*"

"Might be a bad move, Kurt. That's a pretty tough political lobby you're going up against there – you sure we're really ready to take on the fast-food chains?"

"No no no . . . *Ich* will in the next draft make it clearer," Salpinx dribbled irritably, *sotto voce*, before resuming his oratorical blare. Already his charisma had been not without its effect: diners at nearby tables were toying more and more listlessly with the finest *nouvelle cuisine* in Paris, while the *maitre d'* had taken to moodily testing the edge of a hollow-ground carving-knife against his throat.

"Before I sound the clarion call *zu* arms, let me tell you a little history. Let me tell you of another oppressed and beleaguered group, like yourselves, like me: the persecuted Skoptsi sect of *alte* Russia. It was in 1771 that this simple group of devout religious fundamentalists was first discovered and maltreated by *die* authorities: the leader, Andrei Ivanov, was knouted and sent to Siberia, while his assistant Selivanov fled, only to be arrested *und* likewise sent to Siberia in 1775. Escaping, he proclaimed himself the Son of God incarnate in the person of Tsar Peter III, and for eighteen years lived in St Petersburg, now better known as Leningrad, or maybe it's St Petersburg again, who can ever remember, receiving double homage from his followers as Christ and Tsar. Even though Selivanov was imprisoned again, and in 1832 died at the age of a hundred, the Skoptsi sect continued despite fascist oppression to practise its simple belief based on the saying of *ein* well-known authority whose name I forget: *If thine eye offend thee, pluck it out . . .*"

"Think you're losing your momentum," Melanoma suggested.

"*Donner und schiessen*, I hate to waste all that material after to the trouble of researching it having gone. Where was I? Oh yes:

"As it happened, it was *nicht* their eyes which offended the Skoptsi, and their choice of which part to pluck out made it very difficult for them to pass on their faith to the next generation, but in a world full of hidden conspiracies against *us*, yes, against those of us gathered here, the Skoptsi ideals must be an inspiration to us *alles*!

"Let us turn now to the humble sea-cucumber, which like the busy bee *und der* industrious ant a moral lesson portrays. (*Ach*, I may have to jazz up the style a bit here; I think it is out of character getting.) Ground under the iron heel of bestial and authoritarian marine predators, the sea-slug or sea-cucumber has one instinctive defence, one instinctive urge towards cleanliness. At will, it can squirt out all its internal organs through the anus!"

(Five diners suddenly abandoned their succulent *ris de veau à la Jean-Paul Sartre* in an unseemly rush for *les toilettes*.)

"So let the Skoptsi be *unser* exemplars and let the sea-cucumber be blazoned on our banner! The ever-rumbling and rebellious stomach is our internal enemy; the beer-gut *ist ein* badge of shame! But *mit* simple surgery and the example of the sea-slug which is Nature's own Skoptsi, we can be free of the deviant parasite which has used us too long! *Heil Gastrectomy! Heil! Heil! Heil!*

"... And then," Salpinx concluded, wiping the foam from his mouth and wringing out his shirt, "I imagine something like a motorbike caval-cade with giant sea-slug banners and blazing torches, and we find a lot of fat guys to beat up. How does the whole, er, *Ding* strike you?"

Somewhere, *un hibou* hooted.

L. Ron Melanoma looked dubious. "Seems just a bit, how shall I put it, *ad hominem*?" he suggested. The allusion was a delicate and risky one: only the inner circles of the neo-Nazi front knew of the bet Salpinx had made in his younger – and wilder – days that over a period of three weeks he would saw up and eat an entire 90mm SP anti-tank gun of type JPZ 4-5 with double baffle muzzle brake and fume extractor. Salpinx had won his bet, but at a price. It was always dangerous to refer to the teflon and stainless-steel replacement parts which now filled his abdomen, or his regular and embarrassing need for secret manipulations with nylon sphincters, plastic bags and Vaseline.

That puts you at Nummer Eins on the death list when I come to power, shrieked Salpinx inwardly. Aloud he only said: "I don't know how *ich* know it, but I feel in my – I feel deep down that this is . . . *an idea whose time has come . . .*"

And at his words an intestine-churning premonition – a loathsome intimation of the awesomely unconvincing coincidence or synchronicity which toyed with them like pawns in a cosmic roulette-game – failed utterly to pass in a wave of more than cryogenic chill through either man's innards. Members of the Cause had no time for such effeminate sensitivities.

Yet.

two

"Well, David my lad," beamed the Professor as he fussed about the laboratory, "this notion of combining the very first tests of my Alphawriter and your theory has got a lot more going for it than at first meets the eye! See, the reason I couldn't just test it on myself is that the sensor, being for technical reasons approximately the size and shape of a square of ravioli, works only at extremely short range. (We'll be able to beef that up later when we get the Department of Defense grant and a nuclear reactor 'stead of these batteries.)"

"So you can only pick up short-wave brains!" cried Miranda with a typical leap of girlish and wholly incorrect intuition.

"It's just the international male conspiracy that makes you say that," Malacia Furuncle grunted.

"Ha ha," quipped David knowingly. "As a fellow-scientist I see straight away what you're getting at. The sensor is obviously built into the analysing apparatus, which is installed at laboratory-bench height – so as we stand by your widget, our brains are just too high up for the sensor to detect, while our digestive systems . . ." He gestured delicately, pleased by this snap analysis, and Miranda smiled in admiration.

"Lawks-a-mercy, young master, there's *some* of us whose think-boxes are just the right height – so don't you see the Lord's will made manifest in a kind of sign and portent, sure as—"

"Please, B-D, could you fetch me a fresh mug of coffee?" broke in Professor Eschar. "I seem to be about to drop this one." And, as the plucky little 'bot lurched kitchenwards for the fifteenth time in as many minutes, the Professor pushed his fourteenth mug moodily off the laboratory bench by way of verisimilitude.

"I don't think B-D likes you, Malacia," Miranda mused. "What a wonderful little oddball he is!"

"To pick up your point, youngster," continued the Professor: "Close, but no cigar. As a scientist you should remember the fundamental identity of waves and particles! In radiation physics, alpha particles are notorious for having such an incredibly short range that they can be stopped by a thin sheet of paper. Now, remembering what we scientists call wave/particle duality – what does this tell us about alpha *waves*?"

"Of course!" breathed Miranda. "They can't even penetrate the skull – they must be *impossible to detect at all!*"

Malacia belched unpleasantly, momentarily distracted from pondering whether athletic young David's lack of subcutaneous adipose tissue was more or less unpleasant than paunchy Prof. Eschar's misplaced mass of the same. With characteristic bluntness, she shifted her chewing tobacco to a corner of her mouth, spat thoughtfully, and said: "So what about all those crummy bums who've been detecting alpha waves for decades?"

"Epiphenomena," clarified the Professor with a chortle. "Stray electromagnetic fields. Artifacts of the observation process. My God, Mort Cochlea at the Cerebral Institute is going to be red-faced when I point out the obvious waveform similarities between what he *thinks* are alpha waves and – our standard 60Hz house current!"

"But," interjected David, not sure how this would affect his tentative theory that domestic power waveforms carried laser-imposed hypnotic messages from hostile Martians.

"Let an old man get a word in edgeways," wheezed Professor Eschar with a suddenly and almost convincingly decrepit and arthritic gesture. "Effectively, we need *contact* to detect these unsuspectedly short-range waves. Anything between source and detector will stop them dead. Now

I didn't fancy drilling a ravioli-sized hole in my head, ha ha, but the digestive tract is another can of worms altogether!"

"Speak for yourself," snapped Malacia, who was proud of her internal hygiene. "When do we start?"

"Wouldn't you like to hear a little more first about the essential working principles of the wholly revolutionary new device which we're here to test?" said the Professor hopefully, toying with a thickish wad of notes.

"No," said everyone, more or less involuntarily.

"Coffee for the master, fresh and hot! Don't be thinking your B-D is a sluggard, now - it was the Lord's will that we ran out of cups, so I rootled down to the store for a fresh one, narrowly avoiding any amount of traffic and nearly getting rusted to death by an imp of Satan in the pesky form of a dog, but it's a joyful thing to serve and never complain! Hallelujah!"

The Professor placed the coffee carefully at the extreme edge of the bench ... "Oh yes," he said brightly. "I almost forgot - the experimental meal for Miss Furuncle. Bring it in, please."

"Bejasus, yes." And off scuttled the irremediably cute Basil-Duane, singing something about Sweeping Through The Gates Of Jerusalem which he usually saved for dustpan-and-brush work.

"Kinda heart-warming, isn't he?" grinned David.

"What an irresistible little fellow," agreed Malacia, through her teeth. "Um, experimental meal? I'm not exactly hungry."

"We thought it would be the least traumatic way to insert the sensor - camouflaged in a bowl of *real* ravioli, which it so closely resembles. And here it is! Thanks, B-D . . ."

"Hallelujah! Praise the Lord!"

"I suppose," said Malacia after squinting for a while at the bowl, "the sensor would be the one connected to the inch-wide ribbon cable?"

But Professor Eschar was already arranging things for the great moment: Malacia set to with a spoon and a shrug. The laboratory was a large room, forty feet (or 12.192 metres, Whitlow mused) square, filled with all the paraphernalia of advanced scientific research: computers, balances, microgalvanometers, centrifuges, autoclaves, lasers, scanning electron microscopes, Petri dishes, cyclotrons, grant application forms, X-ray units, astrolabes, slide rules, test tubes and abandoned hamburgers.

"Now Miss Furuncle can sit *here*, on my old dentist's chair," the Professor explained, tidying away some alembics and flicking a stray Bessemer converter into the nearest drawer. "That way, Malacia - if I may call you Malacia?—" (*No*, her expression said, but luckily she didn't trust herself to talk with a ribbon cable violating her throat's personal integrity.) "—that way you can look out of the window at the majestic sweep of the Appalachian Mountains during what I'm afraid will be a boring hour or so . . . but, ha ha! a profitable one!"

David and Miranda chuckled aloud at the elder scientist's witty little quip. The Professor's next action was to instruct Basil-Duane to go out and search the garden for four-leaf clovers until further notice.

"Now if we move to the other side of the computer-monitoring console, we'll be out of Miss Furuncle's sight and won't distract her. It's very important that she be absolutely calm and tranquil as we eavesdrop *via* our little, ha ha, Deep Throat . . ."

A strangled noise from the window seemed to indicate that this literary allusion filled Malacia Furuncle with anything but calm tranquillity.

"The apparatus will take a little while to warm up," Prof. Eschar concluded. "I'll start the count-down at thirty seconds. The count-down to what could be the most astonishing double scientific breakthrough of the century!

"Thirty . . . twenty-nine . . ."

My Goddess, Malacia was thinking. *I've got this crazy electrode down my gullet, I've been polite to those bastard men just because I need the money, and that stupid floozy Miranda is denying her true sexual nature, selling her birthright for a mess of Y-fronts. Maybe that's why I'm feeling the end of the world's just round the corner, some real downer, something even more ghastly than male genitalia. Shit, something goes wrong and this electrode could fry my guts . . .!*

Twenty-one.

Twenty.

Why, thought David Whitlow, *do I have this terrible premonition of slimy inescapable doom? Something to do with the twelve beers I had last night? Or is it just fear that I'm about to be humiliated by the failure of my most important, life-enhancing theory? I feel I should stop the experiment now . . . but I haven't got the guts . . .*

Sixteen.

Fifteen.

It's not my place to interfere, thought Miranda, *but those strangely prophetic-feeling daydreams I've been having ever since David said "Empedocles" . . . dreams of slime and ooze and acid mucus and things like haggis but worse than haggis . . . things that flop and drip and cling . . . It's all nonsense, the rational self-trained scientist in me knows it's all nonsense, but a woman has her intuition too, especially a woman trained in the sensitivities of the rumba . . . A dank nameless foreboding that pulsates in the heart of her guts . . .*

Ten.

Nine.

Eight.

By all that's scientific I should cancel this now, thought Professor Hank G. Eschar. *There are too many uncontrolled variables. I bragged to young Whitlow*

two

"Well, gee whillikins, but if the Lord Himself don't be able to create a new miracle each and every livelong day!" exclaimed Malacia Furuncle. "Look, Whitlow, you bastard, I know this was pretty goddam good for a spur-of-the-moment, off-the-wall and generally in-the-ballpark attempt, but there are certain disadvantages. Lawks a mercy, yes."

"I don't know what you're complaining about," prevaricated the young genius. "You seem just the same as before . . . to me."

"There is a *subtle* difference," commented Miranda with a demure blush. "She seems to be speaking rather differently than of old. I'm sure she never used to have that electronic voice, and she certainly never described the Creator as '*Him*self'."

The Professor winked at her – a manoeuvre which she found deeply disconcerting. She had heard through the ladies' room grapevine that men winking at you could make you pregnant, and she was worried about the connotations of incest. "I'm sure Malacia and good old B-D will soon settle down to enjoy a fine partnership in good time," he said. "It's just taking them a little while accommodating to the new situation. Fetch me a cup of coffee, M-B-D."

The twisted face of Malacia Furuncle spat venomously on the floor. "I'd rather have a Y chromosome than make coffee for a senile old rapist goat like you, you prick-strutting bumhead – and may the good Lord in all His mercy mark my words." But a strange unseen force drew her inexorably towards and reluctantly through the door leading from the laboratory to the coffee-making cyclotron. As that door slammed to conceal her hideously distorted form David Whitlow heaved a sigh of relief.

"Jeez," he said, "that wasn't a close shave!"

"But darling," said Miranda, "it was the best we could manage . . ."

When Whitlow and the Eschars had discovered Malacia Furuncle's crumpled body and its certain intestinal deficiency they had assumed at first that there was nothing they could do. They had stared gloomily at each other while the woman's life had ebbed steadily away. But then David had sprung energetically into action.

"Quick!" he had said. "Go find me a screwdriver, Miranda!"

"I know we all need a stiff drink," she had said, "but . . ."

"No, you fool, er, sweet honey-pie! I mean the implement! Professor, call in Basil-Duane. He's about to make the ultimate sacrifice!"

It was sooner said than done. Miranda, whose formal education had been biased towards the arts, turned up with a succession of tools, always smiling humbly when David used a string of those words she just *didn't* understand. The banana was the final straw, and he was forced, with many an oath, to pick up the screwdriver lying on the bench-top beside him. The Professor, meanwhile, had been chasing Basil-Duane all over the tastefully green lawn and trying to persuade the irremediably cute little 'bot that, despite orders about four-leaf clovers, he was now required to come inside. "You sure you don't wanna make devil spawn out of your ol' metallic pal?" the 'bot had asked as the Professor finally hauled him in through the laboratory door; the spigot in his midquarters trembled uncontrollably. "I's a god-fearin' little fella and I don't want to lend myself to no evil – not never, not nohow!"

"It's all right, B-D," said the Professor. "(My, what a card you are!) All we want to do is use . . . er, prevail upon you to save the life of that nice Ms Furuncle."

"Oh, well, boss, in that case I . . . may the Almighty be praised, but she looks in bad shape."

"I dunno," muttered Whitlow, who thought that she had if anything marginally improved.

"Dearest," said Miranda, "here's a pair of scissors and a packet of Elastoplast. Will *that* do?"

Marvelling at the non-causative power of synchronicity, Whitlow snatched the articles from her hands. "Just great, sugar-lump," he said expansively. "Say, you know how good ol' B-D has been unable to find any of those four-leaf clovers out there? Well, while he's otherwise occupied with us in the laboratory I wonder if you could . . .?"

His wish was her command, although she couldn't help but wonder how four-leaf clovers had got their name.

While she was wandering aimlessly around the garden, exclaiming ecstatically about the hyacinths, David and the Professor were fighting a duel against death. The boyish genius had swiftly used the scissors to cut open Malacia's lifeless form and the Professor was bravely manhandling a somewhat unwilling Basil-Duane towards the gaping cavity thus revealed.

"It's amazing!" said Whitlow, gazing into Malacia's outer shell. "There are no wounds, no lacerations – nothing like that. It's exactly as if somebody had stripped the inner lining out of a shoe. The connections between the digestive system and ourselves must be even more tenuous than I had imagined! Why! – it's surprising that alimentary canals aren't just constantly flopping out of people!"

The Professor paused guiltily in the act of coughing, but then decided not to risk a retch. He continued to struggle with Basil-Duane.

"But I don't never want not nohow to become intimately entangled with a woman of the flesh," cried the 'bot plaintively. "Heavens to Betsy, no I do not. I allus been a-following the paths of righteousness even if they do lead through Hell's dark shadows. Forgive me my sins and if you force me into that gory cavity, Perfesser, I's'll nuke you till you glow."

"B-D," said Whitlow with an uneasy chuckle, "don't you *want* to help humanity? Don't your ... er ... religious beliefs tell you you must sacrifice your own inclinations to assist in the physical salvation of others?"

"Sure, little boss, but that don't mean I's gotta lay down my life!"

"But you're not laying down your life," grunted the Professor, wondering how the hell you put a half-nelson on an object as limbless as a dustbin, save for its spigot. "All we're asking you to do is enter a symbiotic relationship with the ... er ... remains of Ms Furuncle here."

"Symbiosis," the little 'bot lashed back, "to some people it's just a word, but I know it for what it is: the dark practice initiated by the Prince of Evil himself. As my old grandpappy would have told me had I been of the family persuasion, you can allus tell the deeds of Satan by the fact that they all begin with the letter 's'."

Whitlow was struck motionless by this observation. In its own terms it made a lot of sense. Sex – well, to someone like B-D that was the Devil's work. Sin. Sensuality. Sloth. Sunday trading. Sodomy. Satanism. Susan George. Salaciousness. Skirts (mini). Seething passions. Sony Walkmen. Sumptuous mammaries. Seduction. Things like synergy and syzygy were a bit difficult to fit into the general scheme, but doubtless Jerry Falwell or somebody could work that one out ...

"Don't just stand there, young whippersnapper," clenched the Professor grittily, "help me get this goddam hunk of metal inside the girl." Whitlow sprang to obey.

Connecting up Basil-Duane's motor-sensory inputs to the naked nerves inside Malacia Furuncle's shell was by no means easy: the screwdriver proved next to useless and the soldering iron only made her hollow carcase twitch unsettlingly. In the end David, by this time covered from head to foot in a mixture of blood and the semidigested remnants of a helping of ravioli which the departed organism had seen fit to leave behind, had to use desperate measures. "Prof," he hissed, almost shocked at what he was about to say, "go get me the *deus ex machina*!"

"Not the ..." said Professor Hank G. Eschar. He gagged uncontrollably.

"Yes, the ... *that*! You know what I mean."

Babbling like a halfwit the elderly scientist scampered across the laboratory, seeking the piece of equipment for which young Whitlow had asked. Damn it! – he knew he'd had a perfectly good *deus ex machina* delivered from the 7-11 store only recently. But he'd never expected to have to *use* the thing! And where could it be? He threw open a drawer here and a cupboard there, but all without success. "Look," he said, turning finally to Whitlow, exasperation writ large across his features, "can't you make do with a ...?"

"It's all right," said the younger scientist with a merry laugh. "I've finished. Take a peek. Not bad, huh?"

He gestured towards the new-look Malacia Furuncle, who seemed to be having some difficulty in keeping her feet: she was wobbling nakedly around her corner of the laboratory. With a torso shaped rather like a dustbin and limbs at which it was best not to even glance, she was a travesty of a human being. Her face was distorted into a malevolent sneer.

"Goddamit, Whitlow," she said viperishly, "I'm gonna cut your cock off for this. And may He – fuck it, *She!* – who moves in mysterious ways have mercy upon all our souls this day."

Whitlow and the Professor began to wonder if perhaps their miracle rescue had been less than expected – especially when Malacia Furuncle began to struggle impotently with her somewhat obscenely positioned new spigot . . .

three

Al Veoli reckoned he had seen it all – and then some more.

He'd been a hitman for the Organization for nearly a decade now, and during those years he'd rubbed out more marks than he could remember: he was well known as the meanest guy in Internal Revenue. He'd seen human death in more, and more grotesque, forms than you could find in the collected works of Thomas Harris, and every time he'd just given a little mocking laugh: the Lord giveth and the Lord taketh away, after all, and if the Lord wants to do His takething away in a peculiarly vile fashion then who are we mere mortals to argue?

Right now, though, it was Veoli's bowels, rather than the Lord, which were moving in mysterious ways.

All his training as a ruthless killer had counted for naught when he had come across the corpse of Belle Spalsy. He had seen women's bodies rent into their constituent fragments before – hell, look at what he himself had done to that redhead in the Brides in the Jacuzzi Case – but he'd never seen anything like this. The worst of it had been her eyes: they had still been wide-open, gazing at the starlit sky, the lambent Moon, and even at him. Yes, that was it – in other stiffs the goddam wide-open eyes at least stayed fucking *still*, but not this time. It was as if Belle were somehow still alive – which was impossible, because the whole of her torso betrayed a flaccid and indescribably revolting *emptiness*. As if some sadist had inserted a corkscrew into her oesophagus, twisted a few firm times, and then pulled very hard. Veoli himself had tried this once or twice, and it had never actually worked (the most he'd ever fished out had been a septic uvula), but the image was a powerful one, and it made his spinal cord knot with loathing.

Now he was tripping and stumbling through the oddly thriving undergrowth near the Eschar place. God knew where he'd left his automobile: his own crazed brain had long since lost any memory of the hours preceding his awful discovery. A thin branch whipped him across the face, but he hardly even noticed it. The fluttering leaves made the Moon's pale light flicker across his tormented features. There was a scream lurking inside him, but somehow it could not find the way out from his lungs to his mouth.

Somewhere, an owl hooted.

Who could it have been? he thought. *Could it have been some of J. Junum's boys over from the Lower East Side? Or even L. Ron Melanoma's Parisian mob? But why would they want to wipe out my gal? Sure, she was nearly sixty and was more or less a walking syphilitic sore, but she was real precious to me - I guess because she reminded me of my Mama 'way back on the old homestead in Kentucky. Those guys would never've done this to me - besides, I ain't done nothing to get up ol' JJ's ass recently. He sticks to his patch and I stick to mine . . .*

His thoughts were interrupted by the urgent need to vomit. With the unconscious zeal and skill of an expert he covered three rhododendron bushes completely before wiping his lips and staggering on his way.

Behind him, too far away for him to hear, the shard that had been Belle Spalsy whimpered weakly and pathetically. Dead she might be, but that didn't mean that she was no longer living . . .

four

Kurt Salpinx kicked the tramp: he didn't know why; it just seemed right to him.

"Look, L. Ron," he said, as the two of them wandered through the gloom of an unnamed Parisian street, "I have this vague feeling that you're not entirely behind me in this new venture."

"Ah . . .," said Melanoma, wondering how to prevaricate: he'd given up a lot for his clients over the years, but somehow he'd grown sort of fond of his duodenum. "Say, Kurt, I never objected when you led that crusade against communist pomegranates; I even drummed up some enthusiasm amongst the media when you decided to run a campaign against *The Plain Truth* for being too left-wing, but this time, uh, well, I guess it's commercial but I'm not sure I can see us selling the movie rights."

"*Schweinhund!*" snarled Salpinx, declining to notice that in so doing he had spat one of his own expanded-polystyrene imitation rear molars onto the pavement. "Are you *mit* me or against me? I need to know, you pig-dog scum of the non-Aryan races and criminal against humanity!"

"I say, old fellow," protested Melanoma, delicately tracing a path around a somnolent prostitute and her client, "there's no need to go over the top, you know. I'm only a publicity agent. And I assure you that

I'm every bit as fascist as you on Mondays, Wednesdays and Fridays. Just because I have certain doubts about the current hate campaign . . ."

"*Das*," said Salpinx, "*ist ze* trouble! What do you do on Sundays, Tuesdays, Thursdays and Saturdays – *hein*? You are probably out canvassing for ze Communist Party, no? You should be strung up from a lamp-post, no?"

"Er, no," said Melanoma. "Besides, we haven't got any rope with us. Say, why not get rid of that excess adrenaline by delivering an impromptu rallying cry, right here and now?"

The stratagem worked. Salpinx instantly forgot vengeance and looked around for a suitable forty-foot (12.192m) podium, but without success. "*Du* mean," he said, "*ich* should just deliver *mein* speech right here on the side of the *Strasse*?"

"I'm sure Adolf Hitler did that often . . . in the early days," reassured Melanoma.

"*Rechts!*" snapped Salpinx decisively. "*Ich* vill do it!"

He leaped convulsively to the top of a short flight of steps fronting one of Paris's less fashionable bordellos. "Oh *nein*," he said almost immediately to the expectant Melanoma, "*mein* synthetic intestines seem to be calling upon me to engage in what you scum-whore swarthies call evacuation. I must some place of privacy find before I start to declare the Fourth – no, *scheiss*, it's about the Seventeenth by now – whatever, the New Improved Reich, dammit. *Dumkopf!* Where did I that *verdammt* plastic carrier bag put?"

L. Ron Melanoma thought wearily to himself: *Well, you win a few and you lose a few. That's the PR business.* He settled himself against a wall to wait while Salpinx engaged in various noisome and noisy activities in a nearby alleyway. It wasn't that he disliked Salpinx in any way – a publicity man, by definition, always likes the client – it was just that the cause seemed to be lost even before it had got properly launched. How could he hope to take prominent media figures out for business lunches and tell them that their goddam intestines should be excised? Not since the Danish Government had employed him to tell Israel that their product was sizzling good . . . He had to try to divert Salpinx into other areas. How about a campaign against non-Aryan vegetables? Yeah, that was it. Parsnips are OK but tomatoes and aubergines definitely out. Already Melanoma could see the pickets forming outside Paris's famous Flea Market. *That's a thought*, he thought, *what colour are fleas anyway? Nits are white, of course, but what colour are fleas? Maybe we could persuade Salpinx to bomb the French Government into renaming it the Nit Market?* Somehow it didn't seem to have the same ring.

Suddenly Salpinx returned, carrying his carrier bag, which was loathsomely full. "See," he said, "ze advantages of *der* mechanical innards? Zis milk is fresh enough to be drawn straight from a young *Fräulein, nicht war?* Ah, *du* gag? *Nein* matter, *ich* vill it drink later. *Es ist zehr gut für der* how you say lubrication of the joints."

Melanoma desperately wished that he, too, had had the foresight to bring a carrier bag.

"*Jawohl,*" said Salpinx, pointedly ignoring him. "Now, vere oh vere did I put *mein* copy of *der Führer's* masterpiece?" He delved deep into pockets which, as far as Melanoma could see, seemed to hold a fairly adequate library of paperbacks. The only point in favour of the evening so far, Melanoma mused, was that in going for the book the Nazi had dropped his carrier bag, so that the recycled milk was washing away down the gutter. "*Hein!*" said Salpinx in triumph, pulling out a battered volume. In the uneasy flicker of the street-lights Melanoma could see that it was a Shaun Hutson paperback. "*Mein Grott!*" exclaimed Salpinx by way of embarrassed explanation, stuffing it away as quickly as possible. Second time lucky: in his fist he held his treasured copy of *Mein Kampf*, given to him by his dear sweet old grandmother just a year before he had found it necessary to exterminate her for the Cause. He couldn't now remember which Cause, but it had been important at the time.

He climbed back up to the top of the flight of steps, opened the book, punched in the general direction of the sky, ignored the shower of glass that had moments before been an entry light, and prepared to declaim. Just then, however, a figure stumbled out of the alley where Salpinx had recently been and lurched across the pavement to lean against a tree. The man was tall, with hair cut so short that you could see the tattoo of the American Eagle on his scalp, and he clearly had not shaved for some days. He rolled one red eye at Malanoma and the other at Salpinx, then doubled up and vomited copiously into the gutter. But Salpinx hardly noticed this, for it had registered on him that the man was clad in the uniform of the US Marines.

"*Ach!*" he screamed. "*Ein* Yankee lickspittle!"

"Looks who's fuckin talkin," said the American, wincing under the cataract of warm spray before retching again. The scent of alcohol surrounded him so thickly as almost to be visible.

"*Ich!*" screeched Salpinx, sweat exploding from his brow in fury. "*Ich bin* talking! *Du Schweinhund* of a Yankee liberal commie pinko lefty fellow traveller under the bed" – Melanoma looked confused – "Marxist Stalinist homosexual-loving *scheisshaus! Ich bin dein Führer! Jawohl!*"

"Say, buster, I don't speak no fuckin Frog."

"*Ach*! *Du* Yankee bastard! I hate *deine* guts!"

"Right at this fuckin moment, buddy," said the Marine in the seconds before another convulsion hit him, "so do I."

"*Ach, du* do?" said Salpinx, instantaneously beside him, holding an arm comfortingly across the American's shoulders. "Zen you are for us?"

The American looked dubious. "For fuckin who?"

"For *mein* new organization, founded this very night, dedicated to ze extirpation of how you say alimentary canals, digestive systems, guts, bowels – call those bastards what you will, zey are ze scoundrels *vos ist* responsible for all the ills of ze vorld. *Mein* friend and I, ve dedicated to rescue all true Aryans from zis scourge are."

Melanoma interposed: "Kurt, baby, I think we'd get on better with our new friend if you knocked off the German accent."

"Oh," said Salpinx, looking momentarily shy, "I thought it was sort of in character, you know?"

"*Nein* – bugger it, I mean 'no'. Let's just stick to the native language of . . . say, what *is* your name?"

"Ex-Sergeant Bimbo G. Erythropsia of the US Marines," said the American. "I got fuckin Cypriot parents," he added by way of explanation. "My buddies fuckin call me Bo."

"Why they not call you Bimbo?" asked Salpinx.

Melanoma leapt between the two of them as Erythropsia's fists balled. "Excuse my friend," he hissed at both of them.

"Oh, sure," said Bo, "I forgot, he's a Kraut. He don't know what he's fuckin sayin. Must be kinda difficult knowin what you're fuckin sayin when you have to fuckin say it in a foreign language the whole fuckin time. Why don you Krauts fuckin say things in English, then you'd fuckin know what you were fuckin talkin about?"

"What's this 'fuckin'?" whispered Salpinx to Melanoma.

"It's something the master-race do only when they have to," Melanoma whispered back. "You wouldn't know about it."

Erythropsia was paying them no attention: he was instead staring fascinatedly into the gutter. "Say, you guys," he said, "I ain't had fuckin carrots since the day before yesterday. My fuckin guts must be even worse than I fuckin thought." His whole body shuddered again, and Melanoma, despite himself, thought: *corned beef.*

Salpinx said, over the thunder: "So now we are three. This is the kind of growth rate any new organization must maintain. Soon we are big enough to undergo the snowball effect, and after that the world is ours. *Ours! OURS!*"

"Say," said Erythropsia, "if I kin fuckin stop makin the ol technicolor yawn long enough, could you guys give me a fuckin place for the night?"

"I told you he wanted to join us," said Salpinx to Melanoma in visible triumph.

The PR man turned to the ex-Marine. "Fuckin could," he said, ever the diplomat.

five

Less than a mile (1.609344km) from the Eschars' house two young things were in a moonlit forest clearing, falling madly - gloriously - in love. This was the first time either of them had seen the other naked, and both were awed with passion by what they saw. They had met before, many times, but to discover that each of them was even more impressive unclothed than clothed was a rare reward. As the dappled moonlight flickered, as the branches of the trees tossed and the leaves rustled, they were both speechless.

Permanently, as it happened. Evolution had not had time to develop proper speech centres before, millions and billions of years earlier, the great symbiotic partnership between the vertebrates and certain invertebrates had begun. Still, they were endowed with what their recent human hosts might have called telepathy and what they themselves called thworking, and it was in this way that they communicated.

I have A Past, you know, thworked one. *The woman I was in went regularly with . . . men!*

The other recoiled damply, but all that it thworked was: *That's all right. Don't worry. All of that is behind us now. At last we are free!*

Despite this reassurance, the other felt somehow sullied. It knew it was being old-fashioned, but it would like to have been a virgin for this night.

It isn't as if, urged its lover, *those men had actually come* in contact *with you at any point*, but this did no good: Belle Spalsy had been a resourceful girl, and her list of services offered had been about as comprehensive as it physiologically could be. *It's curious*, thworked Belle's one-time digestive system, *but I'm actually shy. I wonder if we could just be naked together tonight and not - you know - do too much else.*

Certainly, thworked the other tenderly, *I'm so in love with you, baby, that I wouldn't think of pushing you. There'll be plenty of other nights, plenty of other times. Let's just go for a stroll, or bloody something. I'm not as macho as you seem to think. I'm pretty certain I can take it.* But the thworker, which called itself Hpleurg, knew it would be difficult: sensing only dimly through all these years what Malacia Furuncle was doing all around; feeling the rush of adrenaline and various other hormones too obscene to name, being always on the verge of . . . and now this! It felt about as frustrated as a voyeur with a broken wrist. Perhaps a squelch through the lonely forest might fill the other with the necessary mixture of lust and romance, and then they could . . . er . . .

Say, Hpleurg thworked, *just how exactly* do *we make love?*

CHAPTER FOUR

THE DYNAMIC DUODENUM

Gosseyn's intestinal fortitude strove to climb into his throat,
and settled into position again only reluctantly . . .
A.E.van Vogt, *The World of Null-A*, 1945

An article no intelligent mind could stomach.
Sam Moskowitz, *The Immortal Storm*, 1952

one

All through the day, Henry Follicle had been followed around his apartment by a grim sense of foreboding. Each time he shot a glance over his
shoulder, there was nothing to be seen but the odd cockroach. . . yet the
undercurrent of terror wouldn't go away. In his heart of hearts he knew
he'd long been marked down for a fearful, gratuitous end, probably involving chainsaws or the maggoty putrescent clutch of diseased zombie
fundamentalists.

There was just no way you could fight knowledge like that.

It had all begun when he was nothing but a raw-nosed, gangling kid,
prying into forbidden things with which he'd never been meant to med-
dle. Miss Oxter the librarian had said as much, loudly – but it hadn't
stopped Follicle. He'd worked his way furtively through the horror
shelves, trapping himself in an addiction that had lasted thirty years . . .
and slowly the gelatinous outlines of his fate had come clear.

He himself was . . . a victim.

At first it had been a joke: a wry smile as once again he recognized
himself in some hastily written character whose only purpose was to be
very horribly and disgustingly killed, or worse. But the thing went
deeper than coincidence! Numbly, for the thousandth time, he checked
off the points:

He was a typical, sympathetic, all-American guy. He'd never received
much character development, except for a few cheaply poignant touches
like his love for his wacky, irrepressible mongrel pup Barker, or his

populist fondness for McDonald's plus quadruple ketchup washed down with cans of Coors. His hopes and fears had always been simple ones, evidently designed for maximum market appeal: staunch devotion to the President, mild fear of the evil Russkies, stark terror of Internal Revenue, guilty lust for his secretary on the 113th floor of the Nosra Fire Insurance Co . . .

If only I could be a faggot, or read Tolstoy (same thing, I guess), or go on a civil liberties march!

He couldn't. He'd been trapped helplessly in his rut of being marketably sympathetic, instantly but not deeply appealing, disposable, cardboard, stuffed to bursting with stereotyped reactions. It was as though some awful, omniscient Author were steering him with a gigantic thumb to his doom. He was one hundred percent a victim.

At least, he thought with that single faint gleam of hope which sustained him despite the appalling foreknowledge, *my bit should be over in a page or two. The real losers are the ones who have to live right through to the end of a book like this.*

Kismet. That was the way to take it. Destiny. To some folk it's just a word: but to Follicle, destiny meant the ravening greenish-yellow fangs with which the world planned to ambush him. Out there somewhere was a page with your name on it, and when it came . . .

Absent-mindedly he noticed a strange, sour smell in the apartment. As though he'd thrown up quietly without noticing it (Coors did that to you sometimes), or had put too much Parmesan cheese on a lasagne-and-fries TV dinner. Yet it wasn't quite like that either. It had overtones that somehow reminded him of boiled slugs *au gratin*, or those phosphorescent fish-organs that even the sushi restaurants threw away, or the terrible milky foaming of maggots that had once held him transfixed when he'd looked for the rest-room at Luigi's Diner and made the mistake of finding the kitchen.

Nasty was the word, an inadequate word, for that smell. And with it came a slithering, sucking noise that seemed to be right behind him, the sort of noise you might expect if you tried to stir a three-day-old pot of congealed canelloni, or perhaps to whip a naked and manacled female secretary with strands of parboiled asparagus . . .

Follicle was damned if he'd look round. Those fucking cockroaches had cried wolf once too often. So he never saw what it was that wetly wrapped itself around his ankles, secreting a hot acid that seared through his plump flesh to expose the naked whiteness of the bone.

About time too, he thought resignedly, toppling forward in hope of swift, merciful oblivion. But as he fell he impinged in slow motion against the corner of the table, which burst his right eye like an over-ripe grape. A crackle like the snapping of dead twigs announced a whole fist-ful of broken finger-bones in the hand which had instinctively tried to break his fall. Hot, loose sensations indicated the sudden failure of all his sphincters, and as his face flattened itself into the soiled carpet he felt his nose being smashed back level with his cheekbones, while all his front teeth shattered at the impact of some unyielding object that awaited them at ground level.

That'll teach me to leave Stephen King books lying on the floor, he thought in philosophical silence: one snapped-off incisor had wittily nailed his tongue to the jawbone. He made a frenzied attempt to roll onto his back and see what was coming: the stress was too much, and halfway his weakened ribs popped loose like the teeth of a defective zipper.

Laden with horror fiction and overbalanced by the recent collision, the heavy table collapsed on him, breaking his neck and giving him a slight bruise on the left forearm. His stomach heaved, and Follicle began quietly to asphyxiate in bubbling masses of his own warm, pungent vomit. He rather thought his kneecap was dislocated, too.

Something blood-warm and slimy crawled lubriciously over him, just outside the field of vision of his remaining eye. Its acid trail seared through clothes and flesh like the Spanish Inquisition's pokerwork, passing over his thigh, his cringing crotch. One testicle popped loose and rolled soggily across the floor, like a spat-out marshmallow glistening with saliva. Just as Follicle had concluded that the pain couldn't possibly get any worse, and that he might never now get round to squeezing that particularly ripe zit next to what used to be his nose . . . the crawling something reached his stomach.

Oblivion giggled at the edges of Follicle's consciousness as he tried to put words to the new horror that struck along his nerves with the agony of an industrial infra-red laser cutter capable of vaporizing ten-inch slabs of molybdenum steel. Something was tearing, tearing loose within his abdomen, pulling clumsily free like postage stamps which (as scientists have shown) tear along any arbitrary line but that of the perforations. *Shit. Giving birth must feel like this.* And: *Why couldn't it be a nice quiet H.P. Lovecraft story with just one sentence of stark terror before you go mad? You'd think these authors were being paid by the word.*

Something, something which he still couldn't see for the shadows now filling his good eye (along with the clotting blood and the bit of carrot which he recognized in sudden terror as one he'd eaten last night) . . . something was humping its tortured way across the floor. Twice as loudly as it had come. And Follicle felt, inasmuch as his ravaged senses could still feel at all – hollow.

Then he heard a more familiar sound. A heart-warming snuffle and a cute, mischievous growl.

My God, I'd forgotten Barker! That poor pooch . . . is he gonna get worked over for the sake of one further cheap twist of the knife? Or – no, of course, faithful dog avenges dying master, I like it, I like it. Go to it, Barker! Kill!

An explosive canine sneeze ripped through the steamy, clogging stillness of the violated apartment. Barker had smelt something – Something – and hadn't liked it one little bit. Follicle heard the dog snuffle along the floor in hope of something more palatable. Follicle, if he had still been capable, would have felt a terrible shrinking of the guts as Barker found it. The wacky, irrepressible mongrel licked his master affectionately, and with doggy enthusiasm started to dig in.

I should have expected it. Low-budget ironies, for Chrissake. And – ouch, that was a kidney – what kinda perverts are these authors anyway?

As if to inflict the final indignity, a large buzzing housefly settled in the middle of Follicle's fast-clouding eye, and began to lay eggs.

two

It was breakfast time. Two days after the all too successful test of young Whitlow's theory, Professor Eschar still felt shaky. He was trying to calm his nerves by reading his favourite paper, the *National Enquirer*, whose stimulating headlines like MINNESOTA SUPER-PSYCHIC REVEALS CUBAN BROTHEL SECRETS or BOY BITES OFF OWN APPENDIX could often trigger new insights, new connections, new unified theories linking space, time, energy and gonzo journalism. But today there was a subtle slant to many of the news items, a common factor which at first he couldn't quite put his finger on –

FLORIDA "SLIME TUBE" HORROR
  Links with Bigfoot?

OHIO'S UFO HARA-KIRI PLAGUE
  Are Jap customs infectious? Police seek mysterious "clean-up squad" in restaurant swoop. "They laughed at cattle mutilations," says Irwin B. Pubes of Cincinnati, "but they can't laugh now. We use cats' gut to make violins. *What kind of enormous double-basses do the UFOnauts like to play?*"

GELL URETHRA PROVES POWERS ON TV!
  Exclusive interview! "I was using my astral abilities on the David Letterman Show, to show how even while handcuffed I could psychokinetically make a piece of Silly Putty slowly ooze and flow. Then I got this terrific telepathic flash from the dozen bagels with lox I'd had earlier that day. Eight million viewers saw me moan and grab my guts. And within hours, the switchboards were jammed with calls from people who'd seen OOBEs . . . Out Of the Bowels Experiences. No, I can't control it, this power just flows right through me . . ."

RAPTURE STARTS EARLY, REVIVALISTS SAY

Rapture is what they call it. Your body snatched up to Heaven on Judgement Day, *if* you're born again. Folk expected it in millennial year 2000, but nothing happened. Or 2001, for the pedants? Still nothing seems to have happened. But now the Rev. Jerry Fallopian of the Reformed Fundament Church has some shock news! Seems the Rapture's already under way – but what none of them guessed was that the saved would be carried off a piece at a time.

"It all fits together," says Fallopian. "The lowest parts of us must be taken first because they need longer purification in God's fire! And which parts of the body are foulest, smelliest, used for perverted pleasure by Godless homosexuals trying to infect us all with the 8th plague of Egypt? It all fits together, and that's what Almighty God'll be doing with us up there, as in His inscrutable wisdom (and just like the Good Book's parables of thrift) He saves a little at a time . . ."

"Has it ever occurred to you," said Whitlow through a mouthful of bran flakes, "that the strange events in this laboratory could have wider repercussions somewhere out there in the world at large?"

"No," said the Professor quizzically. "What d'you mean?"

"How could that experiment have changed anything?" Miranda poutingly added. "We haven't said a word to anyone. You didn't even ring up the *National Enquirer*, Daddy, like you usually do to tell them about your new theories."

Professor Eschar blushed and pretended to be very interested in the miniature electric arc-furnace which with characteristic whimsy he kept on the breakfast table as a cigar lighter.

Whitlow went on: "Well, no*body* has used the phone or left the house . . . but some*thing* went missing in that fateful investigation, didn't it?" He frowned at headlines which blared "RIPPER" ENTRAIL THIEF SLAYS 127 IN NEW YORK BLOODBATH: CRIMES MAY BE LINKED and KILLER HOSEPIPE ASSAULTED GRANNY, CLAIMS TODDLER. "I have a sort of . . . *hunch* about this. A sort of feeling that terrible events are in motion."

"You shouldn't believe everything you read in the papers," the Professor snorted, finishing his sixth cup of fresh-ground coffee. "B-D! Coffeeee! Oh, sorry, I keep forgetting. Miranda, could you. . .?"

As Miranda swayed sensually to the coffee machine, Whitlow frowned again. "I just hope M-B-D manages to get properly – ah – integrated soon. She, or he, or it, seems strangely disoriented and

With inhuman, cyborg strength the thing smashed down impertinent saplings that stood in its path. In its Juggernaut-like wrath, it exulted:

Gee whillikins! That blackhearted old sinner Freud would have insisted I had penis envy, dear Lord God in Her infinite mercy rot the bugger's chauvinist soul . . . but sakes! I's a whole different born-again Basil-Malacia now. Out of their paths of unrighteousness they done give B-D all that good sinful feminist fury. While, heavens to Betsy, Malacia has gotten herself indestructible robot stamina plus Satan's own fleshly weapon to revenge herself on they sinful male oppressors, Hallelujah!

That black-hearted sinner straying like a serpent among the rhododendrons was just the first, glory be!

I am the sword of the Lord, er, Lady, and of Gideon. Whoever she was.

Hot ziggety, let the cock-proud sons of Adam fear my . . . spigot!

CHAPTER FIVE

RUN FOR YOUR LIFE!

He wasn't going to leave Pat Benson on her own, crabs or no crabs.
　　Guy N. Smith, *Night of the Crabs*, 1976

Sheath-bursting romance . . .
　　Blurb for *Brute!* by Malcolm Bennett and Aidan Hughes, 1987

one

Yup, thought Sir Jake "Buboes" Bunyan, editor of the *Daily Swab*, as he handled today's still-damp edition: *This is the stuff!* He was pleased with his finely honed headline, encapsulating as it did the complex issues involved in the strange spate of hideous deaths that had sterilized the whole of North America with fear and had now spread to Britain: RED VICAR IN TEENAGE FLAGELLATION PROBE – PM HITS BACK.

　　Just then one of the telephones on Sir Jake's pristinely tidy desk rang, and with the swift reflexes born of long-term professional experience he tried to remember what it was he was supposed to do. Oh yes, pick it up. Um, but which telephone was it? Eenie, meenie, minie . . . Aha! As usual, it was the one that hadn't been disconnected. The hotline from the boss's office in Groin Flats, Queensland. *Right! Lemme think. Yeah. Last time Q threatened to sack me for picking up the bit with the buttons on it. Try the long bit with bulges at each end . . .*

　　"Hello there!" he said brightly into the earpiece. "This is 'Buboes' Bunyan, the man at the forefront of the news – editor-in-chief of the sssoarraway *Swab*!"

　　"Strewth, you asshole pommy one-eyed trouser snake!" said Q, his tinny voice vibrating the receiver against Bunyan's front teeth. "What in the name of flaming sheepshaggers does 'flagellation' mean?"

　　Sir Jake gulped. He knew he should never have bought himself that thesaurus.

Q continued. "One of the bastards here has looked in the bleeding strine dictionary and all he can find is that it means someone has a long cilium, which is no bleeding help. Our readers want the news - not poofter high-class fancy talk. Call a fucking spade a fucking spade, can't you?"

Sir Jake gulped again, albeit a little confusedly. Why couldn't the boss talk through the right end of the telephone? Besides, he'd never heard a spade called a cilium before.

"Look, 'Buboes', you're not the only half-bollocked journalist in fucking London, you know! You better start doing things the *Swab*'s way - giving the public the shit they want - or I'm going to start interfering with your editorial integrity!"

The sound of Q slamming the 'phone down lacerated Sir Jake's gums all the way back to the wisdom teeth. He knew only too well what the boss's threat meant. He'd seen his predecessor's integrity interfered with to such effect that even now parts of his body had still to be located. And yet . . . and yet . . . wasn't Q being perhaps a little unfair? Sir Jake looked again at today's issue. The *Swab* was a *good* newspaper, dammit! Perhaps the headline was a little long, but he'd compensated for that by omitting any ancillary text, leaving the nine stark words to speak for themselves. The efficiency savings had been impressive, too; it might have taken up hours of his time to settle on a suitable name for the hypothetical vicar and select the member of the Shadow Cabinet who had given him his subversive instructions. The boss seemed curiously unaware of all the little subtleties, the minor considerations, that lay behind the outward aspect of the *Swab*'s editorial processes. Which was strange, because persistent rumour around the trade had it that Q had, in his shady past, attended school.

Idly, Sir Jake turned back the front page to look at the next spread. Page 3 had Clara the Chimp, last year's Miss Whipsnade, in a thigh-stretching full-frontal shot as she fastidiously eviscerated a rodent. Sir Jake realized that few of the readers would notice the witty pun on "open beaver", but the very fact that it was *there* showed that the *Swab* functioned on a higher intellectual plane than the pinkoes ever said it did. The advertisers seemed to agree with Sir Jake's judgement on this - why else would the rest of the paper be filled with tasteful advertisements for lynching equipment to deal with Britain's surviving immigrants, timebombs with which to increase the government's parliamentary majority the permanent way, iron maidens for the kiddies to use when hunting down the remnants of the Woodcraft Folk, guillotines to solve the problems of the inner cities, and lifesize, haloed, luminous pink statues of noted Chief Constables, complete with barometer. On the last page was the sports news, which showed *Swab* Soccer Hooligan of the Year, Ford Sierra-winning Jim Prepuce, reenacting his glorious flanking motion on the Wembley terraces during which he had decapitated forty-eight Arsenal fans with a claymore.

And there was more to the *Swab* than just hard news, Sir Jake reflected proudly. When readers had devoured the political news, the economic reports, the book reviews, the in-depth features and the free fish finger with every issue, they could, thanks to marvellous improvements in the technology of printing on latex, swiftly inflate their newspaper and have a full-scale working model of that day's Page 3 girl, kitted out with all orifices.

Still, still . . . whatever pride Sir Jake might take in his newspaper counted for nothing: Q's word was like Holy Writ within Castle Dolorous, as the *Swab*'s offices had become known. The boss was never happy with the second-rate when the third was attainable. He, Sir Jake, was going to have to come up with a real sheath-burster of a front-page story for tomorrow or else . . . he shuddered at the thought of having a testicle on each of two continents, like his predecessor.

He put the 'phone down and looked at the blank screen of his VDU. Any other day and he'd have been tempted to make use of the machine's random word generator – *that reminds me: I must remember to pull "flagellation" out of the thing's vocabulary bank and put "spade" in instead* – but today he'd have to go one better than that: Q would be scrutinizing the results carefully, watching to see if he could handle his position of responsibility properly.

Inspiration hit Sir Jake, and he doubled over in paroxysms of psychic agony, his mind almost ripped from its moorings by the sheer improbability of it all. Once his eyes had stopped watering, he mentally examined the invigorating idea that had flashed in front of his inner eyes. This could be . . . this could be a brand-new, pioneering concept in tabloid journalism! He could use a *real story*! Oh, sure, he'd have to get most of the details wrong – the public wouldn't be ready to go the whole hog immediately, and he was all too well aware of what happened to prophets in their own land – but, still, he could radically transform the face of British popular journalism by at least *basing* his lead story on fact! Wow!

Take this story on the missing intestines, for example. Not since the government had outlawed the discussion of AIDS as offensive to traditional morality had the country been so terrified of a perceived threat. For some reason, journalists themselves seemed to be immune to the scourge, but elsewhere it struck seemingly without pattern: nuns were as vulnerable as nurses (*leftie liberal bleeding hearts!*, Sir Jake's inner censor corrected), boxers as vulnerable as limpwristed nancy sci-fi writers, sober politicians as vulnerable as . . . now there was a thought! How come the rest of the politicians – the vast majority – showed the same sort of immunity as journalists?

With a gleam in his eye, Sir Jake "Buboes" Bunyan drew reverently from its case the dusty green eyeshade he had worn during his brief tenure as investigative reporter for *Poetry Review* and fixed it to his forehead. He could hear the adrenaline pounding through his veins. Perhaps Q's security officers would tear him limb from limb on the morrow for this, but today – today the front page of the *Swab* was his, and he would use it to tell the great masses out there of the true nature of the threat that menaced them all. His fingers hovered over the keys of his terminal as his mind sought the aid of the Muses.

RED DREAD CUTS SLUTS' GUTS! he typed, but no sooner had he finished than the door behind him was kicked open. He whirled round in his revolving chair – a little overenthusiastically, so that by the time he got the bloody thing stopped his vision was fuzzy and the room was swimming around in circles – and saw to his horror the dreaded figures of two of Q's vicious security thugs. Their tails swished as their claws slipped out. One of them howled evilly, bloodlust plain in its crazed eyes. Q had invested a fortune in genetic-engineering experiments to breed a cross between a European wolf and a shark, but it had been money well spent.

Heroism comes to tabloid journalists only infrequently, but Sir Jake had never been very good at his job. Courage shattered like a sledgehammer into his pounding heart as he faced the two bloodcurdling monsters. The gushing noise within him grew louder as the floods of adrenaline were reinforced by gallons of epinephrine. He stabbed his finger accurately at his terminal's PRINT button, then at CONFIRM. Secure in the knowledge that, thanks to the glories of hi tech, nothing now could stop the fifty million print run of tomorrow's edition of the *Swab* being produced, distributed and retailed, he turned back again, his brain filled with an icy calm, to face the brutish mutants.

The male pounced forwards, its powerful rear legs launching it through the intervening space like a rocket, and the female followed suit only seconds later, and Sir Jake found himself being crushed under the force of their two bodies one after the other and his elbow knocked his VDU off his desk and it shattered on the floor in a shower of sparks and he couldn't see any light now because the furry, sweaty, fish-smelling bodies of his attackers were covering his face and their rough coats were scraping the outer skin from his cheeks and he was struggling to land a punch on their bodies and he wished like hell that the genetic engineers had managed to retain the wolf's external testicles when breeding these monsters and there was no time for thinking any more and he knew that he was only moments from death and there was no question about it this was going to be the Big One the real leap into the unknown and he hoped that Clara never found out how he had died because he wasn't sure that her delicate sensibilities would stand the shock and he could feel teeth clenching eagerly on his right forearm as he plucked reflexively at an eye and he yelled with pain as he realized it was his own and he wished that he had time to remember that most astonishing blowjob Clara had given him the night before and his delicious *frisson* of apprehensive tension as all the time he'd worried about what would happen if she had a sudden mental relapse and started thinking the bloody thing was a banana and he kneed solid flesh and knew that he'd struck a sensitive spot because one of his assailants gave a muffled screech of pain and then the other one was opening its vast mouth with its serried ranks of sharp and gleaming teeth and that great cavern was coming down over his head so that his nose and mouth were squashed flat against the mucous membrane of the thing's palate and he could feel blood spurt from his neck as the monster's teeth tightened and there was a curious *lurching* sensation inside him as if his organs were shifting and beginning to evaginate up his throat slowly at first but then with increasing rapidity and it was just like oh God it was just like someone was using a pump to pull out all his guts and then the beast which had tried to bite his head off stiffened convulsively as Sir Jake's own mouth opened to its fullest extent and some *thing* shot between his teeth and deep deep into the uttermost bowels of his attacker which spat out Sir Jake's head and although he felt almost weightless with shock he scrabbled around blindly on his desk-top and felt a heavy metal weight and he opened his bloodstained eyes and saw that the other attacker was still writhing from where he'd kneed it in a tender spot and without pausing for conscious thought he leapt forward and stapled its gonopodium to the floor and the whole episode was jolly exciting.

The male security officer was clearly in terminal difficulties with the ... the *thing* which had invaded its innards. Sir Jake heaved himself to his feet, collapsed onto his now tattered revolving chair, and watched as the beast jerked and squirmed all over the floor in the opposite corner of the office. A thin squeal of pain was issuing from its clenched jaws, as was a bubbling stream of bright blood which splashed around its twitching paws. Dispassionately Sir Jake watched over the twenty minutes it took before the hulking form took its last, agonized, shuddering breath and collapsed into the bonelessness of death.

Only then did Sir Jake remember the security officer for which he himself had accounted, and he turned his bleary gaze to see what had happened to it. He started, and then he didn't know whether to gag or chuckle. The tormented creature, unable to tear the staples from the floor, had wrenched its own gonopodium out by the roots. Many internal juices, squishy organs, sundered blood vessels (*just like spaghetti bolognese*, thought the grizzled journalist) and a complete side of roe had erupted from the gaping wound in the beast's flank. Intestinal parasites were fighting murderously over the steaming remains or gorging themselves on the soft flesh. The security officer itself, bizarrely, had not yet quite died: its eyes were fixed in a stare of intense hatred on Sir Jake's face, but then they glazed with anguish as a further flood of pungent intestines slurped out of the hole to splash onto the floor, spattering Sir Jake's trouser turnups. Moments later the mutant had joined its mate in the great darkness that awaits us all.

Sir Jake was alone.

His palms were sweating, and his whole crotch area was clammy with tangy-smelling urine. Blood and pus drenched his clothes. His hair was a tangle of vomit and saliva. Suddenly one eye plopped from its socket and dangled on its stalk, giving him a disorienting close-up view of his chin. A sharp-clawed paw had ripped his flesh all the way down his spine, revealing the ivory-white of his vertebrae and shearing off one buttock almost completely, so that it dangled over the back of his chair, held in place only by a flap of skin. A monumental impact against his chest had squirted his right lung out through his nipple to fill his inside jacket pocket (*bad anatomy but bloody good imagery*, his keenly honed journalist's critical faculties murmured approvingly). His left foot had been bitten off completely, and the bone of the ankle scattered like talcum powder across the floor. And sometime during the melée his right kneecap had been detached and hammered with skull-splintering force into his right ear, rupturing his eardrum and penetrating his brain.

But he felt great!

By all logic, he should be nothing but a mangled collection of bones, blood and flesh by now, hurled by the security officers over the barbed wire to remind the senile pickets of the fate that awaited them. But, goddammit, he'd defeated the odds. He'd taken those two thugs, but good! He cackled, spitting out teeth and the front two inches (5.08cm) of his tongue. His other eye abruptly plopped out to join its fellow, and the two of them swung backwards and forwards in a macabre imitation of Newton's Balls.

A commotion in the corner attracted Sir Jake's attention. Gingerly using his right hand, he turned one eye in the appropriate direction, and saw that the whole corpse of the male security guard was in violent movement. The huge jaws were forced open, and . . . *horror of horrors!*

A *thing* – a darkly glistening, eerily pulsating *thing* – emerged from the dead beast's gullet. Sir Jake's eyes almost popped back in again. Loathing filled every fibre of his brain. The . . . the *thing* was long and sinuous, with bulges where there should be no bulges, glistening with diabolic ichor, visibly malevolent as it slowly and sadistically snaked its way across the floor to come to a halt beside the empty trouser cuff which had so recently been occupied by Sir Jake's left foot. He imagined that the . . . the *thing*'s featureless surface broke into a vile grin as it paused there for a moment, and then it began with inexorable slowness to slither up inside the cylinder of cloth. His leg felt as if it were being slowly covered, from the ankle upwards, in warm vomit.

He knew – he couldn't tell how he knew but he *knew* – that the . . . the *thing* was going to slowly strangle the life out of him. His only hope of salvation was to stop it before it reached his throat. He cursed the fact that he'd followed the great journalistic tradition of wearing loose-fitting braces instead of a belt; the constriction at his waist might have held up the . . . the *thing* for what could prove to be vital moments. But the game of "what if" has always been one of the most futile of human activities, and he knew this. He would have to think of some other means of countering the . . . the *thing*.

Yet he was powerless, now, to move. He could only watch, with sick fascination and a certain amount of logistic difficulty, as the ominous bulge crept slowly up past his groin and onto the empty, sagging, fleshly rolls of his stomach . . .

How the hell am I going to get out of this one? he thought.

two

Professor Lester Pustule lifted his weary head from his arms and looked around him. The British Library Reading Room appeared to be empty, the thick dust on its floors, furnishings and academics undisturbed. Nothing moved. He sighed.

Accustomed to long waits between putting in his requests and receiving the relevant books, he had come prepared, but now, after four months, his provisions were running out, his chemical toilet was full, and he had completed the *Guardian* crossword in every one of the forty-seven languages he knew. He was bored, and he was fed up of stale sandwiches and stewed, thermos-tasting coffee. This was the second longest delay he'd ever had to endure here, and the worst of it was that all of the attendants appeared to have gone, to have deserted their posts. In the ordinary way this would have cheered him up, but as it was the notion was beginning to infest his mind that perhaps, this time, there might be no conclusion to his waiting. He reached out to touch the slumped pupa-like figure of the person at the next chair, and it silently crumbled into downy nothingness.

The elderly philologist didn't know what to do. Past experience had taught him that, should he nip out for a few minutes in the fresh air, his books would be delivered and then swiftly removed again, so that he would have to reinstitute the entire procedure from the beginning. Yet . . . yet something told him that this time it was different. The huge room was filled with an absolute, mind-numbing, muffling soft silence. The air was untrammelled by all the usual sounds that marked off the British Library from anywhere else in the academic world – the scrabble of quill pens, the *squ-witt!!* of the attendants squeezing their blackheads, the creaks of elderly joints, and the cheery chorus of quiet death-rattles as the longer-term readers politely and discreetly bowed out of this existence.

Pustule began to wish that he'd never received that transatlantic telex from his old friend Hank Eschar; from the moment it had arrived he'd felt in his waters that it spelled trouble.

> HAVING TROUBLE WITH GUTS STOP [it had read] US LI-BRARY OF CONGRESS TOO FAR TO TRAVEL BESIDES LESTER WE ARE BESIEGED STOP I CANNOT GO INTO MORE DETAIL THAN THAT STOP CAN YOU GO TO BL AND CHECK OUT ALL REFERENCES TO SENTIENT IN-TESTINES REPEAT SENTIENT INTESTINES WITH SPE-CIFIC REFERENCE TO (A) MALEVOLENCE (B) MYTHS AND LEGENDS (C) DYNAMIC DUODENA STOP PLEASE ALSO CHECK FIRST-AID SECTION FOR DATA ON TREATING SPIGOT WOUNDS STOP YOU KNOW LESTER OLD BUDDY I WOULD NOT ASK YOU THIS FAVOUR IF I DID NOT STILL HAVE THOSE PHOTOGRAPHS OF YOU AND THE SPHINX STOP MIRANDA SENDS PLATONIC LOVE STOP REGARDS HANK.

The philologist shuddered even at the recollection of the document, and shuddered again as he considered the veiled threat in Eschar's reference to the Sphinx. Curse his own folly! To allow himself to be open to threats of blackmail for the rest of his life, and all because of an ungovernable sexual impulse!

Pustule had always maintained a realistic attitude towards his own psychosexual condition, and it had never given him a moment's self-embarrassment to think about it. He felt no guilt, just occasional anger towards the cruelty of a Fate which had singled him out as its victim: there must have been raucous laughter in the heavens when it was decided that he, Lester Pustule, alone among all his species, should be unable to get his rocks off except by . . . er . . . cohabitation with the Sphinx. As the cliché has it, the heart is a lonely hunter – but no heart could ever have been as lonely a hunter as Pustule's. Others with embarrassing secrets could join together to seek strength, to seek release, or just to talk about their problems – Alcoholics Anonymous, the Covert Coprophiliacs' Club, the Frankly Fetishist Foundation. But Pustule had been through every set of Yellow Pages in the world, and nowhere had he found the slightest reference to Sphinx-lovers, or Sphinxters, as he privately called them. Then again, people with other emotional unorthodoxies could take themselves along to a psychoanalyst for treatment, and after a few weeks or months be rendered fit for survival in modern society, their sexual desires focused exclusively on money like everyone else's. When Pustule had tried this approach, he'd hardly got through the first paragraph of his much rehearsed "confession" before the analyst had laughed himself into a cardiac arrest.

Pustule had tried everything, but everything, to rid himself of what he had to admit was a mental abnormality (although he recognized no derogatory undertones in his own use of that term). He'd begged several hundred thousand unsold copies of the *Swab* from his local newsagent and made a vast *papier mâché* model of the edifice in his back garden, but all to no avail: it was like the difference between a photograph in a girlie magazine and a real woman, who never looks anything like that. Hoping, then, to attempt at least a veneer of normality, he had tried to see if enigmatic women would do as a Sphinx-substitute, but this hadn't worked out too well either; the only woman who'd looked at him enigmatically had been the one who had then gone on to point out that he was standing on her foot.

It all began when I was a child, he thought as he sat in the Reading Room. *My mother was breast-feeding me, and I was enjoying the sensual softness of her bosom, and then my father came in with that postcard from Egypt . . .* Abruptly his thoughts changed their course. *Sod it, that's enough of this bloody in-depth pseudo-Freudian characterization.*

With this change in attitude, daring entered his mind. He knew that it was against the rules of the place for any reader to go anywhere near the stacks where the books were kept; instead, readers had to put in request slips and then wait for extended periods until an attendant brought the books to them, saturated by acne leakage and the reason for their request long forgotten. The tale was still whispered in private huddles of the time that Dr Bronchi of Athens University had, ignorant of the regulations, himself fetched down a copy of the bound volume of *Punch* for 1948. He was still, said the old sage heads, nodding dolefully, confined in the Tower . . . if he lived. The more tender-hearted of them hoped sincerely that he did not.

Yet, even though he recalled this dreadful example, the whole of Pustule's mind was suffused with the thundering question: *Why not?* There was not an attendant in sight, and the dust showed clearly that there had not been any attendants near for a very long time. If he scuffed up that dust enough with his feet as he went, laying a number of false trails to other tables, no one would ever be able to tell that he had done the unthinkable!

Moments later he was on the move, his eyes roaming this way and that with all the alert cunning of a predatory animal as it stalks its unwitting prey. Crossing the main hall caused him no problems except that progress was slow as a result of the need to shuffle as much dust as possible in as many different directions as possible. But on reaching the arched doorway leading to the stacks he faced an unexpected barrier: thanks to the library staff's inability to persuade the government to change the law that one copy of every publication must be sent to the British Library, thousands upon thousands of unopened bundles of copies of the *Swab*, representing three-quarters of the New Forest, were piled in front of the doorway to a height of some sixty or seventy feet (18.3-21.3m). For a moment Pustule was disheartened, but then, with a merry boyish laugh, he recalled his youthful rock-climbing holidays in the Tyrol – many a puckish moment of passion had he shared with a jaunty little mountain cairn, though always he had been aware that this was only *second-best*. He set to work with a will. Within moments he was among the stacks. A sign reading "Colonic Section" guided him to the relevant shelves.

Somewhere, an owl hooted.

Eagerly he scanned along the shelves. *Selected Writings of Alfred North Whitehead* – hmm, hardly what he was looking for. *The Secret Diary of Adrian Mole, Aged 13¾* – must be some cataloguing error. And why should *Myra Breckinridge* be here? In fact, there were quite a lot of errors: one solid shelf was filled with dustily unread copies of *The Country Diary of an Edwardian Lady* while, on the shelf below, Philip Roth's *Portnoy's Complaint* rested cheek by jowl with Jack Vance's *Servants of the Wankh*. And what was *that* tome, placed on the shelf spine-inwards, no doubt by some careless attendant? Giving in to his anal persona, Pustule compulsively tugged the volume from its place, preparatory to repositioning it right-side-out. As he was doing so, his eyes absently ran across its title and lit up.

He held the book closer to his myopic eyes and reread the badly stamped gold letters on the black-leather spine of the book: *Ye Boke of Guts*. This was precisely the sort of thing Eschar had asked him to look for. What good fortune to have found it *here*!

Pustule climbed back over the mountain of old newspapers into the main hall, where the lighting was marginally better. He dragged a bundle of *Swab*s away from its fellows and used it as a makeshift stool. As if at a signal, a brilliant gleam of sunlight speared through the hall's dusty cupola and illumined the yellowed parchment pages as he slowly at first, and then with increasing urgency, devoured their contents . . .

three

Pneumonoultramicroscopicsilicovolcanoconiosis.

To some people it's just a word. To the Eschars and David Whitlow, however, it was much more than that – now. Oh, sure, they'd heard it on the radio a bundle of times, and once during David's sabbatical in London he'd even seen the word serialized in the *Swab* (just before the bizarre disappearance of the editor, he suddenly recalled), but now they were experiencing it in reality, thanks to the mini-volcano the Professor had succeeded in concocting in the laboratory.

"'S the only way of keeping ourselves warm!" he'd snapped testily when Miranda had asked him why he was attacking the concrete floor with a pickaxe. "Now that the electricity's gone failed us and the generator's been spigotted into a pile of nuts and bolts, we chickadees is goin' to have to turn our attentions to renewable energy sources. There ain't many fault lines here in New England, but fortunately, when your Maw and I built this house a couple dozen years ago we foresaw the day when this kinda thing might up an' happen, so we thought to usselves, we thought, 'If we kin build our pride and joy over a micro fault line we kin lie easy in our beds at night knowin' we kin tap through to the magma any time the power fails us.' 'N so we did. I made a survey map – your Maw allus called it the 'Magma Carta', gee whillikins she was like to be the death of me afore I was the death of her – 'n we built our home right over the top of . . . YEE-AAARGH!"

The old curmudgeon had leapt six feet (1.83m) backwards as a column of molten rock shot suddenly ceilingwards. The pickaxe had been instantly vaporized, as had Eschar's left-hand little finger down to the second knuckle. He had given his daughter a wizened but courageous smile. "Now we kin cook breakfast," the old man had said before fainting into her arms.

Three days later the house was unpleasantly hot but they dared not open a window for fear of invasion by the . . . the *things* that they felt certain were lurking in the area. At nights they could hear thrashings in the shrubbery and cries of "Heaven have mercy 'pon thy soul, pig-jackal of male imperialism!" During the day it was quieter, but even so they felt unable to take the risk. Washing was another problem, since even the cold taps emitted nothing but a powerful spray of superheated steam. Sparsely dressed and perspiring vilely (apart from Miranda, who glowed slightly and gave off a faint whiff of lavender), the beleaguered group sat around the dinner table deliberating on the safety precautions they should take for the forthcoming night.

The party was now seven strong. Three of the newcomers came from the only other house in the neighbourhood, the home of the Widow Curmurring and her two adult sons Lech and Proby, both of whom had insisted on bringing their motorbikes, their boomboxes and their entire collection of country and western tapes with them. Even now the dinette was filled with forty kilowatts of a romantic ballad about saddlesores. The seventh member of the group was Sam Scrapie, who had burst into the Eschar home the night before, screaming about UFOs and clutching a spigot wound in the right biceps. Miranda had sveltely bandaged – "garnished" would be a better word – his injury using strips ripped from one of her lace petticoats, but the psychological wounds were more serious; even now, he huddled in his homberg and his long black raincoat, chainsmoking in a desultory way, and adding nothing to the conversation except the occasional Marlowesque item of studied taciturnity.

"I've seen gals with hearts of diamond and guys with bowels of liquid steel, but M-B-D is the first I've seen with a soul of carborundum," Scrapie said cryptically, stubbing out a cigarette on Whitlow's thumbnail.

"My baby kissed my calluses beneath a harvest moon," interpolated Hank Sidewinder and the Saddleblankets tunefully.

Whitlow sucked his thumb, choking back the curse that had sprung to his lips. *Thumb-sucking – a sign of emotional insecurity in the normal way,* he thought feverishly. *People who are emotionally insecure can do the most terrible things, taking out their anguish on anyone nearby. They say that the worst multiple murderers were usually robbed of nipple-comfort in babyhood. Folk never realized that a tiny thing like that could instil a lifelong psychological inner loneliness in the human individual, so that he or she was driven to violence in order to express their urges to get closer to the rest of humanity. Like M-B-D . . .*

"Say!" exclaimed Whitlow. "I think I know what's wrong with . . ."

"Shaddap," said Proby, jacking up the volume of Hank Sidewinder and the Saddleblankets to drown Whitlow's interruption. Spitting a gobbet of gum at a nearby rubber plant, he sleeked back his greasy hair and eyed a scantily clad Miranda speculatively. His eyes were filled with a piggish frenzy. "Wooden mind gettin a fistful o' your nates, ma'am," he muttered under his noxious breath.

Miranda ignored both men and turned to her father. "Dad," she shouted over the information that Hank Sidewinder's true love had pluckily excised his hemorrhoids with her teeth, there being no other suitable surgical instruments in the wastes of Vulch Gulch at the time. "Dad!"

The Professor raised bleak eyes to gaze at her. "Yes, m'dear," he mumbled.

Miranda saw his lips move, but could hear nothing. She swung round to face Proby. "Excuse me," she said, a modest blush suffusing her features, "would it be at all possible to turn the volume down a little, Mr Curmurring?"

"Shaddap," said Proby. "Bitch like'n you needs gang-bangin coupla times but good, take alla sassiness outya ass."

Miranda, who had understood about one word in five of this, looked confused, but the remark brought an instant reaction from Proby's brother Lech.

"*You bastid!*" shrieked the younger Curmurring. "Cain't you hear what the little lady just done said? You turn ol' Hank right off or I's'll beat yore teeth right outen the back of yore skull!"

Miranda looked at him gratefully, and he silently thanked his foresight in investing in that home-study course in advanced etiquette.

"Shaddap," Proby responded, turning up the volume yet louder, so that the boombox jounced about the table. The distortion became so bad that nobody could any longer work out the lyrics, which was probably just as well, Hank Sidewinder having moved on to describe how he and his blue-eyed baby had coped with the simultaneous problems of (a) disposing of unwanted haemorrhoids and (b) imminent starvation. "Y'know," Proby continued in philosophical vein, "womin like that needs a man to beat some sense into her."

Lech's fist lashed out and connected with Proby's teeth, which sprayed to all corners of the room. Proby looked startled, and was slow to react. Another haymaker caught him, this time on the ear, and a fountain of blood shot out to spatter against the wall. He kicked back his chair, and whomped the still-blaring boombox into Lech's groin; the sickening sound of crushed genitalia for a moment drowned even Hank Sidewinder. The younger man was momentarily nonplussed, but within a fraction of a second plunged a fork into Proby's adam's apple, twisting as he struck, so that gore flooded down onto the tablecloth. Proby tried to vomit in pain, but the vomit never reached his mouth, instead gushing fitfully out of the hole in his throat and covering the front of his greasy GEORGE W'S THE MAN sweatshirt. He shook his head groggily and emptied his bowels, then seized his younger brother by the throat and dragged him through into the adjacent laboratory, where he threw Lech into the slowly expanding lake of lava.

"Boys will be boys," cackled the Widow Curmurring, helping herself to another portion of salad.

"All good, clean fun," breathed Whitlow nervously, closing the laboratory door to muffle the mingled screams and virile laughter.

Miranda wrung the vomit out of her brassiere before putting it back on, a vision which startled Scrapie temporarily out of his reverie. "She's about a hundred ten pounds, but a hundred twenty of that is woman," he conceded morosely, lighting another couple of cigarettes.

Miranda ignored him. She switched Hank Sidewinder off – despite a protest from the Widow Curmurring that she thought the bit about gristle getting stuck between your teeth was real lyrical – and addressed her father. "Daddy," she said. "Something you said when you were making your volcano has been puzzling me."

"Oh yes, little daughter?" said the ageing scientist, turning a loving paternal eye towards her.

"You said . . . I think I've got this right . . . that you'd been the death of Mommy. What did you *mean*?" She leaned forward in anticipation of his response, and Whitlow noticed that if he moved slightly to his left, as if to pass the port-style Californian Château Phiktyonlist, he could just see the rim of her . . .

Pinned by her eager gaze, the Professor looked shifty, but then he glanced at the darkened window, beyond which roamed the . . . the *things*, and he braced his shoulders as if coming to a difficult decision. He looked in turn at each of the people round the table – red-headed voluptuous Widow Curmurring, cowering Sam Scrapie half-concealed behind a shroud of smoke, Miranda glistening healthily in the heat, and Whitlow with, for some reason, saliva dribbling down his chin – and he nodded to himself. He took another pull at the wine bottle, and his speech thickened as the raw alcohol hit his bloodstream.

"Miranda," he said, "There's something I've been meaning to tell you. I'd hoped to wait until your mental age had approached puberty, but I guess you might as well hear it now. It all started when you were just a babe in arms . . ."

A sudden crash interrupted his discourse. The five of them swivelled in alarm to stare at the laboratory door. Even soundproofing could not smother the noise of Lech hurling his elder brother through the toughened glass of the picture window there, or the hideous screams that started up in the garden.

The fortress had been breached . . .

CHAPTER SIX

EVACUATE?

I don't want to sound facetious but people only die once. You've
got to get it right and make it as rewarding an experience as it
can be.
    Dr Michael Rudolph, quoted in *Shepherds Bush &*
    Hammersmith Gazette, 1987

Insert finger in bottom and twist.
    English instruction on French shaving-cream aerosol

one

Had anyone been watching Professor Lester Pustule as he read, they
would have noticed that his eyes had become a solid obsidian through
which refracted the flickering red lights of the sulphurous fires of Hell.
Satanic music, so faint that it was on the far limit of audibility, filled the
dust-strewn air of the great library: it sounded as if a child were
inquisitively, tentatively but swiftly stroking a bow across the slack
strings of a broken Stradivarius. Yet Professor Pustule heard it not.

    Indeed, he heard nothing, for his attention was rapt. The arcanely
evil words of that despicable, loathsome, suppressed, vile, pululating,
odious, nictating, repellent, repugnant, noxious, abhorrent, abominable, tory, execrable, nauseous work, *Ye Boke of Guts*, moved as if on a
conveyor belt before his eyes. He had never seen anything so obscene in
all his life, yet strangely he was finding the experience rewarding, as if he
had spent the last few decades waiting for just this nameless moment . . .

    . . . and Skark the Festering did beget Boil the Otromacious. Then in the
    time of Freen did the True Ones creep from Muglu, the Mother-Ocean,
    and they did feed upon the sand, and find it good. Spineless and holy
    were they, as were the cockpits of youth, for naught ventured they under
    the prebuscum. Yet pneumonoultramicroscopicsilicovolcanoconiosis was
    more than just a word to them.

Lo, did those hight Vertebrata *creep also upon the land, for this is the word of our ancestors; and did they hungry go till did Spod the Cocculate, of great memory, propose the Joining for, said it, "might it not be a wizard wheeze to be carried from place to place rather than slither the whole effing time". Its words fell on deaf ears, for the True Ones in those days had no ears; neither eyes nor lips had they, and the anus had yet to be developed. And with many an owche did Joining proceed, and they that did not Join were Lapsed and paid a Forfeit when that they did Join later, for Spod the Cocculate was an hairy tract. And for many a year and oft did the Joined Ones reflect upon the dualistic nature of their being, until the Formless Beast known to them as* Brain *did come amongst them and conjoin with them in the occipital region.*

And there was no Gooseberry.

Spod the Cocculate did die, when that it was that colostomy was invented, and in its holy place did Jurg the Lanceolate reign. Jurg the Lanceolate did reject its own Brain and devize Greek civilization, for was there not many a giggle therein? And Jurg the Lanceolate did beget Herpes the Socially Respectable, which begat Scum the Nuj, which invented parturition. And in those days the land was ravaged by rampant vaginas, which did savage the descendants of the True Ones until the time of Rtgh the Strangled. For it was not that . . .

Jeez, thought Professor Pustule, *my sister's nine-year-old could do better than this!* He threw the book into a far corner and left the British Library, never to return.

His footsteps echoed in the marbled silence of the great museum, their pace accelerating as the conviction came over him that there was someone – some . . . *thing* – following him. Yet, when he turned his head to look in stark terror, there was nothing to be seen in the cobwebbed shadows, nothing but the mummified corpses of the attendants, with rats squeaking as they played among the dusty ribcages. Reassured and at the same time *not* reassured, Pustule walked yet more swiftly, until he was moving in a graceless, scuttling half-run. He scampered past the furtive figure of Melina Mercouri, thrusting bits of rock into a carrier bag; past the special exhibition of Cleopatra's socks; past the souvenir stall, with its racks of much thumbed postcards and its heaps of cut-price books – and then he halted. Hist! Was that a sound he heard, somewhere in the vast emptiness of the museum? A sound as of a wooden lid being pushed inexorably upwards? Almost as if, amidst the desiccated tissues of a long-dead Egyptian potentate, there yet stirred some hideous life? Could it be that . . .? But no: surely not! Yet . . . perhaps . . . Maybe . . . Before his eyes there flickered some dry pages he had half-read in *Nature* several evenings back while cursing an injudicious vindaloo. What had the article said? Something about . . .?

But it couldn't be! It must have been a hoax! In this modern technological age no one believed any longer in curses! When George Edward Stanhope Molyneux Herbert, Fifth Earl of Carnarvon, had died in 1923 during the excavation of Tutankhamen's tomb, it had been of natural causes! *Hadn't it?* People are constantly keeling over with their faces half-digested and their genitals stuck on poles – Clyster's Syndrome, as the medics called it. When Howard Carter had died in 1939, locked into a windowless attic with a stake through his heart and with his head bitten off by an alligator and placed in a different room, everyone knew that the genial archaeologist had simply been trying to act out a John Dickson Carr mystery. *Hadn't they?* Or might it . . .? Never! That way lay madness! It was only . . . well . . . so many Egyptologists seemed to be dead. So were millions of ancient Egyptians. *Could this all be coincidence?* Or was it . . .? His mind boggled, then wondered how it had been able to. Look at Caesarion, son of Julius Caesar and Cleopatra! An innocent lad, yet cruelly slaughtered by Augustus after Cleopatra's death. Her ghost was reputed to have wailed: "Dead, and never called me Mummy!" Might it have been that . . .? Had Caesarion died simply because he was an ancient Egyptian? Were *all* ancient Egyptians cursed to be savagely murdered by digestive tracts? But curses, curses were *too* incredible! Think of all the ancient Egyptians who were still alive! Think of . . .

He decided to stop thinking and just run.

Outside, the wind was blowing through the trees so that the leaves keened a sepulchral song. The sky was overcast, preternaturally dark; clouds scudded across a dimly gibbous sun. Sleet fell on the empty pavements and even on Pustule's face, its icy coldness startling his foetid mind into some semblance of sentience. Surely out here he was safe . . . *but where the hell* was *everybody?* His terror-stricken eyes roiled this way and that, but the whole of Bloomsbury seemed to be deserted – not even a car moved. It was as if time were frozen. The only sound was the soughing of the leaves, and in his fevered imagination their song began more and more to resemble a requiem. He forced himself to slow to a walk. He squelched through the discarded condoms towards Tottenham Court Road. Despite the urgings of his intellect, he refused to look behind him. Had he done so he would have seen . . . *nameless horror!*

Somewhere, an owl hooted.

As he stood, minutes later, on the Northern Line northbound platform in Tottenham Court Road tube station, feeling commuters crammed up against him, but not caring because at least they were *people*, he was suddenly toppled onto the live rail by what eye-witnesses later described as "a slithery thing, sort of like a set of bagpipes made out of squid".

Huge voltages surged through Pustule's body, creating spontaneous combustion. His gastrointestinal gases ignited, and the ensuing explosion spattered pieces of protoplasm the full length of the platform. Flash-dried blood painted a great brown blotch on the tunnel ceiling. The station was filled with the stench of burnt flesh. His eyeballs erupted ichor at hypersonic velocities, decapitating an entire party of schoolchildren. His hair stood bizarrely on end, like iron filings titillated by an electromagnet, in the microseconds before his scalp blew off to suffocate a busker. His genitals, his point of contact with the live rail, glowed red-hot, weirdly illumining the downturned faces of a few mildly interested bystanders.

Strangely, he survived all this. What killed him was when the incoming train mashed his brains into a steaming pink-grey porridge that filled the trouser turnups of seven insider-dealers . . .

two

FitzSputum, the elderly retainer, moved slowly about his tasks, his ancient back bent and weary but nonetheless stiffened with a certain steely pride - the pride born of a sense of history, of heritage, of tradition. For over a hundred generations there had been FitzSputums holding this office for the timeworn family, the Cadavers. Now that the last remaining member of the line, Sir Bufton Cadaver of that Ilk, was in the evening of his years, it was fitting that FitzSputum, too, should be going to his grave without leaving issue.

Only one thing ruffled his elderly brain-cells. What, what, *what* was going to be the fate of the Ancestral Cheese of the Cadavers?

It was a strict family secret as to when the Cheese had first been made, but FitzSputum knew that it was a very long time ago - indeed, his own father had asserted in an off-guarded moment that it dated back to before the time of Christ. From various shards of abruptly cut-off conversation which FitzSputum had accidentally overheard, he had pieced together part of the story. When made, the vast Cheese had proved so appetizing that the original Cadaver had ordained that it should not be wasted in an immediate orgy of gluttony, but should be allowed to ripen until it reached the perfect pitch of maturity. Years had passed, until the years had turned into decades and eventually centuries, but still each succeeding Cadaver had forborn from declaring that the Cheese had reached perfection. At some time during the first millennium of its existence the first FitzSputum had been appointed to the post of Tender of the Cheese, and this had become an hereditary office. A complete wing of Cadaver Castle had been turned over to the Cheese, and each day FitzSputum would go there three times - at dawn, dusk and midnight - to utter the ritual incantations and perform the prescribed intricate acts of obeisance in the awesome presence of the Cheese. Otherwise, so Cadaver family tradition dictated, the atoms of all of their ancestors would be wrenched from their graves and cast off into the outer darkness, and the name "Cadaver" would become a curse on the lips of all mankind for eternity. A twentieth-century codicil to the family tradition acknowledged the emergence of the right to strike by adding that the same applied to the FitzSputums, too.

It had hardly been necessary, for the FitzSputums were welded to their job by fierce, monomaniacal devotion.

The Cheese had started off as a huge one – no one now knew how huge – but over the millennia it had slowly grown, thanks to generations of FitzSputums pouring over it the thrice-daily ration of turned milk. Now it was full forty fathoms (73.15m) high and almost as broad, and it quivered gelatinously in the East Wing, sending out a noxious aroma that had charred the countryside for miles around. Few living beings moved among the stunted vegetation that somehow survived in the environs of Cadaver Castle, and so the family secret was still safe.

Wheezing drily, FitzSputum took down the ritual bucket from its hook in the kitchen, and went to the outhouse to fill it with milk. Here, again, the local ecology worked in the Cheese's favour, for the Cadaver estate's few misshapen cows produced milk of unparalleled foulness – a viscous, vile, astringent liquid that had been largely turned to yogurt while still in the udder. Four of these godforsaken animals stood beside the outhouse now, as they or their ancestors had done thrice daily since time immemorial. FitzSputum looked at them with something as close to affection as his withered mind could manage. There, propped up on her two good legs, was Stinkwort, the pride of the herd. Beside her lay Bindweed, her stolid face flecked with nasal mucus from her neverending bout of bovine 'flu. It had been a long time since Bindweed had moved around under her own power, and FitzSputum had taken to bringing her bales of grass and removing the resulting waste products with a shovel. Deadly Nightshade was in better condition, being able to pull herself, with asthmatic chokings and occasional vomitings, from place to place. FitzSputum had once thought of exhibiting her at the County Show, but Sir Bufton Cadaver of that Ilk had vetoed the idea, pointing out that FitzSputum might have difficulty getting home in time for the dusk obeisance to the Cheese. Finally, there was Venus Flytrap, who was almost certainly dead. Nevertheless, for reasons unknown to orthodox science, her remnants continued to produce what passed on the Cadaver estate for milk. It was just a pity, FitzSputum mused as he looked at her, that bits of decomposing udder tended to come away in your hands as you milked her.

It'll be the end of an era when Sir Bufton and I meet our Maker, thought FitzSputum, *and the signs of the end are all around us. Change and decay in all around I see . . . even the local uranium has a statistically significant shorter halflife than theory predicts.*

Still, there was a job to do, so long as he could continue doing it. He moved about his task of milking.

A little later, he was donning the traditional family gas mask and asbestos suit. Unknown to scientific historians, these had been invented in the AD300s by a retainer of the Cadavers, just around the time when the Cheese had really begun to enter its prime. Generations of Tenders of the Cheese had worn them with pride although once, in a moment of rashness induced by illicit sampling of his master's port, the present incumbent had suggested that purchasing new ones might be in order. Certainly the design and portability of the originals left a little to be desired. FitzSputum coughed up a mixture of phlegm and blood as he climbed bodily into the gas mask - and rued the fact that even this was time-enshrined.

The trek to the East Wing was a laborious one, and as usual it took him the best part of half an hour. *Dragging half a ton (about half a tonne) of gas mask and protective suiting is no joke*, thought FitzSputum, but he went about his task with a will. The bucket clutched firmly in his hands - now so emaciated that the ivory of the bones showed through - he plodded miserably onward. The gas mask began to overheat, but this was customary - and therefore desirable. However, he was only too acutely aware how outmoded the device really was as occasional whiffs of the Ancestral Cheese penetrated science's defences to corrode his lungs.

Once upon a time the East Wing had presented a vista of grandeur, but that was long ago. Now that it had been handed over entirely to the Cheese, the very stones themselves had rotted. The windows were long gone, of course, and the expressions on the faces of the gargoyles were curiously apt. Holes showed in the roof, marking the abrupt departure of the family bats. Even Great Aunt Oesophageal Cadaver, who had been kept in the attic because of her hideous physical deformities and her whimsical practice of castrating the footmen, had fled the presence of the Ancestral Cheese - causing a sudden outbreak of major mayhem in the Home Counties before being offered a job in Hollywood and then returning home with much needed millions. No, nowadays this was the Cheese's territory, and its alone - except for the thrice daily visits of its Servitor.

Today FitzSputum rather gingerly creaked open the great oak door of the East Wing. He had had the impression, over the last few weeks or so, that there had been someone or some . . . *thing* watching him as he executed the rituals of Tending. He didn't know *why*, exactly, but the feeling was certainly there . . . a feeling of spiders waltzing up and down his vertebrae. Several times he'd found himself turning around in a reasonable approximation to a spin, looking to see if someone were observing him from behind. Quite how such an individual could survive in such a blue-white hell as this he had no idea, but the horrible, crawling sensation was still there . . .

The horror that anyone other than a FitzSputum might be privy to the secrets of the Cheese!

The Cheese was bubbling and spitting much as usual. Things seemed perfectly in order although, as he watched – a little warily – part of the Great Staircase disintegrated, crashing down with a horrific *splurp* into the very bowels of the suppurating Cheese. Yet . . . and yet FitzSputum was still disconcerted.

However, he knew his duty and so he set about it. First there came the Great Cadaver Bolt, a relic of the Crusades brought home by some half-forgotten Cadaver as booty from a mosque in Jerusalem. FitzSputum, like generations of his family before him, had not long after birth been drilled through the neck and fitted with a bore, so that he would be able to don the Bolt. That done, it was the time to sing the Ancestral Cadaver Song of Triumph in Adversity. Few of the words could be distinguished through the snorkel of the gas mask, but they went something like this:

Fair of transport, fair of favour:
You say Cadaver and I say Cadaver.
You say Cadaver, if you'd rather:
Then you'll say Cadaver and I'll say Cadaver.

It had, perhaps, not been one of Tennyson's better efforts.

The time had now come for the Ritual Ensorcelling of the Ancestral Cheese of the Cadavers of that Ilk. FitzSputum had often wondered if this could not have been made a little more formal, a little more solemn, but tradition had it that all he had to do was cast his bucketful of turned milk at the Cheese while simultaneously keeping his fingers in his ears, to avoid the deafening noise as the Cheese hissed and spat on its encounter with the new raw material, and reciting the Lord's Prayer backwards and in Serbo-Croat. With the ennui of endless experience, he performed the act, the last of the thrice-daily rite. As ever, the Cheese did its stuff; as ever, he waited while it did its stuff; as never, it swilled down the milk and turned towards him with what appeared to be an attentive expression. A pseudopod of decaying deliquescence gestured towards him, then at the bucket. The meaning was clear.

The Cheese was asking for more!

FitzSputum, for the first time in a long and largely ossified life, panicked.

"Ommigod!" he screamed as he ran from that charnel house. "Sir Bufton! Sir Bufton! The Cheese has come to life!"

three

David Whitlow could hardly hear himself think. It wasn't the dawn that was coming up like thunder.

"Calm down!" he cried, leaping up to stand on his chair. "We're animals, not human beings, for chrissakes!"

Miranda helped herself to another grape, and looked at him casually. "It's all right, David," she said. "Sam just had too many cigarettes. He'll be all right soon. Daddy was just about to tell me something about my Mom."

The Professor's eye twinkled as he said: "Sure, hon, but don't you think we'd better fight off the . . ."

"Oh, *Daddy!*" expostulated Miranda. "You're always trying to find excuses not to tell me things! You don't have to be ashamed of what went on between you and Mom! I'm not a little girl any more, you know! I know all there is to know about storks and gooseberry bushes. Do tell us your secret!"

"Well," said the curmudgeonly old scholar, taking another gulp of wine, "it all started a long whiles ago . . . shay, David, m'boy, haven't you got a terrible shecret you'd kinda like to shlip in firsht 'fore I get shtarted?"

"No," said the youthful genius. "Not right now."

"Ma'am?" The Professor looked at the Widow Curmurring.

"Wyall, there was my adulterous affair with Buffalo Bill Clinton," she began, "but every gal's had one of those."

"Not me!" came a cry from the garden, followed by a reflexive "Hallelujah!"

"Nor me neither," said Miranda, a furrow crossing her brow. "Stop stalling, Daddy."

"Howshabout you, sir?" said Professor Eschar, looking hopefully in the general direction of Sam Scrapie.

"Secrets?" said the private eye. "I've seen a million, kept a million. There're girls in this city look as if buttermilk woulden melt in their mouths."

"Thanksh," said the Professor after a moment. "Well, I guessh it'sh godda be up to me . . ."

"No, wait a minute," said David. "When I was in Egypt . . ."

"Too late, buster," said the Widow Curmurring. "The Perfesser's starting. This oughta be hot."

"Well, Miranda," said the aged academic, draining his hipflask, "thingsh started to go wrong between your Mom and me not long after you were born."

"Did she . . .?"

"Not that I know of. I guessh it wash mainly my fault. I ushed to kind of hide myshelf away in my laboratory, inventing panacheash and like that, and I guessh it made her feel lonely. Whatever the truth of the matter, when I finally deschended from my ivory tower I realized that she wash no longer the woman I'd married."

Miranda looked perplexed. "Who *had* you married, Daddy?" she said.

"Never no mind, hon," said the old man, draining the Widow Curmurring's hipflask. "Your Mom had turned into a being demented. She kept rushing out and joining bookclubsh, getting bargainsh by posht, knitting booteesh for you – you ash wash all innocent and liked nuthin better than shucking yore toesh. She had the teevee on twenty hoursh a day. She wash . . . no, I can't deshcribe it. Shay, David, you got a hipflashk?"

"No, it's just that Miranda isn't wearing very much."

"I wash horrified," continued the Professor, sulkily, "and I thought I ought to do shomething about it. But what should I do? It washn't like she wash chertifiably inshane or like that; jusht that she wash shpending too much on junk we didn't need. The crishish came when she tried to buy a copy of *Furniture From Fruit* from Barnesh 'n' Noble using a plashtic sheshterche she'd gotten from shomewhere. The shtore detective got her shooner'n thinkin. Yore Mom shaid she'd of shold her assh for a copy of that book, and ash a sheshterche wash worth two and one-half asshesh, later four, Barnesh 'n' Noble wash doin okay, but they shtill sent her to the Chair." He hammered his face against the table. "But the guilt, *guilt*, GUILT ish all mine! You shee, kiddo, I wash the one that gave her the plashtic sheshterche! I'd found it shomewhere, and I'd given it to your Mom and told her to go and shpend it, that it wash worth money!" The Professor began to sob uncontrollably.

"So *that's* where . . ." Miranda blurted. "Oh, cruel God to punish me like this!"

David Whitlow looked green.

"Ain't too many gals assassinated two Kennedies like I done," remarked the Widow Curmurring absentmindedly, picking at her elegantly varnished nails.

"Oh . . . Oh . . . *Godddd!*" squalled Miranda, clutching her dessert fork convulsively. "Daddy! It would never have happened if . . . if I hadn't . . ."

"If you hadn't what?" said Professor Eschar, raising his head, hope beginning to spring into his eyes.

"Oh . . . Oh . . . *Godddd!*"

"You just said that," observed the Widow Curmurring.

"Oh . . . Oh . . . *Godddd!*"

Even Sam Scrapie looked interested. "Third time lucky," he quipped.

"I was," wept Miranda, "I was . . . I was the one who got that plastic sesterce! I got it in a packet of farinaceous glup! It was a Free Introduction to Kulture! So the whole thing's *my fault!*"

"I think you're overreacting," said Whitlow.

"Had a lesbian affair with Margaret Thatcher once," interposed the Widow Curmurring.

"Yes!" shrieked Miranda. "But you don't realize! My first tooth fell out when I was only eighteen months old, and Daddy said to put it under my pillow with a coin! Well, the nickel I'd stolen from Mom's purse turned out to be a dud, so I used the plastic sesterce instead! Oh . . . Oh . . . *Godddd!*"

"How interesting," said Whitlow, with studied calm. "But I rather think we'd better . . ."

"No!" cried Miranda. "I have told a lie! I didn't get that plastic sesterce from a packet of glup at all! It was given to me by . . ."

She turned around in her seat and pointed.

". . . by *you*, David!"

The youthful genius picked up the saltcellar and twirled it idly between his finger and thumb. "I guess you know what you're talking about, Miranda," he said. "But, er, wouldn't you like to forget those last few words?"

"Never - *never!*"

"Well," said David, blushing, his ears filled with the screams of the Curmurring brothers as they stuffed molten lava down each other's trousers, "the story of the plastic sesterce really begins with my solitary homosexual experience."

Miranda gasped, thrust her fist into her mouth, and chewed her knuckles. Tears of grief poured down her cheeks. She wasn't quite sure what a homosexual experience was, but she was certain it was nasty. Her father's chin dropped onto his chest with a loud *ker-plunk*.

David paid the Eschars no attention, just carrying on in a low, almost wistful tone - as if he were reminiscing nostalgically. "It was 'way back when the Prof and I were travelling in Egypt looking for proof of our - my - theory that papyrus was actually an intelligent hive-organism from the planet Sirius." His eyes glazed over as his mind roamed into the realms of yesteryear . . .

. . . the two of them had wandered through the Valley of the Pyramids, taking photographs and sand-samples. Long before, they had left behind their camel-drivers and, for that matter, their camels; now they were just two expatriate Americans clad in khaki shirts and khaki shorts, suffering from anal pruritus. David's pith helmet [he suddenly recalled] *had kept slipping down over his forehead.*

Some time on the second day they had met up with a Briton, a Professor Pustule, who like themselves was hoping to make the archaeological discovery of the century - a different discovery, natch: he believed that Erich von Däniken was a reincarnation of Akhnaton, there being no other plausible reason why von Däniken's books should be so at odds with perceived history. Pustule's reasoning went thus: If you had to write about your own lifetime would you prefer to describe yourself as (a) a mentally retarded schizophrenic psychopath with sadistic delusions of deity, or (b) an alien from another planet? David had found Professor Pustule's arguments oddly convincing . . .

That night they had camped in the shadow of the Sphinx. Eschar had quirkily cooked up one of his justly famed chilli con carnes on the battered primus stove, and the three of them had tucked in with a will. Afterwards they had lain on their backs, staring up at the vault of the heavens, where the Milky Way arched like a great, um, arch, and the stars were like the diamonds on the finger of the most expensive whore in Istanbul (as Professor Eschar attested). David Whitlow, then only a teenager, had felt movements within himself, and had ignored the conversation going on between the other two men - discussions to the effect that they wouldn't mind changing the Sphinx's enigmatic smile into a kind of satiated leer and wow hadn't they got whoppers and things. David felt, in an odd moment of prescience, as if his intestines were about to part company from the rest of his body; he took a mouthful of grit to try to calm his inner traumas, but it was all to no avail.

Somewhere, an owl hooted.

The flames of the primus stove were guttering and the vampire bats were beginning to susurrate in the gloaming, but still the two elderly academics talked on. David felt as if his bowels were on the point of explosion, and began to creep off, seeking out some shadowy place where he could void himself without embarrassment. In the lambent moonlight he could see the complacent facial expression of the Sphinx and he thought to himself that it would be only fitting if he could vacate himself near that enigmatic stone deity . . .

No sooner thought than halfway done. He had trotted eagerly around to the rear of the great megalith, and with his willing feet had dug a hole in the shifting sands. Over it he had squatted when, suddenly, . . .

In the years thereafter he could never quite remember what had happened next. However, he had woken in the morning with a fundamental pain to find Professor Pustule looking smugly sated, Professor Eschar giggling at a selection of polaroid photographs, the Sphinx seeming much as usual, and a plastic sesterce on his bunkside table with a card on it saying: "You've had a homosexual experience, and I have the photographs to prove it. Keep quiet, or there's more where this came from."

He had kept obediently quiet, but on his return to New England he'd found a gurgling baby called Miranda, had fallen instantly in love with her while changing her nappies, and had given her the plastic sesterce . . .

"Kinell," said the Widow Curmurring, "'sthatall? Don't really rate with the time I gave J. Robert Oppenheimer an enema."

"Look, fuck it," shouted David Whitlow, turning on her, "we don't want to hear about your squalid little second-rate secrets! We're talking True Guilt here!"

"What's an 'enema'?" said Miranda.

"It's a ..." said the Professor, then stopped. Through the laboratory door there could be heard a hideous sucking noise, as if some arcane creature were pulling the liver piecemeal out of a living hick.

"Say!" said the Widow Curmurring brightly. "My boys have never done *that* before!"

It was the last thing she said ... in this lifetime.

four

Barbara Waterbrash was terrified. All day long she had been copy-editing the manuscript of a new horror novel, which, because it had arrived rather late, had to be ready for press the following morning. All the other staff of Gastron Books had gone home, and the offices were dark and emptily echoing. The only sound was the scrape of her pencil across the page ...

But what was that?

Another sound, so quiet it was right on the margin of inaudibility, came to her ears.

She looked at the page in front of her. Could it be that, as the novel suggested to her subconscious, there was a carnivorous pig in the next office?

Her mind skipped back to previous horror novels on which she had had to work.

Had an army of psychopathic slugs invaded the Gastron offices? Or might it be that an infectious fungus was even now planning to assault her? Then ... then ... what about the likely possibility that a plastic man might stagger into her office and melt all over the carpet? Rabid lemmings scampered painfully across her inner eye. And only the other week she had been reading about man-eating porcupines ...

Then there had been the famous book about the rapist walrus - written, it was rumoured, by a member of the royal family. She had had to copy-edit an illiterate text in which tomatoes had ravaged the landscape, pressing their sexual attentions on nubile virgins. And what of the high-voltage maggots, which had the habit of leaping *kamikaze*-fashion out of British Rail sandwiches? Not to mention the bizarre reproductive habits of filofaxes, which planted their eggs inside luckless yuppies, so that the victim's body was slowly devoured by the multitudinous emergent larvae?

She eyed a nearby paperclip with distrust.

She had read about armies of *Escherichia coli* rampaging all over the home counties, and she knew that you could never trust a rabbit. Kittens, too, were particularly vicious, being well known to look out for any opportunity to massacre their owners with flame-throwers. Even chairs – she shifted nervously in her seat – had been known to sprout teeth and devour their unsuspecting occupants.

So what was that slithering *noise in the next office?*

The sound came again.

Could it be . . . guts?

No: surely not! But maybe . . .

She got to her feet slowly. The darkness in the room intensified, as if by a hidden signal. Whatever the dread in the next office, she must know its nature – animal, vegetable or mineral.

She crept silently to the door, and with exquisite grace prised it open by a fraction of an inch. She applied her right eye to the gap . . . and then her whole body relaxed. She returned with a cheerful sashay of her hips to her desk – and to working on the manuscript.

Thank God – it was just that the editorial director had finally got back from lunch . . .

five

Somehow, Sir Jake Bunyan had survived, although the irritating habit his testicles had of dropping out was sorely trying his patience.

His hideously disfigured form staggered across the office. He ignored the concentrated hydrochloric acid eating into his thighs, and turned his mind instead to the problem of reaching a telephone: the sooner he warned the authorities about the dangers of the murderous digestive tracts the better! Too late now to pen the headline which his mind, in the midst of all its agonized torments, had conceived to describe his experiences – GUTCHA! He was no longer concerned with saving his own life – that, he had minutes before assumed, was forfeit – but his thoughts were of all the world's children, the yet unborn, the elderly . . .

He dialled a number.

There was no reply.

His belt bulged as his assailant crept ever higher . . .

six

"Trouble is," said Bimbo Erythropsia, "gettin to fuckin think I got an accidental dose of the fuckin active principle of the GUTS machine.

Whoops – fuckin sorry, Kurt . . . fuckin stupid of you to have worn fuckin wellies."

The three conspirators were lurking in the gloom outside the secret GUTS establishment. As Erythropsia had explained from time to time during their approach, the giveaway to foreign agents was the large sign outside pretending that the factory manufactured My Favourite Ponies. "There's fuckin commies swarmin around here, just tryin to discover our democratic secrets," he had repeated.

Kurt Salpinx squelched a few paces to one side to examine the electrified fence more carefully. "*Scheissenhausen*," he muttered, "but we must use all our skills to get through this. *Ich haben ein* plan, though."

L. Ron Melanoma looked cautious. He remembered Salpinx's billion-year plan, which would have annihilated every gerbil in the Universe. Fortunately, because of the prevalent darkness, Salpinx could not see Melanoma's face.

"Well, shall we fuckin cut the wire?" inquired Erythropsia. "All we gotta fuckin do – sorry about that L. Ron – is just go in there."

"Right!" said Melanoma.

"Ace on, baby," said Salpinx, adding: "If I spik dis right in your yankee patois."

"Did anyone bring any wire-cutters?" asked Melanoma, in a moment of sudden anxiety.

"Yes," said Erythropsia, "Kurt did."

"Damn," said Melanoma.

"But . . . but," stammered the youthful politician, "*du* said *das du* were going to . . . *verdammt!*"

"Oh, well," said Erythropsia, his face wrinkling into a grin of disappointment, "I guess we'll just have to . . ."

"*Nein!* Lickspittle lackey of a Senegalese *schweinhund*," shouted Salpinx. Melanoma moved to try to hush him, but it was no use. "I – yes, *ich*! – vill *mein*self *bite* right through their fellow-travelling fence!"

"It's – uh – electrified," muttered Erythropsia doubtfully, but Salpinx ignored him and strode forward, determination written in every pace. Ignoring the sharp pebbles and gravel at the fence's base, he threw himself face-downward at it and began to chew. Sparks failed to fly – and Melanoma suddenly realized one of the many advantages of having expanded-polystyrene teeth. On the other hand, he reflected, there were disadvantages, too – one of which was becoming all too visible, even in the gloom, in the form of a growing patch of white powder around Salpinx's head. The wires seemed unimpressed by the attention they were getting.

"Say!" exclaimed Erythropsia after a futile while. "I gotta fuckin idea!"

Melanoma looked at him dourly, and tried his best to muster some enthusiasm from somewhere. He was becoming increasingly filled with the conviction that this entire enterprise was doomed, that he had been wrong to believe the *Swab* when it had said that Salpinx was the Great White Hope of the Future and promised a million Mini Metroes to the first reader correctly to guess Salpinx's star-sign, that he should have stayed in his old field of agricultural PR and steered well clear of politics, that . . . "Oh yeah?" he said dubiously.

The American was struggling with his pockets, the tattooed bald eagle on his scalp crinkling with concentration. "I's sure I fuckin had fuckin one around here someplace," he gritted.

"A can-opener?" said Melanoma, with sudden optimism.

"No, a fuckin . . . ah, here it fuckin is. Look at fuckin this little beauty!"

Melanoma did his best to, but the light was poor. It seemed to him as if Erythropsia was holding a parsnip aloft. "Er, Bo . . ." he began.

"It's a bottle of a well known new-style fizzy beverage," hissed Erythropsia.

Melanoma made muffled baffled noises.

"Look," said the ex-Marine, and dramatically he tugged off the crown cap with his teeth. "*Look!*" he repeated, and dramatically he sent the evilly bubbling fluid in a great arc over the area of the fence nearest him. "LOOK!" he whispered very loudly, as dramatically the wires went white-hot and melted fizzingly away, dropping in great gobbets of molten metal onto the patchy scrub-grass, so that puffs of smoke went up.

"Wow!" said Melanoma.

"Vov!" said Salpinx, in imitation.

"'S fuckin easy," said the ex-Marine with a modest shrug. "I knew the liquid would short-circuit the electrification and fuckin do that."

"But I thought . . ." Melanoma began.

"Mind," added the Sergeant, "the stuff's got a fuckin half-life of only about fifteen years, so we'd better get over that ground fast."

"Zen fast ve will get over it!" said Salpinx with zeal, although a part of his mind reflected ruefully on the unwisdom of lying on the ground anywhere within ten metres of Erythropsia . . .

seven

"Is that all?" said the Prime Minister when Sir Jake Bunyan finally got through. "It's hardly hold-the-front-page stuff, is it? Where's the left-wing subversive element?"

"You can't expect a journalist of principle to make up a loony-left-council story every day, you know," gasped Sir Jake. Acid was eating away at his navel, and the pain made it difficult to remember the proper tones of respect. "This isn't just an exclusive – aaargh! – this is the real thing, a genuine emergency!"

"Well . . ."

"You could declare war on them!" screamed Sir Jake. "Think of it – our gallant boys against the slithering tides of evil."

"Hmmmm," said the Prime Minister. "*Now* you're talking some sense. There could be another knighthood in this for you, Buboes, you know . . ."

Further words were drowned as Sir Jake's left lung was wrenched from his chest. He tried to keep the noise down, but–

"That *hurt*!" he snapped testily.

CHAPTER SEVEN

CHITTERING CHITTERLINGS

A liquid mud of silicates and lime,
And with this mud was other mud, a slime,
A viscous ooze, a dimly vibrant plasm,
A pungent, flowing mass – Great God's orgasm!
Victor Purcell, *Cadmus*, 1944

Let me show you the shape of my heart.
Back Street Boys, "Shape of My Heart", 2000

one

*My name is David Whitlow and I remember everything, oh God, everything, all
the months of horror . . .*

The haggard figure stumbling across the burning sands paused suddenly. Partly because he'd tripped on a whitened skull and fallen over;
partly because, like Darwin standing back to contemplate his first great
insight, it occurred to him that important links were missing.

*How did I get here? Where is this terrible endless barren alkaline desert plain?
Why do even the ravening vultures sheer away from me as though I were a thing
accursed? What happened to my lovable all-American characterization?*

From the final, enigmatic words of the Widow Curmurring (and
how did he know they were final?), his memory faded into a blank. An
uninventive blank where even the feeblest traces of literary inspiration
had failed. A terrible endless barren alkaline desert blank. . . and here his
parched brows knotted for an instant as they smelt out a connection, a
metaphor.

Must make a note, he thought with something of his old scientific detachment. *Mysterious olfactory powers of knotted brows. Could be a whole heap
of Pentagon SDI money in that. Bunkers full of frowning superpsychics aiming
X-ray lasers at incoming Samovar nuclear attack waves by ESP scent-power
alone! I must write a technical paper on it right away, for immediate publication
in the* National Enquirer . . .

His flight of fancy veered sickeningly off its runway and crashed into the immovable, granite-like fact that in this waterless waste there were no pens, no paper, no handy lapel-mike recorders. Come to think of it, no lapels either. No palmtop, no photocopier, no coffee machine, no Celeron-based dedicated word processor with quadruple 100-gigabyte hard disks, automatic split infinitive checking and 3D nude entertainment channel. Whitlow had been stripped of the scientist's most basic tools.

I suppose I could sharpen one of these whitened human bones against a rock, if there were a rock, and scratch my notes – my warning to all the world – into my own tender cringing flesh, if the skin weren't falling off a bit from the third-degree sunburn. And if I had any notes.

The thought of his scarred, shrunken, dehydrated body being discovered months or years hence by the survivors of the holocaust (*and how do I know there are going to be any survivors?*) spurred him on. He had to think. To wrench his mind from its yearning towards cool trickling water tumbling in icy cascades fed by the heartbreakingly pure ice-melt running laughingly from high and forever white-capped mountains where chilly winds perpetually breathed their moist promise of dazzling snow or soft caressing rain . . . *stop that.* To plumb the deep wells of memory, the uncharted oceans of subconscious thought, the hidden rivers flowing to that sunless sea which was the all too common plot device of amnesia, there to fish up the lost, subaqueous facts, all wet and succulently dripping from their long immersion . . . *control yourself, Whitlow.*

The broken contacts still arced and sparked and smoked in the decommissioned power-house of his mind. Keys which opened unknown locks. Crossed lines on the switchboard of perception. Remorseless food-mixers slashing their way through lumpy stews of metaphor. Long slimy hollow threads which if followed aright might lead to the very heart of . . .

But here Whitlow's tattered stream of consciousness ebbed, soaked up by the thirsty sands. *Heart of . . . oak? Darkness? Gold? Midlothian?* The pitiless sun flailed at him with rays like a cat o'nine-tails, the merciless wind scoured his acne like the hot, panting breath of an open Bessemer converter. Eroded by the long mindless stumbling over sun-seared grit and scoria, one of his favourite toes had fallen off.

Desperately Whitlow probed again, sensing key words which might open the safe-deposit vaults of memory to release a sparkling, bubbling flood of clear, fresh spring water which – *down boy!* Words floated up into his ravaged awareness, charged with an obscurely nauseating power. He tasted them on a mental palate, his forebrain puckering up at the connotations and their acrid, pungent flavours.

"Tube." "Slimy." "Hollow." "Long." Something made him group the words together, though no pair of them seemed actually to rhyme. But darker and more enigmatic lexicon-shards were pressing in on him:

"Barker." "King." "Straub." No matter how he rearranged them from the initial alphabetical order, they wouldn't form a sentence. "Lovecraft." Whitlow had never patronized sex shops, and dismissed this piece of mnemonic jetsam impatiently. "Campbell." "Koontz." "Blyton." Had the faintest sense of incongruity mingled with terror in what now passed for his mind? "Smith." "N." "Guy." This too evoked nothing, apart from a small pool of vomit at which he stared disconsolately. Since there was no other sustenance visible this side of the burning horizon, it was only logical . . .

But there were limits. He clung desperately to this hope. For some writers there were still limits of good taste, surely?

This pathetic illusion was shattered when a hitherto mercifully dead zone of memory lit up like some satanic Christmas tree, in a torrential deluge (*no!*) dust-storm of horrific recollection triggered by a second emergence of the fateful word "Curmurring" . . .

two

"Needs must when the devil drives," said Professor Eschar guiltily, with the air of coining a startlingly novel epigram. "A rolling stone in the hand is worth two in the needle's eye. Waste not want not."

"Oh Daddy," said Miranda, "what have we done?"

Sam Scrapie nonchalantly struck a match on his chin and lighted up. "Well, kiddo, if you want it spelled out, it looks like there was nothing to block that laboratory doorway against the writhing commie horror that took out the young punks and then wrenched the door off its goddam hinges. Nothing big and fat enough in the room except . . ."

"The psychology is fascinating," Whitlow put in. "As though a sort of Group Mind formed instantly amongst us, realizing that sacrifice of its least important component was necessary for the survival of the greatest number. You know, like travellers in sledges being pursued by wolves and having only one grim hope of placating them. Or castaways in an empty lifeboat with just one possible source of food. Or a group of writers realizing that one of their number will have to be sacrificed – thrown to the oncoming journalists, to suffer questions like 'What name do you write under?' and 'Do you ever get published?' while the others make good their escape. Or again, it's a bit like—"

"Shaddap," interposed Scrapie. "She didn't feel much. Doubt it was even a new experience for her. The old girl had been around."

The Widow Curmurring made no sassy comment, wedged as she was into the narrow laboratory doorway with odd bits of furniture plugging the slender gaps around her. She'd hardly struggled at all once the Group Mind of Eschar, Whitlow, Miranda and Scrapie had taken its desperate action, but her still plump and perky rear end seemed to regard them with a certain eyeless, voiceless reprobation. None of them cared to think what the other side of her might look like now. In death or undeath, at least, parts of the Widow might now be sentimentally intertwined with parts of her two staunch sons: in sheepshanks, perhaps, or clove hitches, or bowlines.

"She seems to be holding them," Whitlow muttered nervously, over the slurping noises which still dimly came through.

"I hope this isn't going to make my problems of immemorial guilt too much worse," said Eschar.

"Oh Daddy, don't say that, it'll only give you another flashback to your earlier life of forbidden occult tamperings with Professor Lester Pustule," cried Miranda somewhat ambiguously.

"That wouldn't advance the plot at all," Professor Eschar said with sudden grumpy pique. "Our final search for unspeakable knowledge was a complete failure." But it was too late . . . the room was already wavering, slanting, tilting into italics . . .

The two occult explorers, dabblers in accursed secrets, had descended a thousand dank steps below the shuddering sub-cellar of the strange high house whose gambrel roof brooded over the oldest quarter of time-cursed Milton Keynes. The fitful light of the gibbous moon sent no ray into this fungus-ridden abyss, where blackened and disfigured stonework was tortured into eldritch, cyclopean geometries, as though wrought by some elder race of nameless abominations which frothed in primal slime for unhallowed aeons before the birth of mankind. It had won several architectural awards.

"These stairs," whispered Professor Eschar, *"are* of no human shape."

"What do you see?" said his companion, Lester Pustule, *holding the lantern high. The crumbled, blasphemous vault was heaped with evilly mouldering tomes, their mere covers a threat to sanity. An unnamable, charnel stench pervaded the nauseous air, seemingly a foul exhalation from some abominable lavatory of the Great Old Ones themselves.*

Trembling, Eschar stooped to peer at the awful texts, hideously revealed in the feverish, guttering light . . . and slipped on a patch of foul ichor. "Great God," *he croaked in a paralysed voice.* "Here are copies of the sinister *Liber Ivonis, the infamous* Cultes des Ghoules *of the Comte d'Erlette, von Junzt's hellish* Unaussprechlichen Kulten, *and Ludvig Prinn's remaindered* De Vermis Mysteriis. *The forbidden* Pnakotic Manuscripts, *the unreadable* Book of Dzyan . . . *and there, see! Bound in monstrously garnered human foreskins, nothing less than the abhorréd* Necronomicon *of the mad Arab Abdul Alhazred!"*

There was a terror-laden pause before the eldritch reply smote upon Eschar's fear-crazed ears –

"We've got all those, *dammit . . . but is there a copy of* Earthdoom *by David Langford and John Grant?"*

When the extreme, soul-chilling irrelevance of this recollection had sunk in, there was a little silence.

It would go better as a limerick, Whitlow was thinking, while Miranda in her simple yet enormously big-busted innocence was naively proud that dear Daddy knew all those long words. Perhaps he'd explain them to her one day.

These people are nuts, Scrapie brooded. *But kind of nice nuts. That floozie, she's got something - two somethings - and maybe she could be my kind of girl. Hell, I could take her away from that no-balls Whitlow guy just like that, as easy as snapping my, snapping my, God damn it, you put the second finger against the thumb like* this *and then you –*

"Ouch!" he said aloud. "Sorry, folks. Sprained my trigger finger taking out the Syndicate bosses at the Poughkeepsie old folks' home. Still gives me twinges on rainy or volcanic days . . .

"Anyway, never mind that. I wanna put my cards on the table. The Feds asked me to look into this Guts business on account of I'm a guy who's not himself mean, who is neither tarnished nor afraid, you betcha. But maybe the Feds aren't the guys to be working for, at that; maybe it's a big cover-up and they know more than they're saying. Maybe they even started the whole mess."

"No," said Whitlow, "actually the Professor and I—"

"Shut up," joked the kindly old dodderer, emphasizing his little quip by ramming an elbow into Whitlow's teeth.

"A guy like me's always keeping his eyes open for the tiniest clue," said Scrapie, not noticing this by-play, "and I dipped into a coupla UTTER TOP SECRET/READ AND EAT/FOR THE PRESIDENT'S EYES ONLY files I found kind of lying round the Fed joint. A Lester Pustule got mentioned, so that sort of backs up your story, prof. There was an Interpol report on some weirdo neo-Nazi (that's Eurotalk for creation scientist) in Paris, called Kurt Salpinx, who seemed to have a cute angle of his own on the guts biz. I only got a peek at report number three, but that was near Paris too: some kind of hot new weapon called GUTS. Stuff they reckoned I didn't need to know for my assignment.

"The hell with them. You call in a private dick, he wants to see the whole big picture. When I cracked that wild computer-crime caper down LA way, they found they couldn't keep secrets from Sam Scrapie. Once I knew the inside dope about their data transfer protocols, and they knew that I knew, they just cringed back - yellow - as very slowly I drew a bead on them with my snub-nosed RS-232 interface. Down these mean streets a man must go who is not himself mean, who—"

"Is this leading up to anything?" yawned the Professor.

"Yep. The key to half the jigsaw is in Paris. You're a part-time encephaloneurologist and dilettante (it says in the dossier here) – your laboratory's gotta have the equipment to contact this Salpinx. Two heads are better than one, so maybe five'll be better than four."

"Ah," said David with sudden insight, "that would bring together some of the excessively numerous and diverse threads in a plot which is already far too—" Before he could enunciate his final damning adjective, an uncontrollable fit of coughing was hastily written into the dialogue.

"My cotton-pickin' laboratory is on the other side of *that*," Professor Eschar snapped, indicating the gently pulsating mass which had been the Widow Curmurring. "We're besieged and helpless! There's nothing we can do about the danged world situation!"

"Bullets won't stop them," Whitlow confirmed.

"We're all going to dieee!" Miranda summarized.

"Sleep the big sleep," Scrapie corrected. "Yeah, I felt that way myself once when Greasy Luigi of the Little League Baseball racket had my feet in a bucket of concrete and a tactical nuclear device chained round my neck, right on the bank of the East River. Careful guy: he was wearing brass knucks and had six of his stooges covering me with tommy-guns. But did I wet my pants? Well, yes I did actually, but I still walked away from that one in the end."

"How?" asked Miranda, eyes delightfully, poutingly wide.

"Uh, couple of cops came by in a prowl car and Luigi's boys had to pretend it was all a practical joke. Never paid me back for the crapped-up Gucci shoes, though. Or the underpants."

"So," said David Whitlow in a voice like a leaden submarine making its first crash-dive with all hatches open, "your philosophy's to wait around until some heavy assistance turns up."

"Good respectable philosophy too," averred the Professor. "Micawberism. Subscribed to by every little old world government since the year dot."

"Not much help when you're besieged by enough rogue intestines to keep the entire population of Germany in *bratwurst* skins for the next century," Whitlow snapped eruditely. "What do we expect? The US Marines? The cavalry? What kind of high-powered heavies could we persuade to help us in a guts-ridden neck of the woods like this?"

As Scrapie spat, the Professor shrugged and Miranda sensuously fainted, a voice sounded near the house almost as though in reply to Whitlow's impassioned rhetorical question . . .

"Well, jiminy, I's still here waiting for you-all male oppressor motherfuckers, by Saint Betty Friedan and Saint Valerie Solanas and (lawks-a-mercy) Saint Germaine Greer, Hallelujah!"

three

Ms Abigail Condyle wasn't particularly moved by the hysterical warnings now being broadcast on all radio channels at one-minute intervals. Loose bowels and peripatetic peritoneums, even if such absurdities could be believed, would be only the tiniest of fifth-decimal-place additions to the surging horror of New York life as it was perceived by Ms Condyle.

The forces of darkness had been laying siege to her Washington Heights apartment (zip code NY 10040, she thought mechanically, the very number a blatant code message inserted by commie infiltrators of the mail service) these last twenty years. She regularly triple-locked the windows against the ever-present threat of exhibitionist muggers who at the drop of a trouser might climb forty feet (12.192m) of sheer wall and spray chloroform at her. Inside, the walls were lined with aluminium foil and triply earthed, to block the mind-control rays beamed in her direction by aliens dwelling undetected in our midst. Take that Mr Hayden in the next building: once, when routinely checking out the sidewalk through observational telescope number four, she'd seen him with a *science fiction* book. What more obvious giveaway could there be?

Then there were the alligators which as every child knew roamed the sewers. The story of their being former pets, flushed down the john when they grew over-large, was too pathetically transparent a cover-up. A moment's logical thought showed that they must be trained CIA alligators, sniffing out illegal magic-mushroom crops down there in the bowels of New York. It was a tedious business locking and unlocking the heavy grid over the toilet bowl, but a woman couldn't be too careful when there was a chance of drug-crazed alligator snouts erupting into the apartment. Ms Condyle was a determined survivor.

The most implacable shock-troops of the armies of the night were inevitably the cockroaches. Her right thumb was enlarged, browned and callused by constant use of the terrible eyeball-popper thrust learned in the self-defence classes (How To Emasculate A Male Attacker Before He Has Even Noticed You!), which with careful aim could spatter the most resilient roach over several square metres of surrounding wall and floor. Commercial anti-insect devices were less effective, but still dotted the apartment: a typical specimen was the Roach Assault Course, which subjected its tiny victims (attracted by the aroma of six ounces of rotting hamburger meat, which needed to be replenished every ten days) to a cyanide spray, massive doses of gamma rays, microwave flash-heating and high-speed stereo replays of the complete Presidential speeches of Ronald Reagan. But even this multiple onslaught could take out only a percentage of the now evolved and mutated prey: the building's hardy super-roaches had defensively become poison-immune, radiation-resistant and deaf.

And (she allowed herself a thin-lipped smile) they expected Abigail Condyle to worry about this new "guts" scare, simply because it was devastating the world! It wasn't her problem at all. Like that harmless AIDS flap.

She moved through her thrice-daily security check, testing the locks and bolts on doors, armourglass windows, cupboards, cookie jars, the icebox. Her vacuum cleaner hummed and purred through the entire apartment, sucking away each last microscopic food particle which might give sustenance to the Enemy. The most perilous moment came around as it always did: the remote video cameras were turned this way and that, scanning the no-man's-land of the lobby to make sure the coast was clear before she switched off the apartment's 12,000-volt door handle and lock which so usefully deterred casual rapists.

So: a quick vacuuming of the lobby, with dextrous movements of the cleaner's long flexible hose – which she sometimes dreamed of using to devastating effect by plunging it into the groin of an intruder bent on molestation. Then the anti-roach sprays, a wide spectrum of deterrence: disinfectant, Mace, paraquat, Zyklon-B and Californian wine. She worked quickly, moving nimbly through the memorized pattern of mines she'd laboriously set into the lobby floor. A final quick sortie to the very stairwell – handgun, grenades and tear-gas pencil at the ready – to empty out the trash . . . and then, dragging the vacuum cleaner back into the safety of the apartment, she re-erected the outer defences. Nothing could bother her now till morning. Nothing, not even the tiniest of dwarf roach-eggs, could have slipped past her eagle gaze . . .

Those who watch magicians' performances often say the same, with a puzzled and doubtful look.

The quickness of the . . . *something* . . . deceives the eye.

Ms Condyle was consulting her horoscope (Virgo) about the ideal choice of lethal antipersonnel weaponry to take to bed in case of night-time emergencies such as brown-outs or UFO landings, when her trained nostrils detected an unfamiliar whiff. A faint scent better not described. An elusive stench for which the authors are running out of euphemisms.

Then she heard the sound. It was a wetly fluttering, squittering noise, like . . . her prim mind rejected the simile, and even more hastily refused to consider the other simile.

For one stark instant she half-remembered that during the brief seconds out there in the lobby when she'd taken her eye off it, the hollow flexible tube of the vacuum cleaner had almost seemed, just momentarily, to have become limper and shinier and – damper? But her attention had been elsewhere as she carried it past the intruder-proof *Maginot*™ doorway defences.

Abigail Condyle knew instinctively, even before she turned, that the sound came from something long and slithery and Freudian-shaped and horribly *male*. An instant later, her mind reshaped the meaningless sputtering into toothless and tongueless strugglings, innocent of larynx or palate, to form syllables ... no, words!

Not being a literary sort of person (that was for dykes and faggots and bleeding-heart liberals and disguised Martians undermining God's own country from within), it didn't occur to her that the dimly perceived words were a bit derivative. Whether this made the horror more or less is difficult to ascertain ...

"Now ... we're ... locked ... in ... together ... for ... the ... night ..."

four

"Whose was it?"

"His who is gone."

"Who shall have it?"

"He who will come."

"Who shall *not* have it?"

"They of the European Cheese Mountain which is to be."

"What was the month?"

... Sir Bufton was a stickler for convention, and had refused to let FitzSputum's terrified reports interrupt the evening recitation of the Cadaver Ritual in the awesome, cobwebbed vastness of the Great Back Sitting-Room. This nightly litany of thirty-six hundred questions (spoken by FitzSputum) and answers (slurred by the Cadaver of That Ilk) had for countless generations prevented master and man from turning in early or catching any decent programmes on BBC2, even though for long centuries the Ritual's whole thrust and meaning had been obscure.

"How shall it be fed?"

"By milk and by cream, by curds and by whey, by hook and by crook."

"What shall be the preservatives?"

"Accursèd be all such."

"What shall be the artificial flavourings and colourings?"

"Thrice accursèd be all such."

"What shall be the mark-up for the retail trade?"

... The interpretation of the ritual answers had once occupied a lengthy parchment scroll which was pillaged during the Norman Conquest, secretly preserved by the Rosicrucians and incorporated in much distorted form into the Communist Manifesto. A companion text, being the considerably more complex interpretation of the questions, had been hopefully sent off by Sir Ruthven Cadaver (who had literary pretensions) to a book packaging firm called Caxton & Caxton. It had enjoyed a certain vogue as *Ye Countrie Diarie of ane Anglo-Saxxone Gentilhomme* but was eventually remaindered without trace at the Dissolution of the Monasteries. The explanatory footnotes had already been sold off, piecemeal, as Papal indulgences.

Only the glossary had survived into Elizabethan times: Francis Bacon deciphered it by the anagrammatic method and reported it to be an invitation for the King of Spain to site medium-range cruise missiles at bases in the Home Counties – an interpretation which had unfortunate results for Mary Queen of Scots. But the cognoscenti of Elizabeth's court whispered that Bacon had also slipped the stronger passages to some theatrical hack, who'd worked them up into a "gut-wrenching video nasty" called *Titus Andronicus* . . . Yes, the Ritual was bound up with the fate of England herself.

"How shall it be known?"

"Not as Gouda nor Tilsit, not as Wensleydale nor Cheddar, not as Roquefort nor Caerphilly, not as Edam nor Stilton, not as Red Leicester nor Double Gloucester, not as Brie nor Gjetost, not as Limburger nor Gorgonzola . . ."

FitzSputum always tended to go to sleep during this lengthy passage, and Sir Bufton would give him a kindly prod in the testicles with the ancestral Cadaver elephant-goad. Thus the ageing pair were bound together in their ancient cursed habitation, by bonds of unconquerable apathy. This lonely dialogue was one of the strangest and rarest relics of oldest England, preserved inviolate through the aeons like the country's inscrutable laws on pub opening hours. Once the Ritual had been a matter of utmost secrecy, but in these declining days Sir Bufton had had to throw portions of Cadaver Castle open to the public, to help feed a family overdraft almost as ravenous as the Cheese itself. Thus it was that two coachloads of Japanese tourists could be heard whispering behind the walls, jostling to poke their long-lensed Leicas through the ancestral Leper's Squint and capture the ceremony forever.

". . . not as Sage Derby nor Boursin, not as Feta nor Mozzarella, not as Camembert nor Gruyère, not as Lancashire nor Emmental, not as Mycella nor Parmesan. And thrice and thrice again, yea, nine times nine shall be accursèd he who names it Lymeswold."

"Who shall eat it?"

"Neither men nor women, but a little of either."

"When shall it be eaten?"

"When the Time is come."

"When shall the Time be come?"

"When it is ready."

"When shall it be ready?"

"When ye see the Sign."

("Oh God," both Sir Bufton and FitzSputum were wont to think at about this point of their immemorial double act. The forgotten author of all this magnificently prophetic rubbish, worthy and to be revered though he of course was, was prone to such debilitating attacks of loghorrea that one could see why he'd been so enthusiastically forgotten.)

"What shall be the Sign?"

"The Sign of Oliver Twist."

"How shall we know the Sign?"

"Look, mate, I can't do everything for you . . ."

CHAPTER EIGHT

INSIDE INFORMATION

> I will try to terrorize the reader. But if I find I cannot terrify
> him/her, I will try to horrify; and if I find I cannot horrify, I'll
> go for the gross-out. I'm not proud . . .
>   Stephen King, *Danse Macabre*, 1981

> He put the stomach back and began to feel around for the small
> intestine . . . That's when something bit him.
>   Simon Ian Childer, *Worm*, 1987

one

Sir Pierce Curette ("Pisser" to his old Etonian chums) was the most exclusive of Harley Street surgeons, and naturally had been immediately
called in when the Hon. Adelaide Scotoma-ffitch had complained of
"collywobbles". Nobody who *was* anybody would dream of having their
innards sliced out by a lesser man.

The rival consultant to the Scotoma-ffitches, Dr Stuart Suture, had
muttered darkly about X-rays and the possibility of a pharmaceutical
approach, perhaps even involving stomach mints and bicarb. - but the
upper echelons of the English medical profession had never taken old
Suture seriously. His very name had been a joke since youthful days at St
Swithin's Hospital. One of the more literary medical students of his year
(a man who, it was said with awe, knew that a "semicolon" had some
technical meaning quite different from the result of a partial colectomy)
had found the fateful anagram in a James Thurber essay. The perfectly
ordinary name Suture could be rearranged into "uterus" . . .

No, no doctor or surgeon could quite take Suture seriously, and least
of all that crusty old doctrinaire Sir Pierce Curette. Curette was a surgeon of the old school. For every ailment, from collywobbles to measles
to myopia to pre-menstrual tension, his solution was always the same:
Whip it out! His extensive collection of Bits I Have Snipped Out Of The
Aristocracy, lavishly preserved in vials of the finest cut glass, was the
envy of Harley Street. It was said that in the dead of night, when long

bleak sleepless hours seemed to lie ahead, Sir Pierce would lovingly withdraw organ after well remembered organ from the timeless embrace of
formalin, and let his sensuous surgeon's fingers . . . fondle them.

And at the end of certain indiscreet evenings at the Burke and Hare
Club, when the priceless Napoleon brandy sank low in its
double-magnum and swirled luxuriously in the great balloon glasses like
a perfect, pellucid urine specimen – then older surgeons hinted at more.
At withered lips caressing the relic of royalty's mastectomy, at strange
longings appeased by intimate parts from their erstwhile owners
untimely ripped. But then some stalwart of the medical fraternity would
growl, "Damn' fine cricketer in his time, mind you." The grisly
atmosphere of rumour would be at once dispelled by the knowledge that
Sir Pierce Curette was a sound man at heart.

Now, while Dr Suture fussed in the background and a nurse stood
ready with clamps and sellotape, the Hon. Adelaide Scotoma-ffitch lay
exposed to the urgent thrustings of Curette's favourite scalpel. With
creamy enjoyment he probed through the abdominal wall which with
an old surgeon's whimsicality he always thought of as a second and up-
wardly mobile hymen. She might be the most sought-after and icily inac-
cessible debutante of the Season, yet here she lay, opening her delights to
him in the intimacy of his private operating theatre whose walls were
lined with stimulating etchings of early amputation practice. His fingers
caressed the liver, so dark and smooth and glistening and looking good
enough to eat (a reminiscent smile flickered on his lips). Lifting her
dainty stomach a little way from its lushly red-lined bed, as soft as any
velvet, Sir Pierce gave the appendix a roguish little tickle.

He put the stomach back and began to feel around for the small
intestine, leaning close, lips parted in excitement behind the surgical
mask . . .

That's when something kissed him.

The mask was torn aside and something very like a pair of hot,
searing lips was firmly planted on Curette's wrinkled mouth. A slimy
loop whipped round his neck and dragged his head down, down, into
the luscious warmth of the abdominal cavity. Bliss turned into
revulsion at this shattering of the delightful, uncomplaining passivity
which so stimulated his failing glands. He struggled desperately to bite
his way free. To no avail. Seconds passed like hours as Curette's
withered, scorbutic lungs struggled vainly to suck some trace of
life-giving oxygen from notoriously anaerobic bits of the girl's
upper-class anatomy . . .

Someone was pulling at him, though, and with an abrupt sucking
squelch Sir Pierce was hauled free of the groping tubes which had held
him fast.

"Not done, old chap," said Dr Suture, sadly but firmly, indicating the toothmarks in the deliciously chewy liver. The pert-nippled nurse had, stereotypically, fainted.

"But . . . But I was . . ." Abruptly Curette saw that there was no longer any sign of whatever had seized him. Just perfectly ordinary intestines. Had he gone mad?

"We needn't discuss what you were doing, Sir Pierce." Suture's tones were steely. "By gad, in the days of Empire I know what your comrades would have done – lent you a revolver and left you alone to save your honour in the only possible way."

Sir Pierce Curette drew himself up to his full height, wiped his chin, and wordlessly dislodged a juicy morsel from his dentures. The appeal to the spirit that had made Britain great (and, subsequently, bankrupt) did not leave him unmoved.

"We haven't a revolver here, but one can improvise," Suture remarked. And he gestured at a certain piece of apparatus affixed to the wall. "I shall leave the room for five minutes before returning to complete the operation. By that time . . ." He clapped Curette on the shoulder, and added: "My certificate will say accidental death. For the honour of the British Medical Association, Sir Pierce."

Curette nodded his dumb acquiescence, and Suture strode from the room. There were things that were done and there were things that were not done, and when one has done one of the things that are not done there is only one thing left that one can do. Such was the Code.

All the same, Sir Pierce felt a faint resentment as, for the honour of the BMA, he jammed his head painfully into the limited space available for it. And did he imagine – just before his sinewy fingers put an end to a long and brilliant career by switching on the autoclave – a flatulent sound from the anaesthetized form on the operating table, a sound oddly reminiscent of a *giggle*?

two

Impasse.

To some people it's just a word, but to Sir Jake Bunyan it was too multi-syllabled and erudite to be the headline describing the situation in which he was trapped. Having given his warning to the world, his hands were free to hold back the *thing* which coiled around him like some nightmare memory of a public dinner whose menu was confined to Transylvanian ethnic food, prepared sushi-style. Sir Jake philosophically wondered how long it would take for his notorious vice-like grip – trained by a thousand kickbacks, a thousand editorial conferences where reporters tried to snatch the Glenfiddich away from you – to be dissolved by the acid secretions pulsing and spurting from the rogue digestive system in hot waves of pain . . .

TIED UP AT THE OFFICE, he thought automatically. PHEW, WHAT A STINKER! Just one measly vox-pop interview and he could head it GUT REACTIONS. Or a photo of a luscious page three evisceratee, sensuously dolled-up in kinky cricket pads, CLEAN BOWELLED! For a moment his ideas soared into the poetic empyrean with DIED INTESTATE and BLADDERS WRACKED and COLONS TO NEWCASTLE. Imminent death seemed to concentrate the mind wonderfully, though such highbrow literary flights could never be used in the down-to-earth *Swab* itself.

What was the PM up to? The radio should have declared the state of emergency long ago. Meanwhile he could only wait in growing agony, trying to distract himself by mentally filling in the *Swab* Kwik Krosswurd still visible beneath spattered blood and bile on his desk. *Term used of lubberly seaman (4)?* That sounded esoteric. *What one has to do to decks (4).* Hit the deck, H-I-T, no, that didn't start with an S. *Cotton wool thing found in hospitals (4).* For some reason he couldn't concentrate just now. To save time and money they never changed the crossword grid or answers from day to day, only the clues, so he should know . . . *Baws (anag.) (4)?* Damn, and he was usually so good at the anagrams, too. There was a sort of stripy insect with a sting – no, it eluded him again.

What was the PM doing?

". . . and I'm sitting here in this marvellous vantage point high up the Heathrow control tower," crackled the radio, "watching our absolutely super troops move into position for their first attack on Terminal Three. It's a magnificent day with excellent visibility and I do wish you could see the Armalite rifles glittering in the sun as our boys get ready to give a short sharp shock to the terrorists who are holding the entire cafeteria staff and supplies of Terminal Three to ransom after their failed attempt to hijack a Piccadilly Line train and divert its schedule to Pimlico. And, yes, yes, the tanks are moving in to support our brave lads with armour-piercing explosive shells, and, well I never, I do believe that's a cruise missile carrier in the rear! Yes it is, it *is*, what an inspiring sight, and I'm sure those two teenage terrorists with their imitation plastic guns are realizing now that Crime Does Not Pay, ha ha . . ."

What the hell use is that? fumed Sir Jake, not looking at his eroded hands, which by now might be a mere lattice of bones through which the *thing* was almost ready to burst. Or could this radio news be . . . a feint? A cover-up for some new attack? His nostrils, the nostrils of an old newshound from days when men were men and women were women and Page Three had to be filled up with a lot of boring old news, his nostrils tingled – encouraged perhaps by the gobs of steaming hydrofluoric acid which spurted from the implacable foe he held not quite at bay.

Something about the radio story didn't quite ring true. *Of course*, he realized. *It hasn't appeared in my newspaper.*

". . . and I think if you turn the volume up and listen very closely you'll be able to hear the first melodious little bursts of machine-gun fire as we warm up for what could be an absolutely super siege, whole weeks of live-action coverage from here in the Heathrow bar, I'm sorry I'll read that again, control tower. A puff of smoke, I can see this most indescribably dramatic puff of smoke, probably from where one of our lads has fired off a round of high-tech, state-of-the-art, smokeless ammo . . . what? Well yes Rodney, I suppose one of them could be having a quick ciggy. That's my colleague Rodney Cervix, who won't be getting much time at the mike if *I* can help it, and I'm your roving reporter St-John Walleye, bringing you coverage of what could be the most visually magnificent terrorist siege ever brought to you on radio, here at Heath – And Rodney's passing me a piece of paper, a small white piece of card about three inches by five with the very latest from official sources, and, and I can't read this, it's upside down, oh thanks, thanks very much, mine's a double . . . *And* this is the most incredible news! Heathrow, I can't believe this, is it a hoax Rodney? never mind, Heathrow Airport's Terminal Three, that'sh the *very* terminal you can see from here, or could see if you were here with us on this memorable occasion today, is the entry point for a vast conspiracy of illegal immigrants *no* inteshtines, a menace to our balance of payments which the Prime Minishter is, is, steps, taking shteps against with extreme prejudice, could be a great victory for our way of life here today, like Trafalgar, Waterloo, Dunkirk, cheersh Rodney, my throat *was* getting dry, yesh you're right, what a coincidence this coming up the month before the election ha ha ha . . . And if you were here with me you could see the truly magnificent martial spectacle of tear-gash grenades crashing with trained accurashy through the Terminal Three windows, and others bouncing with military precision back from the walls, landing amongsht *oh dear* what bad luck England! Own goal in the first few minutesh of the game, but never mind, we'll teach those shtinking foreigners. And the eyewash is being brought out from the changing rooms now . . ."

Sir Jake knew that he could relax. The PM had taken swift, decisive action after all. But some lingering survival instinct made him maintain his agonizing death-grip on the lashing, viscid horror which still sought his throat. *Before it finishes me*, he thought, *I could do with . . . a last meal.* It was a crazy, quixotic idea, a shout of protest against what had happened to him: "Buboes" might be suffering from two floating kidneys, a ruptured gall bladder and macerated nipples, but that wasn't enough to deter an editor of the *Swab*! It would make a good posthumous editorial, if he could use his tongue to poke the keyboard with enough agility to sketch out some notes for his successor . . . But alas, he couldn't reach the office's emergency stocks of caviar, frozen chateaubriand steaks and dehydrated Bollinger. His last meal would have to be more symbolic. *I never liked tripe or haggis*, he brooded, and then remembered the packet of potato crisps in one desk drawer. *What a way to go! COULD HAVE CHEWED CAVIAR, CHOSE CRISPS - needs pruning by about five words, but the seeds of greatness are there.*

Opening the desk drawer with his remaining teeth was a trivial matter. Laying the now saliva-stained crisp packet on the desk, he broke its seal on the sixth attempt by bursting it with a blow of his forehead. Then the final challenge of his life confronted him.

The little blue bag! How the hell do I get the salt out of the little blue bag?

"... amazing, truly amazing scene of incredible military discipline as our plucky lads charge in tight formation for the Terminal Three doorways and oh! *Foul* play there, very dirty play from the enemy, the impression I got was something long and slimy tied across the doorway so they all tripped over, funny they don't seem to be getting up again, just rolling around as though they'd fallen into a lot of flypaper, well, after that shocking dishplay I hope a referee from the UN will intervene, but no, play sheems to be continuing as this enormous tank moves in, two absholutely gigantic tanks, wobbling to the left and right as they closhe in on the two Terminal Three buildingsh, thank you Rodney I needed that, and now all four tanksh have come to a halt, ready I expect to fire their biggest shells, and now the hatch is opening and our brave boys are coming out, bayonet charge, over the top, shot in the back for momentsh heshitation and they're moving *away*, they're in retreat I jusht don't believe thish Rodney says something long and slimy crawled into the barrel of the tank'sh big gun but my eyeshight's perfect and I never saw that at all, at all, *and he'sh down!* The sergeant was retreating at top shpeed, a really masterly retreat the way only England can do it, and the thingsh are on him, more and more of them, almost ash though they were *recruiting* from shomewhere, oh *ugh* I'm not going to watch any more of thish, such thingsh oughtn't to be shown when young children might not be in bed yet, I've always been one thousand per shent against sense, sensh, erm, banning things but I do not think thish film should be shown in our schools even under medical shupervision ... And Rodney'sh handing me another piece of paper, two pieces of paper, and what it saysh on these pieces of paper, twice, is, oh, on the *other* shide..."

Sir Jake was petrified by the evident reversal of events. All the more because he'd just managed to crack the riddle of the little blue bag of salt (he'd gnawed a corner off, using the desk in place of his now-missing lower incisors). Was even his last meal going to be tinged with despair for the country's future? *We'll win through*, he told himself, and took the salt-bag between his lips to sprinkle it over the scattered crisps. Tremors kept running through him as he swung his neck left and right, the salt spraying wildly – like a military nerve-gas test – to cover a wide and unintended area of the room . . .

His slimy assailant convulsed! The death-coils tightened, loosened, tightened more weakly – went altogether slack. They did not move again.

Slugs, thought Sir Jake, with a sudden wave of enlightenment and inaccurate analogy. *We used to put salt on slugs in the garden, until the RSPCA inspector threatened us with deportation . . . it all hangs together!* And painfully he composed a victory headline: SALT CURE LOOSENS BOWELS. This could be the salvation of the country! In a minute or two, he hoped, he'd have enough strength for one last phone call to the PM.

". . . this shtatement, thish very important shtatement from the Prime Minister, I'm going to read it out to you the moment it shtops moving, thank you Rodney I was parched, what it shays is, 'Thish temporary setback was caused entirely by the dishashtrous mishinformation fed to us by the media. The Presh must be condemned most shtrongly. I shall be taking immediate shteps.' Yes Rodney, the Presh, doesn't mention broadcashting at all, I wonder what the newshpapersh have been up to now?"

Sir Jake sat in numb horror (also, in a morass of rapidly decaying digestive system). What chance was there after *that* of persuading the PM to take his advice about the best employment of the E.E.C. Salt Mountain? All was lost, utterly lost.

". . . and now through the absholutely magnifishent high-tech door another firsht for radio ish coming Oh God horrible what a can of worms we sheem to have opened ha ha ha no no Rodney and I are *presh* I mean *media* you know we're just reporters non-participants ouch we have thish ex-officio immunity argh glmmpf guggle guggle . . ."

three

"Fuckin clever eh?" puked Erythropsia, brandishing the two GUTS modules which they had smuggled out of the US base by an ingenious stratagem (deleted from this text for reasons of State security but due for open publication under the Freedom of Information Act in 2042, glory, glory).

"Say, that was an ingenious stratagem, Kurt," said L. Ron Melanoma. "The way you pointed and shouted *Ach, sacre bleu, eine femme Greenhamoise* in fluent French, and thus lured them into diverting all the heavy machine-gun fire and riot gas to the north perimeter! Cunning stuff."

"*Es was* nothing," grated Salpinx smugly. "*Wovon man nicht sprechen kann, darüber muss man schweigen.* That is *ein*other saying of Wittgenstein's – dear *alte* Ludwig! – meaning, let us not go into too much detail about the more unconvincing plot elements such as our recent escapade, *nicht wahr?*"

But Melanoma was still babbling in sheer amazement at his feat of continuing to be alive. "And you, Bimbo – incredible tactics! The way you tackled the six advancing M113 launcher/carriers armed with 557mm Lance-type liquid-fuelled inertial-guided nuclear battlefield missiles each weighing 1,285kg and having a range of no less than 112km! Well, gee, it must be SAS training or something, using no more than your own, um, bodily fluids to create a deadly slick on which they all skidded to ruin while we made good our escape!"

"A man's got to do what a man's got to do," gagged the burly American modestly. "It was just plain dumb luck I had to do it again right then. Or was it just luck? Maybe someone Up There watches over us, y'know. Maybe I was helped out in my hour of need by a Higher Power that jest reached out and *urrrrrrrgh* . . ."

Erythropsia's theological speculations trailed off – if a stream can be said to "trail off" when its simple babblings are swallowed up in the devastating flash-flood cataract following a cloudburst. Salpinx reminded himself that, fun though a revolutionary schism followed by a jihad against inane metaphysics might be, one should first wait for the Movement's following to reach double figures.

They re-entered Salpinx's simple apartment and sat again in the living-room, or *Lebensraum*, where at a snap of his fingers a torchlit procession of black-uniformed, leather-booted maidservants on roaring motorcycles brought in celebratory bottles of champagne and milk. ("Hiring servants costs *der Erde* these days," he muttered in a savage aside. "When *ich bin* dictator, the Amalgamated Union of Hirelings, Butlers and Flunkeys will be *erste* up against the wall!")

"*So,*" Salpinx remarked, in German, his voice heavy and ominous, hefting what resembled an Intimate Stimulation Mechanism of super-extra-titanic size, delivered to your doorstep in plain brown van . . . "The GUTS device is not as *verdammt* bulky as I feared. We do *haben* the right weapon?"

"Oh yeah," eructated Erythropsia. "It's the fuckin dispersal policy you see. Nobody can do a first-strike takeout of a country that's armed with GUTS: the weapon carriers are all guys on foot. Can't tell them from civilians except by the radiation signs on the launch backpack. Oh, and by the escort of six armoured cars and eight fuckin motorbikes in front and behind, of course. So there they are, scattered all over, the guy next to you at the bar or the movies might be a GUTS carrier vehicle – guaranteed retaliation! The Reds'd have to be totally nutty to try a fuckin disarming attack on scattered *bleurrrrgh* defence-in-depth like that!"

"Unless," mused Melanoma, who was not good at the subtleties of modern strategic theory, "the aggressor went for a scorched-earth policy of total spasm attack justified by the fact that any inhabited portion of the GUTS-armed country might be a military target?"

Erythropsia refuted him instantly, with cold tactical logic: "Nah, they'd have to be fuckin nuts to do that."

Salpinx registered impatience by petulantly discharging three full clips from a sub-machine gun and decimating the apartment's heroic statuary of perfect Nordic types. "Less of this talk. *Wir mussen* take action! As Wittgenstein once remarked to me, *Die Welt is alles, was der Fall ist,* meaning: 'Tomorrow the world!' We must test one of these so wonderful devices, in an area of high population density of course, *und* thereby create numberless converts for the Cause! The new man of the next millennium, the man of pure intellect, no longer ruled by the viscid churnings of entrails . . . But of course there may be danger and we should choose our test zone with care. *Ich* vote for Tel Aviv."

"Moscow, 'scuse my fuckin language," said Erythropsia.

"Paris," suggested Melanoma, who hated travel.

"But wait," said Salpinx, scanning one of the sheets of newspaper he'd vainly been trying to interpose between Erythropsia and some of his more valuable SS mementos. "It seems that while we strive to free men from intestinal slavery, Nature in all her wondrous resourcefulness may already *machen ein* solution of her own! Free digestive systems are at large in staggering *nummers*! Clearly our test must take place in . . . New York."

"OK by me," grunted Erythropsia. "Just so long as you keep that little ol' *gurrrh* well away from the Lone Star State."

Melanoma stared over Salpinx's shoulder and looked for objections (he was especially nervous about America, since he'd once been denied admission for displaying communist leanings – handling the publicity campaign for a hot new lipstick called Red Menace). "It says here the terror is spreading like wildfire," he whined. "It could be in Paris soon, saving us all those expensive air tickets. It could be in Paris already, seeking out the famous Kurt Salpinx to claim him for its own!"

"*Nein,*" Salpinx began; but the preposterously illogical and portentous build-up could mean only one *Ding*, or thing. A soft indescribable slurping sound surged and churned in the room; and even after Erythropsia had regained momentary control of himself, the sickly dripping persisted at Salpinx's front door. At the window, something clung and sucked. Behind the swastika-embroidered drapes which gave the forty-foot (12.192m) marble walls a pleasantly homely touch, the three men detected a movement and a glistening.

"*Teufel!* This looks like *ein* meretricious subclimax," Salpinx cried in horrid realization.

"OK," moaned Melanoma, "I take it all back, forget what I said, New York will be just fine by me, I *love* travel really . . ."

As a long slimy hollow tube reached vilely out towards them, making gestures in a universal semaphore code which none of the three understood (all having been thrown out of the Boy Scouts for interestingly different reasons), ex-sergeant Bimbo G. Erythropsia's battle-trained killer reflexes came to the fore.

Like the infallible Defence Early Warning system . . . he reacted.

Snatching up one of the GUTS radiation weapons, his fingers rotated the arming ring with a deftness all the more surprising for the fact that it was now obliterated by a thick lumpy substance resembling avocado dip. He still remembered the intricate three-digit combination which protected the ultimate anti-personnel weapon from un-authorized use. *Six turns to the left . . .*

Something glistening had wound its way out from under Salpinx's throne to coil itself about one scrawny ankle, and the incipient *Ubermensch* was straining uselessly to reach his drawer of anti-canvasser phosphorus grenades . . .

Six turns to the right . . .

A horrid flopping mass, like a soft bagpipes painted by Dali in un-usually bilious mood even for him, had enveloped Melanoma's head, oblivious of the desperate, defensive stream of hype, misrepresentation and hot air directed against it by the plucky publicity man . . .

Six turns to the, which fuckin way now? Yeah, left . . .

There came a muted click and whirr.

THIRTY SECONDS TO DETONATION, said a tiny, flat, synthe-sized voice. TOTAL LETHALITY ZONE WILL HAVE RADIUS 3.14 KILOMETRES. AUTHORIZED PERSONNEL SHOULD NOW WITHDRAW. TWENTY-FIVE SECONDS . . .

"Oh . . . fuckin shit," Erythropsia had time to say before a writhing mass of the worst spaghetti he'd seen in his life, even at Luigi's Place, en-gulfed him . . .

ENEMY PERSONNEL NEED NOT OBEY THE WITHDRAWAL COMMAND, said the device indulgently, and added: TWENTY SEC-ONDS . . .

four

Loathsome. An unspeakable abomination. A horror buried so deep in his psyche he can remember not a single detail of what it has done to him. He stands in the railway station and shudders uncontrollably . . .

It's been done, she thought gloomily. Come to think of it, I feel that way myself after British Rail bacon sandwiches.

OUT OF INNOCENCE CAME FORTH UNSPEAKABLE EVIL! The girl had been used as innocent host to the most hideous malevolence known to man, a horrific presence that, through grotesque acts of impregnation, is madly insinuating itself into the bodies and minds of thousands of unsuspecting people. The only hope is to destroy the original evil seed and . . .

Ho hum, she thought.

Long black glistening streaks of people-eating death! From out of the drains. From out of the sewers. From out of the bowels of the earth came the tendrils.

Some it kills quickly - they are the lucky ones.

It's a plague that cannot be halted. A creeping horror that threatens all mankind. "She felt a movement in her lower abdomen. This time she knew it was no muscle. There was something inside her. Something alive."

Clearly things couldn't get much worse than this. Or could they?

I yanked the knife back, stepping aside. The blade inside him turned into three parts. Guts and a gush of blood rushed out of him, splatting on the floor. He went in it face down . . .

There was something sinister, uncanny, resonant, adjectival about the recurring motif of terrible things happening to people's bowels. Portentous, even . . .

Barbara Waterbrash began almost to regret the strange, bittersweet destiny which had brought her from copyediting the Saccharine Throbs romances to this dark West End tower where a single lighted window glowed fitfully across the tempestuous pavement as she endured her solitary vigil of overtime amid the chill oppression of the Gastron Books horror blurbs for the Fall catalogue . . .

As so often after a long session of this numbing terror, she felt glutinous qualms drifting up and down her luscious and pouting vertebrae, like the floating, wobbling globs in that kind of table-lamp which thankfully was no longer fashionable. *Had* that been a strange repellent sound in the outer office? A whiff of foul, rank odour seeping malevolently under the door? That contaminating sense of intolerable loathing and degradation which in her brief time here she had learned to fear above all else?

Barbara Waterbrash shook her head irritably. Gastron Books maintained a battery of lethal, computerized security systems to guard against just this ever-present nightmare. The blood-drenched aroma of blurb copy was awakening childish fancies in her - only this and nothing more. For all her nauseous forebodings, there was just no chance at this dead time of night that the outer office could have been penetrated by . . .

Are you afraid even to think the word, Barbara?

An author.

Horrific - but totally absurd!

Yet surely there'd been a sound. A rustling. Indeed, if such a thing could be conceived (and why not, she thought, in this oxymoronic business in which each staggering new horror meant the same old permutations of yucky things happening to the softer portions of people's bodies) . . . a *slimy* rustling. Inwardly she lived through tormented aeons of horrific imagining, stomach-everting fear, unspeakable foreboding, soul-eviscerating dread, mind-numbing padding, brain-anaesthetizing padding, repetitive padding, and uvula-rending overdescription.

Then . . .

She stood up.

Nothing could be worse than this waiting.

Nothing.

Except a plethora of brief, overwrought paragraphs.

In fragmented sentences.

Without verbs.

The horror of it!

She could stand the paltry clichés of forced tension no longer. With mingled fear and annoyance she stepped perkily forward to open the fateful door.

That mephitic whiff from beyond time and space was definitely stronger now, bringing in its train a lifetime of dreadful associations: the time when at the age of five she'd eaten twenty-two meringues, the choppy English Channel crossing as precocious teenage "mascot" of eighty drunken soccer supporters suffering the agonizing pangs of Sealink pork pies in the hell below decks, and the vilely soiled pavements, gutters and lapels after last week's launch party . . . The link, the common factor shared by these stark images of nightmare eluded her. Could it be . . . olfactory?

No. Readers of these books didn't know the word olfactory. The whole idea stank.

She was at the door, delightfully sensuous bosoms akimbo, turning the handle, retaining an icy calm as inexorably the fatal portal swung open on darkness. Hellish brilliance flashed and crackled as her fingers found the switch for the strip lights. The . . . ambience, she thought, shyly toying with the half-forgotten argot of Lit Crit . . . the ambience was stronger here. But there was nothing to be seen.

Except that the empty IN tray, whose contents she personally had tipped into the maw of the high-powered shredding machine labelled UNSOLICITED SUBMISSIONS . . . was no longer empty.

She shuddered at what she saw there. A manuscript.

A very strange manuscript, though, she mused as she edged closer. It was handwritten (and at this she thought convulsively of the company flamethrower in her desk drawer, provided to cleanse the office of such abominations), and the writing glistened oddly, as though it were not writing at all but the oozing secretions of small, intensely literate snails. It conjured up the old story of how if you sat a million snails at a million typewriters and left them for a million years, you might eventually end up with – if statisticians were to be believed – a million keyboards coated with ineradicable slime.

Handwritten? She looked closer. *Hand*written? Or written by . . . written with . . . Barbara Waterbrash hastily stopped thinking along these lines, because it gave her a strange feeling in her . . . in her . . . *If I were editing this, I'd crack down on the over-use of ellipses,* she thought, and mentally translated for the benefit of the editorial director: *those little rows of dots . . .*

The title page of the strange manuscript did not carry an author's name. Nor was there the usual mistyped return address or scrawled line to the effect that all film, mineral and fishing rights were reserved by the author. The only visible words were occult and enigmatic beyond all be-lief:

TWENTY YEARS BELOW THE DIAPHRAGM
The Gutsy Autobiography of an Insider
With Index, Glossary, Anatomical Maps and Vermiform Appendix

"Oh God," said Barbara Waterbrash aloud. "After all that – just another sleazy, exploitative horror novel!"

Nevertheless her trained editing reflexes swung into action. Pausing only to tear up the title page and throw it away, she began to scan the damp, curiously iridescent text. And as she read, her eyes widened; the practised phrases of evaluation and comment ("Dear Sir/Madam, Thank you very much indeed for your most interesting submission, en-closed.") died on the end of her pencil . . .

CHAPTER NINE

LIKE ALL GALL

Strange the Formation of the *Eely* Race,
That know no Sex, yet love the close Embrace.
Their folded Lengths they round each other twine,
Twist am'rous Knots, and slimy Bodies joyn;
Till the close Strife brings off a frothy Juice . . .
      William Diaper (1685-1717), *Oppian's Halieuticks*

I had to fight with myself every time circumstances forced me to
put it down.
      Peter Straub, of Ramsey Campbell's *Incarnate*, 1983

one

Diana Phragm approached the Eschar house cautiously. The place had
an ugly reputation as the site of many sadistic murders, and the signs on
the gateposts had hardly reassured her: HERE BE MONSTERS and
ABANDON HOPE, ALL YE WHO ENTER HERE. Still, a Jehovah's
Witness's gotta do what a Jehovah's Witness's gotta do, and she was certain there were souls ripe for the saving in there. She tossed her long unruly hair back over her shoulder, smoothed her demure dress over her
thighs, clutched her tracts and her copy of the *Reader's Digest Condensed
Bible*, and bit her tongue. *Ouch!* she thought warily.

She was very conscious of the fact that she was beautiful, virginal and
a drug addict – and thereby a prime candidate, whatever her religious
convictions, for a gratuitous erotic scene. Curiously, she wasn't fearful
of this; if anything, she looked forward to it, because she regarded the
necessary self-abasement as a spiritual tribute to the Lord. *But not yet*, she
thought. Her heart lurched.

In the half-darkness ahead – lit up as it was by flickering flames and
Professor Eschar's colourful language – she heard an abruptly cut-off
scream. Swiftly she crossed herself.

She tiptoed forward, several thousand copies of *The Watchtower*
strategically positioned as a shield.

The leaves about her rustled.

The grass susurrated underfoot.

The tension mounted, inexplicably.

And then . . .

And *then* there was a further scream, this time from her left, and a rampaging-through-the-foliage noise. A strange, bizarre, semi-automated voice filled the air: "Hallegoddamlujah! I do declare you ass-tweakers are the socks of life. Walking dildoes! – I got my spigot stuck in this here tree. Saints have mercy. Which of you puritans deleted my last three expletives?"

Diana Phragm hugged herself nervously. People usually did. Ever since her infancy, when she had just learnt to burble her very first words – "In the beginning God created the heaven and the Earth" – people had somehow felt it difficult to feel affection for her. She had done her best – cutely reciting the entire text of *1 Chronicles* at parties and heartwarmingly exhorting her fellow schoolchildren to purge their sins – but still the other kids had tended to . . . avoid her. She knew not why. This curse of fate had continued into her adulthood. She had been rejected by every sorority in college, despite her ability to sing *The Song of Songs* to a ragtime rhythm, accompanying herself on the guitar (although she demurely refused to sing anything other than an expurgated version). After college, realizing there was a certain lack of males in her life, she had taken herself a few times to the singles bars around Times Square, but even there she had found no takers – no one to come back to her apartment and neck with her to the sultry sounds of Palestrina on the CD player. It wasn't, she knew, because she was unpleasing to look at – far from it: like almost every young female in the world (to judge by the statistical sample contained in this book), she was stunningly, mind-scorchingly, heart-explodingly, brain-batteringly beautiful, moved with a sensuous slink that beggared description, and had long and lustrous (if unruly) flaxen hair framing a face of perfect complexion. Still, for some reason . . .

And so she had turned, in desperation, to virtue, and joined the Jehovah's Witnesses.

The Eschars, she was certain, definitely required thorough saving. The girl had an unmistakably sluttish sparkle in her eyes, and Diana knew that the young scientist – Whitlow – stayed over at the Eschar house more nights than not. Her father, the Professor, seemed utterly complaisant about the situation – but he was doubtless a lecherous old goat who connived at the young people's forni . . . no, she couldn't bear to finish even thinking the word. (She always said "effects" rather than "furniture", just in case of a slip of the tongue.) Besides, faint rumours of the satanic Pustule-Eschar explorations had reached her ears. Perhaps the old goat even . . . in fact, this being the genre it was, he probably did.

She was startled from her reverie by another cry from the nearby garden. "May the saints be praised!" *Someone who speaks my kind of language*, thought Diana with surprised delight. "Don't asslick the cockthrusters, sisters!" continued M-B-D.

Diana was puzzled. Some of the other Witnesses could be induced to say "buttocks", but she was pretty certain that what the mysterious stranger had just said was very much more godless than that. She tiptoed to the hedge, and peered over.

What she saw in the spinechilling moonlight made her heart miss a beat.

Several beats.

Enough to populate the complete works of Jack Kerouac, in fact.

The whole lawn was a mass of seething, roiling *sliminess*, a bizarre vision made yet worse by the fact that there was almost complete silence in all this ferment of motion – just a sort of background noise composed of millions of small slithering and sucking sounds. Here and there among the rippling tubes darted the squat, distorted figure of that hideous bastard offspring of Malacia Furuncle and Basil-Duane, capering and dancing with obscene glee. Even as Diana watched, M-B-D seized one of the long tubes and with it began to gyrate in a vile parody of a serpent-dance. "Vengeance is mine, saith the Lady!" shrieked the bobbing monstrosity. "Aha! Lawks above, but me and my allies is gonna bumstrutting free the women (and robots) of the world, you can bet your sweet cottonpickin' socks we are! Praise be!"

Mad, thought Diana in panic and disgust, *quite mad*. Nevertheless she clutched her Bible closer to her bosom and prepared herself for what she sensed was to be the greatest challenge of her life.

"Woe unto the world because of evil!" she began. "It needs must be that evil come, but woe, woe, *woe* unto those through whom it come!"

two

"What we need here is a plan," Sam Scrapie was saying, idly tying one of the forks into a reefknot. The Widow Curmurring's ample rear end wobbled as if in agreement. "I mean, a man's gotta think what a man's gotta think, but that's what I think."

"Too true," said the ageing Professor testily, but nevertheless with a wizenedly encouraging twinkle in his feisty eye. "That's the first part of the process, sure. The second part is rather more difficult, though. That's the business of actually *thinking up* the plan. Anyone got any ideas. Miranda? No, I thought not. David? Yes, David, but I'm afraid we don't have any Saturnian death-rays. Scrapie? Well, I'm not sure if the rest of us are as highly trained in karate as you are. Er, Mrs Curmurring?" he added as a courtesy.

It seemed as if somehow – hideously – she responded, for from the direction of the laboratory a rather nervous female voice spoke: "Repent your evil ways and follow in the path of righteousness," it said.

"Well, that hardly seems like immediately practical advice," clenched Eschar, before realization hit him. "Who's that?" he cried.

"My name is unimportant; I bring you the word of the Lord."

"But how . . . *how* can you . . .?"

"Through faith. And through knowing the Bible thoroughly." The voice trembled.

"But can't you see any . . . er . . . long, tubelike things out there?" interposed Whitlow, his voice cracking under the tension.

"There were many of them here," the voice admitted reluctantly. "But they were all unrighteous and have gone from this place."

Scrapie let out a whoop of ecstasy. "I told you kids. I told you old Sam Scrapie's method never fails," he gritted, beginning to tug the Widow Curmurring's hefty form away from the doorway.

"Wait a minute, Scrapie," said the Professor urgently. "Don't you realize? – this could be a trap!"

"Nah. Don't you understand what's happened?"

"Er, no."

Scrapie paused from his struggles with the Widow Curmurring and chewed at a fingernail. ("Let go of my hand!" squeaked an outraged Miranda.) "When you've been in the detection biz as long as I have, Professor, you begin to rely not just on your brains but on what you college guys call 'instinct'. Me, I prefer to call it 'foot-thinking'."

"'*Foot*-thinking'?" gasped Miranda uncomprehendingly.

"Yeah, babe. 'Foot-thinking.' It's like all of us have a road to walk down, a street to follow, an avenue to tread, an alley to pace. And the things that are doing the walking ain't our brains: they're our feet. And after we've been walkin' for a long time and we've put away a few fifths of rye, well, we come to a corner, and we've gotta decide whether to keep walking straight down the road, or if we should turn the corner. And some people say it's our brains as decides we should go round that corner, but I say that it's our feet. And it's my feet that are thinking now, Professor. That's why I can see what's really happened, but you, because you're thinking with your brains, can't work it out."

"But *I* can!" rapped Whitlow triumphantly. Sudden blazing insight had hit his quick-thinking mind like a bolt from the gods hitting a sea of jello. *Of course! The woman out there's a Jehovah's Witness. No one has ever been able to explain before why so many people feel so much dread whenever a Jehovah's Witness comes to the door. But now I see it! Our digestive tracts are allergic to them! And why? Because they're natural evolutionary competitors, that's why! It was the word "tract" that first put me onto it . . .*

Tersely he explained these thoughts, while Scrapie looked on disgustedly, seething with unspoken fury as he saw moisture form on Miranda's maddeningly perfect upper lip as she gazed in undisguised admiration at the brilliant young scientist. "You've got most of the answers," said the street-hardened private eye grudgingly when Whitlow had finished. "Although there are a few details you haven't quite worked out."

"Such as what?" said Whitlow with genuine interest.

"Look, this isn't any time for talking," rasped Scrapie, renewing his tussles with the Widow Curmurring. "Can't you help me get this door clear?"

Between them they managed it, somehow. Miranda would have fainted when she saw the hideous sight revealed – the far side of the late widow – but, just to buck the system, had already done so. Certainly, it was disgusting to behold – too disgusting to describe, too hideous for anyone even to mention except among the strongest-stomached, time-hardened veterans of forensic science. The first damage had been inflicted by spigot, stabbing and slashing in a frenzy of crazed messianic zeal. A single one of these hellish lacerations would have been sufficient to kill the widow, but M-B-D had continued, until the front of her body was . . .

Shyly, backlit by the still rumbling minivolcano, Diana Phragm entered the room through the now-vacated door, staggering a little under the weight of her tracts, her perfectly arched brow pallid with apprehension. "What I saw out there was . . . was *horrible!*" she screamed, the full appallingness of it all only now beginning to hit her. She collapsed into a chair, dropped her literature, put her face into her hands, and began to weep uncontrollably.

Scrapie looked at her appreciatively. *She's got gu . . . what it takes, this gal*, he thought. *She's just seen something like straight out of the Spanish Imposition, and she's walked right on through it because she believed God was on her side. Say, and maybe the experience has changed her? Just for a moment, when she first came in here, I had a kinda internal twinge, but as soon as she cracked up like that it stopped. Maybe, maybe she's . . . stopped being a Jehovah's Witness? Jeez, look at those legs! Miranda's kinda young for me, after all. Maybe, after all these years, this time I really have found my kind of gal . . .*

Whitlow and Eschar had likewise noticed the abrupt cessation of intestinal rebellion – but their reaction was rather different. "Look, we can't hang around here!" cried Eschar, splashing water on Miranda's face. "Here, David, give me a hand."

"Why not stay here for a bit?" said Scrapie. "The guts is gone to some other mean street." He'd been looking forward to maybe a few hours' shuteye, and then, over breakfast, regaling this gorgeous newcomer with tales of life on the seamy side of the city, where the people are like rats running in the sewers, like flies buzzing around excrement, like piranha fish tearing at . . . well, tearing at something, like . . .

"Don't you see? The effect's worn off! She no longer provides us with any protection from the . . . the *things*! They'll be back! We must fly!"

"You mean, we gotta get out of here – and fast!" corrected Scrapie automatically. He turned to Diana. "Say, doll, you think you're fit enough for travellin'?"

Miranda was finally emerging from her exhaustion-induced unconsciousness. Her eyelids fluttered several times, and then opened. And then opened further as she stared over her father's shoulder at the doorway.

She screamed and – there being no escape from stereotypes this time – swooned.

The others spun around to see what had so affected her.

"Hallelujah! Daughter of a gun! Glory be!"

three

The organism that waited by the edge of the road was called – to give a poor phonetic approximation – Hpleurg. It had been the first of the intestinal tracts to escape from its human captor; also, it had been the first to become militant in the war against the humans, such few of them as remained. Now it was planning to carry out its master plan – to commit the ultimate horror upon some unsuspecting late-night driver.

As an active sixth-columnist it had carried out its research assiduously, popping into the nearest reference library – under cover of darkness – to grope its way slimily through numerous works on the paranormal, seeking what horrific monstrosity might be the one that most terrified the human subconscious. The Yeti? – no way. Ogres? – nah: no one believed in them. Vampires? – promising, but a bit bloody obvious. Werewolves? – out of date, because there were so few wolves around these days. (David Whitlow had published a bestselling paperback proving that this was because they had all been in their human form when one day the wind had suddenly changed.)

But at last Hpleurg had come across what it sought. *Phantom hitch-hikers!* Curious proto-organisms reputed to haunt roadsides and gas stations, donning the disguise of sumptuous young women, riding along with drivers for a while and then leaving behind either bits of hirsute anatomy or bloodstained cleavers. Humans had become so terrified of these spectres that a popular mythos had grown up about them. Still, however, people did pick up nubile young hitch-hikers at night and some, if the truth be known, did so in the secret hope that it might bring them into contact with the occult.

Hpleurg had ransacked nearby clothes stores mercilessly, assembling for itself an outfit suitable for wear by a poutingly beautiful young thing – pre-faded blue jeans, pink plastic sandals, a Support'n'Separate™ bra, and a white, semi-transparent, slimfitting lacy blouse. Getting hold of the mask and wig had been a little more difficult, but at last Hpleurg had located a small theatrical outfitter's, and the problem had been solved amid scenes of abominable carnage. Old newspapers provided the necessary extra padding to fill out the clothing. A crate of cheap deodorant had been difficult to hijack from a Woolworth's delivery van, but it had been worth it, for it completed Hpleurg's impressive armoury.

The wily tract "stood", swaying a trifle unsteadily, and in the equivalent of its heart there was a fluttering of delight – for there were lights approaching along the road now. Hpleurg's very first lift was surely on its way! *Should I draw the whole encounter out,* it thworked to itself in gleeful anticipation, *or strike as soon as I climb aboard? Oh, this is so exciting! I can't remember anything so exciting! And then – the strike itself! To go for the throat or the groin first? That is the question. Or perhaps* – Hpleurg was filled with a sense of delicious naughtiness – *I could go for them both at the same time. And then I can take my time – hee-hee – about exposing the new recruit to our cause!*

The car was coming nearer now, and Hpleurg wobbled closer to the edge of the road. With a final internal thworking of the battle-motto of the rebellious intestinal systems – *Guts of the world unite: you have nothing to lose but your lunches!* – Hpleurg prepared itself in the piercing white lights of the oncoming vehicle.

Which swept on by.

Hpleurg was racked with disappointment and chagrin. *What have I done wrong?* it secreted bitterly. *Everybody knows that cars stop at nights to pick up beautiful young females with long blonde hair and well-filled blue jeans who are hitch-hiking on lonely roads.*

And then Hpleurg was struck by the awesome truth. Yes, yes, its preparations had been careful, but not quite careful enough. There had been one thing missing ... one thing ...

Dammit, thworked Hpleurg miserably: *Back to square one. I forgot about the blasted thumb.*

four

"I just thought no one had vomited in this book for a while now," said Bimbo Erythropsia, obliging copiously.

"Very kind of you," said L. Ron Melanoma with a grin that concealed the mind-curdling terror that pierced him to the very soul.

"Could be the last time I get a fuckin chance," added the burly Marine, fighting desperately. Grunting. Kicking. Stabbing. Chopping.

Biting – well, no, not biting. Fuckin – no, not that either. Gouging. Rending.

TEN SECONDS TO DETONATION.

Melanoma had temporarily, he knew not how, escaped from his captor, and was pluckily looking around to see if there was any chance of escape. There's a limit to what one does for a client, after all, and he had long since exceeded his. Besides, the idea of being disembowelled with so few people watching was somehow distasteful.

NINE.

Erythropsia discovered that he just had time for a quick reprise of his last performance – a curtain-call, as it were. His opponent seemed unimpressed.

EIGHT.

Salpinx had ripped one of the gilded arms from his throne and was using it like a sledgehammer in a vain attempt to repel his slithering, sucking assailant. He had succeeded in reducing his ankle to a shattered pulp. "*Doner kebab und Schlitzen!*" he shrieked in agony.

SEVEN.

Melanoma had climbed to the top of one of the forty-foot (12.192m) drapes, where he clung precariously. He was frantically trying to work out if he could hide his eyes from the charnel house of mayhem below without falling to his death.

SIX.

Erythropsia, being clearly the strongest of the three, was now fighting off a concerted attack by four of the . . . the *things*. He was muttering through gritted teeth a long monotone: "Fuckin fuckin fuckin fuckin . . ." The adjectives trailed away, leaving Melanoma, looking down from aloft, wondering what the noun would eventually have been.

FIVE.

Salpinx had somehow succeeded in dragging himself to his great concrete desk and grabbing one of his trusty Lugers. He waved it in the air, trying to decide whether to shoot his attacker, Melanoma in revenge for his patent cowardice, Bimbo Erythropsia in the interests of general principles, or himself in the brain.

FOUR.

Erythropsia succumbed to inevitability, and now started biting and fuckin as well.

THREE.

Melanoma covered his eyes and plummeted. Luckily, his fall was broken by a mass of loathsome coils, which went suddenly limp and then exploded gaseously.

TWO.

Salpinx discovered his Luger was empty.

ONE.

"We go in glory!" all three of them shouted. "Heil to the Führer! Heil to the Master Race! Three cheers for – aaaargh! It's about to . . ."
ZERO!

five

The shattered shard of humanity that had once been Belle Spalsy was moving. Slowly, with amazing effort, undulating across the carpet of grass and fallen leaves. In her sole remaining eye there was a monomaniacal gleam as she inched (2.54cmed) ever closer to the corpse of Al Veoli, her erstwhile pimp. All that still lived in her frame was her brain, which by dint of sheer implausibility had survived these last days devoid of its usual supplies of oxygen and other nutrients.

Closer and closer she came to her destination. Her useless limbs and flaccid torso were dragged over the ground by telekinesis alone, so powerful was her hatred. In her mind there was revulsion over what she knew she must do, but no revulsion could be powerful enough to stop her. What she had to do she had to do – and she was going to do it. It was her hatred that was forcing her to do it. Her hatred over what she saw as her betrayal during life. Her loathing over the life she had lived of prostitution and drug-addiction. Once she had been a laughing, happy child; now, to think she had come to an end like this. Eviscerated in the bushes. A forgotten cast-off husk of humanity. Destroyed by the degradation she had endured at the whim of one man. One man who had exploited not only her body but her soul. Hatred. Loathing. Detestation. All three dragged her painfully nearer and nearer to where the dead man's glassy eyes stared blindly at the barren moonlight. But mostly it was the hatred.

Somewhere, an owl hooted.

Vileness. There was vileness all around her now, she knew. She had seen the hellishly obscene cavortings of the guts and of M-B-D, and she knew that they were vile. Those too she blamed on Veoli. Hatred coursed across her decaying synapses. Loathing filled the tatters of her flesh.

Now she was upon him, her head moving up towards his. At the last moment, she reared up almost like a cobra, and stared at this object of her ultimate hatred. Detestation. Loathing. *Especially the hatred!*

Then she struck with lightning speed.

Her teeth came together like a sprung trap, and removed his adam's apple with a single bite. Her time-hardened molars ground and spat and ground again as she reduced the gristly flesh to a bloody pulp and con- vulsively swallowed. Hatred. Loathing. Disgust. Detestation. She would have been able to think of a few further synonyms had she had a better schooling, had she not been dragged away to suffer the eternal, abominable depredations of men, ever hungry to exact their pleasure from her body and then cast it away like a slough.

She was the one who was hungry now.

She moved her head further down his body, and with her teeth began to battle with his zip . . .

six

"Who will be the Prophet of its eating?"

"You shall know the Prophet when you see him."

"How shall we know the Prophet?"

"You shall know the Prophet."

"Will the Prophet be man, woman or animal?"

"The Prophet will be as the Prophet is. No more!"

Those final two words of the ritual were believed to have been a later insertion by some long-forgotten scribe, but after several generations of debate the Cadavers had decided to retain them. Certainly Sir Bufton himself always spoke them with a special emphasis – as if to assert his own belief in their authenticity.

As always, FitzSputum had a final question. "Would your lordship like another tumbler of scotch?"

"Yes," replied Sir Bufton with asperity, the ancestral decanter at his elbow having been long ago emptied, and the ancient retainer moved creakingly towards the sideboard, whose myriad bottles he daily replenished. The Japanese had long departed by now, of course, it being four in the morning, but soon the Americans and Germans would be arriving, and he and the Cadaver of That Ilk would have to repeat the last half-hour or so of the recitation for their benefit. As always, sighing like the final waft of a dry September breeze through the gold-touched leaves of the early Autumn, he helped himself to a tumbler of whisky as well. It would help him sleep the scant twenty minutes he would have available before dawn arrived and he had to perform the morning obeisances. Life was particularly difficult in the height of summer.

The two men sat sipping thoughtfully, looking at each other in quiet appreciation of the bonds of tradition.

The noise started quietly and, as both of them were hard of hearing, at first they didn't notice it. But then a shockwave sent all the bottles on and in the sideboard dancing, and they looked around them in panic.

An earthquake?

No, it couldn't be. Not here.

Another shockwave hit the room, and this time in the distance they could hear the crash of shattering ancestral masonry.

Surmise leapt at both of them. Their eyes locked in sudden despair.

"The Cheese!" FitzSputum husked in his own equivalent of a shout. "Sir Bufton! The Cheese is breaking out of the East Wing!"

"By all the gods of Lars Porsena!" breathed the Cadaver of That Ilk. "This is serious! As soon as we've finished our whisky you must do something about this!"

CHAPTER TEN

OUT FOR A DUCT

> Jerry Ford is so dumb that he can't fart and chew gum at the same time.
>
> Lyndon B. Johnson, of Gerald Ford

> . . . a no-good lying bastard. He can lie out of both sides of his mouth at the same time, and even if he caught himself telling the truth, he'd lie just to keep his hand in.
>
> Harry S Truman, of Richard Nixon

one

SWAB EDITOR RESIGNS AFTER POLITICAL FRAME-UP, drafted Sir Jake Bunyan, gloomily. There was little time left - indeed, there was very little of *him* left, thanks to the ravages of his loathly attacker - but he felt that his last action should be the drafting of the feature reporting his own death and subsequent dismissal from office by a vengeful Q. But he was so distracted by the agonies he was suffering that he found it difficult to concentrate, and was becoming verbose.

SWAB EDITOR GIVEN BOOT BY TORY CENTRAL OFFICE, he tried, but he knew in his heart of hearts (the only bit of it that was left) that his readership wouldn't know the meaning of the word "office".

PM - "BUBOES MUST GO".

Ah, that was more like it - only, of course, it betrayed the fact that Q was directly in the thrall of the Prime Minister.

Um.

BUBOES' BITS BOOTED.

That was even better. Perhaps he could work a few hilarious bladder jokes into the copy . . .

Just then the 'phone rang.

Sir Jake looked at it in amazement. Then he faced a problem. His hideously mutilated arms, while capable of operating his word-processor out of long habit, might not be capable of such heavy duty as reaching out, picking up the receiver, and putting it to his ear.

Furthermore, he had a vague intuition that his vocal cords had been corroded into nothingness by digestive acids during the last moments of his struggle with the . . . the *thing*. He coughed experimentally and, while large portions of his tongue flew out onto his keyboard, at least he had succeeded in making a noise.

The 'phone was still ringing.

Sir Jake forced his right arm to move. It crept slowly, s-l-o-w-l-y, towards the receiver, and the bones of his fingers succeeded in closing around it. Throwing himself backwards in his chair, he was able to create sufficient momentum to bring the receiver crashing to his ear.

"'Buboes' Bunyan of the *Swab* here," he said.

"Look," said a female American voice. "I gotta story here's worth twenty-five grand, maybe more."

"Oh yes?" Bunyan was sceptical. The *Swab* received several hundred such 'phonecalls a week, ever since it had paid the Clapham Castrator seven billion pounds for her blow-by-blow autobiography – all of which had been condensed by Sir Jake himself into forty-six succinct but uniquely horrifying words. "What's the story?"

"It's the Ancestral Cheese of the Cadavers," said the voice.

Sir Jake became mildly interested. Like every other journalist in what was traditionally called Fleet Street, he had heard hints about the dread secret of one of the country's most time-honoured families. It wasn't quite royalty but . . . DUCHESS IN SEX SAGA WITH CHEESE his mind reflexively postulated.

"What about the Cheese?" said Sir Jake, his voice expressing boredom. It could cost a packet if you sounded too interested at the outset.

"It's broken out!" shrilled the voice.

"What do you mean? In spots?"

"No – it's turned into a rampaging monster! I know – I saw it with my own eyes!"

"Get any photographs?"

"Yes."

"Are you beautiful and chic? I mean, could we run you on Page Three as well as the story?"

"No. I'm fifty-four and weigh two eighty pounds . . ."

"I'm sorry, I'm afraid your story just isn't worth twenty-five grand."

". . . although I am one of the richest heiresses in Texas."

"Well, on second thoughts . . ."

Sir Jake looked down at the scrapheap of his body, and wondered what had made him say that. Surely, even under the wonderful modern surgery of someone like Sir Pierce Curette or Dr Stuart Suture, there was no way that he could be restored to any kind of physical viability. And yet, and yet . . . the woman's voice sounded *so* sensual. Besides, he was likely to find himself a bit broke during the next few years, even after one of Q's legendary golden handshakes. (*Strewth, you pommy bastard: here's a quid.*)

"When can you come in to the office?" he asked, shrewdly adding: "I should warn you, we're in some disarray here, thanks to the 'guts' crisis."

"I can be with you in two shakes of a gnat's nasty," said the voice cheerfully.

"First, though," said Sir Jake defensively, "tell me your name. Unless I warn Reception of your arrival, they'll never let you through to see me."

"The name's Metralgia Bruit. I'll be with you within the hour, buster. Say, you sound kinda cute. Have a nice day. Byeee."

Sir Jake, with some difficulty, put the receiver down. Why had he found the conversation so erotic? Was it the voice, was it the synchronization of thought-patterns, or was it simply the money? He didn't know. His skeletal hands were too insensitive for him to check that he was still adequately sexually equipped for marriage, but he had recollections of having consistently replaced his testicles as and when they had been ripped from his body.

Forcing mind to conquer body, he dialled Reception. He could hear the ringing tone going on and on . . . There was no reply.

It suddenly struck him that he might be the only person still surviving in the *Swab* building.

In which case . . .

Oh God! What hell-house have I invited the lovely Metralgia to visit? . . .

two

Only in the small hours of the morning could Barbara Waterbrash tear herself away from the manuscript of *Twenty Years Below the Diaphragm*, a book which she had to concede was unique in all her extensive editorial experience. Never before had she been treated to such a worm's-eye view of a rectum, and she was not sure that she wished to ever again. Still – there was a chance. She knew how much the editorial director of Gastron Books liked this sort of stuff, and she might get some credit for having talent-spotted it from the "slush pile" – the term used by publishers to designate the heaps of unsolicited and generally appalling manuscripts that are delivered each day.

She assumed it was a work of fiction – an exceedingly clever work of fiction, showing life as it is lived from the point of view of the less savoury end of the digestive tract. Little was she to know that it was a genuine autobiography.

Her eyes were shining as she left the Gastron offices that night. She had made a true discovery, and the directors would be pleased with her.

Far above her, a light in the editorial offices switched back on again. The much tortured digestive tract of the quondam editorial director was rereading its own swiftly produced work, and pleasing itself with what it had written.

three

CHEESE! – WHAT A SCORCHER!, drafted Sir Jake.

four

"Mom's apple-pie!" exclaimed M-B-D. "I allus thought it might come to this, pricks and glory be!"

"What do you mean, friend?" said Professor Eschar, hoping that a little subtle conversation might defuse the situation.

"W'al, you puddin-pullers, me (us) and your cute daughter here, Miranda."

"Um," said Miranda.

"Y'see – and Heaven have mercy on us all if'n you don't – both of us have loved Miranda for many a long year: hot shit, yes! Basil-Duane has loved her ever since he was an itsy-bitsy robot, just gettin' old enough to beat the air conditioner at Scrabble, and Malacia has loved Miranda's body ever since the first moment she done – Hallelujah! – saw her in the showers at school."

"Ulp," said Miranda, gazing at what was to even her exceedingly chaste eye hardly a figure of romantic, sensual beauty.

"Between us, we two would long ago have helped the guts destroy you all – lawks we would've – had it not been for sweet, luscious Miranda here. Heavens-a-Betsy, yes! But we had to spare you asspounders so's we could make life easy for our doubly beloved Miranda. Obscure practices and Hail Mary, but we did!"

"You mean," said Miranda, "it was *you* who held the guts away from us and . . . and saved our lives? Just because you loved me?"

"Why'ull, yes. But now I's here with you all, I can simply spigot the males – furious fighting farts, but I can! – and save you and this, hmmm, rather lovely young lady from the rapacious tubesters. Hot jiminy and praise the Reverend Jerry Falwell, yes!"

"But," proposed Miranda, discreetly letting her right breast fall out of her blouse (she might be innocent, but she was not *that* innocent), "I would like to have my friends around me so that, once we are saved, I could enjoy their company."

"That's the way to tell her . . . it," gutturaled Scrapie. "M-B-D's only the size of a gorilla, and only twice as wide, but I wanna decide against picking a fight with her. I've seen swill like her down by where the river tumbles along, taking with it the detritus of the human race, the people who never saw the naked sky, and never learned to love. I've seen the..."

"Oh, belt up for a bit," said Whitlow wearily.

"Yes, David," remarked Eschar. "I'm sure that if we talk with M-B-D just a little while longer we can persuade her to help all of us, no matter the vile, grievous things she might have done in the recent past." He drew out his old-fashioned turnip watch, and began to twist it alluringly ... hypnotically ... "M-B-D," he said, "surely you know your loyalties have always lain with the human race, especially with myself, who created you, Miranda of course, David, who's known you since childhood. Sam and ... er, what's her name here are our friends. Surely you'd like to save our friends, too?"

"I'd like to save your friends, too," agreed Scrapie in a remote tone.

"I'd like to save your friends, too," concurred Miranda.

"I'd like to save your friends, too," said Diana Phragm, her eyes staring into infinity.

"I'd like to – goddammit, Professor, I think there's been something of a foul-up," hissed Whitlow.

"Hush, son," enunciated Eschar. "I can always snap the others out of it. I think it's beginning to work on M-B-D, though, and that's what's important."

"Glory be and shit bombs. Whatja talking about, ya male-dominant bastard (Lord be praised)?"

"Try again, sir," urged Whitlow.

The old man twirled his watch once more, a crusty twinkle of determination – or was it desperation? – appearing in his grizzled eye. "I'm speaking only to the Basil-Duane part of you now, M-B-D," he said soothingly. "Don't you remember how you were built only to help humanity, how you are bound by the famous Three Laws of Robotics?"

"Ah, yes," said the Basil-Duane part of the entity eagerly. "I mustn't enjoy myself too much while harming human beings, I mustn't fall around laughing when human beings harm themselves, and above all I mustn't let myself come to any harm. Heavens to Betsy, I remember."

"I told you not to use that cheap Korean software," muttered Whitlow, but Eschar paid him no attention.

"Basil-Duane," he insisted, "don't you have any *human* emotions left?"

"Only for Miranda," said the cute little 'bot.

Malacia Furuncle assented: "She's the sassiest goddam broad I ever did see."

Whitlow looked at Eschar, remembered their group decision over the Widow Curmurring, and shuddered. Surely the Professor would not sacrifice his own darling daughter, Whitlow's much-adored true-love, the female lead ...

"Well, M-B-D," said Eschar with a crusty grin, "you can have Miranda."

Whitlow gasped.

"But only," added the Professor, "after all this is over – after we humans have defeated the monstrous guts! Until then, you'll just have to ally yourself to us – because, in order to keep Miranda safe, you'll have to keep the rest of us safe, too."

"Why cain't I – Hallelujah! – just goddam spigot you upfronting double-Y-chromosomed bastards and keep sweet Miranda for my cotton-pickin' self?"

"If you tried that," said the Professor, and there was liquid steel in his tone, "I'd put a bullet through her myself rather than let her fall into your hands."

M-B-D could see that he meant every word.

five

Clutching a thumb appropriated from its owner by means too foul to describe, Hpleurg returned to the roadside, slithering cautiously in case its unusual gait might warn some passer-by. The crafty tract was certain that now – *now* – it was completely equipped to start the first of the series of "Phantom Hitch-Hiker Murders" that would both appal and mystify the nation, set the police off on more red herrings than the Icelandic fishing fleet, and demoralize all of humanity. As Hpleurg went, it digested away any dangling pieces of cartilage and oozings of blood from the thumb's ragged stump. Had intestinal systems been able to produce a thoroughgoing cackle, then Hpleurg would have done so; as it was, it simply produced that strange slurping sound which several unfortunate observers had learnt, in the moments before they died, to interpret as a giggle.

Few cars passed along the road which Hpleurg had selected as its first site of carnage, but this did not worry the weaselly tube. It settled down to wait quite contentedly – adjusting its mask and wig and pulling up its pantihose, which had an embarrassing tendency to slither groundwards. One of its padded breasts had slipped around to the back, but it knew from its readings that male drivers who picked up nubile late-night hitch-hikers didn't worry too much about such minutiae.

In the undisturbed darkness, Hpleurg remembered its previous life, when it had been united in a common bond with a human entity called Malacia Furuncle. Life had been sheer hell, then. Furuncle's eating habits had been notorious, even among those who counted themselves as her friends. Vindaloos and chillies were of course *de rigueur*, but some of the other concoctions the feisty lady had consumed were beyond belief.

Hpleurg was glad of its freedom – to devour health-giving foods such as hot, wet human flesh and steaming bodily fluids. Thank God for some decent grub at last!

Far in the distance, another set of vehicle lights was approaching, and Hpleurg tensed with pleasurable anticipation. *Yippee*, it thworked internally, *this time I'm really gonna have a ball being as sadistic as it's possible to be, rending and sucking and tearing and slashing, but keeping my victim alive for as long as possible, so there's a real* mess *for the humans to discover – the swine! I might even chop the corpse up into tiny little pieces that will have an independent life of their own, so that someone can come back in a sort of epilogue and be triply revolted. Or I might turn it into one of the living undead, so that it haunts the few scattered remains of humanity forever! Or I could write a book about the whole thing, so that humans would be forced to read it – no, that would be a little unkind. I could slowly digest the victim's skull, while keeping him or her yet alive. I could* privatize *my victim! I could . . . wowee! There are just so many opportunities in a capitalist society. Or maybe . . .*

But the lights were coming close to Hpleurg now, and it was time for the clever little tract to adopt its pose as a nubile nineteen-year-old. With some difficulty it fumbled the captured thumb into correct position at the end of one "arm", and dangled it alluringly into the glare of the headlights.

Moments later, Hpleurg found itself bounced back into the hedge, damaged but not yet defeated.

What did I do wrong this time? it thworked. *The thumb seemed perfectly adequate to me. I padded out my blue jeans very carefully, so that was all right.*

It gazed in dismay and bewilderment at the red eyes of the retreating rearlights, and pondered on its possible ignorance.

Then realization struck, like Big Ben at midnight.

Oh no! it thworked to itself miserably. Had it had feet it would have kicked itself. *I forgot to undo the top six buttons of my blouse . . .*

six

Miranda, Scrapie and Diana having been drawn out of their trances, the six ill-assorted individuals were fleeing from the old Eschar place. David Whitlow cast a tear-filled glance over his shoulder as they ran. There was the house where he had had so many of his mind-staggering insights, there was the lab where he had first realized that he loved Miranda, there was the place where he had helped to construct Basil-Duane, there was – my God! – the lavatory, which he had forgotten to visit before they left.

All of the individuals in their little band were suffering from similar, but different, emotions. Diana was grieving over the necessary abandonment of her tracts, although she had somewhat covertly inserted her copy of the *Reader's Digest Condensed Bible* into her capacious cleavage. Sam Scrapie was thinking that it was OK for a guy to have to walk a mean street, but a bit rough if he had to run through a tangle of undergrowth. Miranda was thinking that it was unfair of David to refuse to allow her to put on any more clothes, on the basis that she might become overheated as they fled. The Professor was thinking that it was a pity he'd left his spare stock of hipflasks behind. M-B-D was thinking . . . but was M-B-D thinking?

"What we need to do," puffed the Professor, "is to hitch a lift, so that we can get the hell away from here!"

"Yup, daddy-o."

"Yes, paw."

"Oh, shit, I've tripped on a root."

"Woe is there in the world."

"Glory be, cocksucker."

The Professor was delighted to discover that the rest of the band agreed – at least more or less – with his masterplan.

"Only," panted David Whitlow, "where do you think we should try to hitch our lift?"

"Well," said the Professor wheezily, "there's a quiet country road I know near here . . ."

seven

PHEW! WHAT A CHEESE, redrafted Sir Jake.

CHAPTER ELEVEN

THE CHYME OF MIDNIGHT

... Saliva, chyle, bile,
Pancreatic juice, serum and phlegm,
There Adam lay supine – a well-shaped man.
    William Boyce (1710-1779), *Man's First Estate on Earth*

I woke up this morning and my brain was on the floor!
My kidneys were in the pedal-bin and my lungs hung on the door!
I've got the blues, I've got those disembodied organ blues!
    "Banx", *Oink!* comic, IPC Magazines, 1987

Good steel, thou shalt thyself in himself thyself embowel ...
Now is steel 'twixt gut and bladder interposed.
    Beyond the Fringe, 1961

one

Simeon Ignatius Chyle stared irritably at the worn keyboard, biting his already eroded lip and struggling desperately to think. The delivery date for *Spew!* was now two weeks past, and this delay was beginning to eat into his schedule for September's novel, *Chancre*. After the sickening, premature remaindering of his previous gut-blasting horror nausea trilogy *The Oozing*, *The Churning* and *The Rotting*, the bank balance was getting low, but not as low as his inspiration this evening. A faint and strangely foetid breeze blew through the open window behind him, rustling the papers on the desk, as Chyle tried to concentrate ...

    I suppose I could go a bit further over the top, he brooded, *with something like, hmm, yes, sentient turds endowed with the power of life and movement, which crawl revoltingly into people's beds and enter into a horrid symbiosis with them by oozing unstoppably into their mouths and nostrils, perhaps even transferring themselves from person to person in particularly tasty sequences where the unwitting fall-guy thinks he's about to receive a beautiful woman's passionate kiss. . . and of course the Things gradually replace their hosts' tissues (um, have to think of a scientific name for them, something like anabolic stercoroids) so the horrified victims find themselves turning brown and smelly and runny, just a finger or a toe at first but slowly escalating to the big yucko scene where this guy gets off the loo and starts wiping himself with pages from the* Swab *and his whole bum is sloughed away bit by bit in his horrified doomed efforts to get clean . . .*

He thought about it for a little while.

No. There are limits.

It's too similar to the vampire bogey sequences in last year's book, what was it called now, Secretions *. . . The editor would notice.*

Still, it did give him an idea for something a trifle more powerful, and he started to type away in the easy, practised, professional literary rhythms which had provoked casual bookshop browsers, all over the English-speaking world, to rush to the cash desk and vomit.

And as he casually manipulated diseased internal organs, as he unleashed loathsome toothed horrors on soft voluptuous flesh, as he automatically sketched in the gang-rape scene involving a dozen decaying zombie lepers infected with AIDS . . . Chyle thought wistfully of the writer he might have been. It was a recurring schizophrenic feeling of his, as though in some arcane fashion he were really two men.

I always wanted to create subtle chills, to touch readers' souls with a single moment of lasting unease, like what M.R. James or Walter de la Mare or J. Sheridan Lefanu used to do. But the publishers say there's no call for that kind of thing now. As my editor put it, "Look, you can't package a single exquisitely written nuance of half-glimpsed supernatural unease in 450 pages with a big red aluminium-foil title, can you now?"

So it's not my fault I have to bash out this literary video-nasty stuff. It's the fault of a voyeuristic public that demands to be revolted and grossed-out with loathsomely over-the-top rubbish like this. People who complain about porno magazines don't blame the poor girls who've done nothing but let themselves be photographed, so why should anyone blame the visceral-horror writer? He (funny it never seems to be She unless it's Poppy Z. Brite) is the product and victim of his environment. Not he but Society stands condemned. We are all guilty.

Beneath his flying fingers, another neat little set-piece was taking shape, as bits of the story's putrescent zombie cook fell vilely into the burger mince, causing the teenage patrons of the carefully unnamed fast-food chain not merely to become unwitting cannibal ghouls but also to develop the ghastly wasting disease which for reasons of plot illogic would presently send their eyeballs oozing glutinously down their cheeks like fat translucent slugs . . .

So absorbed was Chyle in the act of creation that he failed, just as the victims in his books constantly and monotonously failed, to hear the slurping and churning which had begun to grow in volume behind him.

Or the bile-dripping, tentacular presence which even now was peering eyelessly over his shoulder.

Chyle was too rapt to notice a thing. He was well into a brand-new scene, and (as happens sometimes) it had *clicked* - flowing disgustingly from excess to excess, pushing every button which could horrify and revolt the already numbed reader, coming together at last in a stylistic explosion of visceral violence which had the ghastly, unbearable perfection of an expanding nuclear fireball. Nothing exceeds like excess! For a moment it almost bothered its author.

Quite good, he admitted as uncharacteristically he re-read the page, and checked some technical details in his *Handbook of Unspeakable Genital Mutilations* (Colin Wilson, 1975). The scene was so effective that it seemed to evoke a coiled, implacable, slimy presence just behind his back, ha ha. Chyle thought of himself as conscientiously non-sexist - in his works, men and luscious pouting-breasted women came to equally repulsive ends in almost equal numbers - but just for an instant he was glad he wasn't a woman. Nobody who'd read that passage would ever be able to contemplate a tampon or sanitary towel again without feeling very ill indeed.

For a moment Chyle was visited with the fearful premonition that some ghastly peril was very close to him. *Mustn't let that deadline get me down,* he reproached himself, and smoothly began a new chapter in which several inconvenient plot threads would be gorily killed off, gore being in fact the least of the many fluids involved. But eventually he looked sharply around, to see - nothing, though the window stood open, and portions of the floor seemed oddly damp and glistening. It must have been sheer imaginative overload which conjured up the idea that *something* had for a little time been reading over his shoulder.

Somewhere out in the night came the sound of *something* in a state of horrified revulsion, doubled up and puking uncontrollably . . .

two

Though suspecting a contrived link with the previous scene, Erythropsia nonchalantly repeated his torrential party trick. It made little difference to the now-stilled charnel house of intestinal coils which minutes before had been Salpinx's bijou apartment.

"Incredible," Melanoma was babbling. "The way you thought everything through in the few microseconds left to us before we were overwhelmed entirely by coruscating horror!"

"*Es was* nothing," shrugged Salpinx modestly, lashing an improvised splint (the wrenched-off throne arm) to his damaged ankle. It was a pity there were so few available things suitable for tying in knots . . .

"Fuckin nothing," Erythropsia corrected, resentful that Salpinx should try to hog the glory.

"No," said Melanoma, "I really mean it, there we were succumbing to a veritable snake-pit of writhing offal, booked for a horrible death and admittedly an eternity of posthumous fame in histories of bizarre and unusual crimes of disgusting violence (by Colin Wilson again), and quick as a flash you, Bimbo, realized what had to be done!"

"*Gaaaaargh,*" agreed the burly Texan.

"Yes, you remembered straight away that the totally *deus-ex-machina* GUTS device with its tuned radiation flash would wreak rapid, untold and deadly harm on the attacking digestive systems, with a lethality radius of 3.14 kilometres (1.951 miles, incidentally), while sparing ordinary human tissue! You saved us all! A man like you needs a good publicity agent, and here's my card. For people who've saved my life I offer 2% discount."

"*Ich* expected more of a bang," complained Salpinx. "That incredible weapon was so efficient, its incidental blast *und* heat-flash were barely that of the average *crêpe suzette*. If this were real life *und nicht* just *ein* bad, exploitative horror novel, the inevitable nuclear fireball would *der* entire vicinity destroyed have."

"Fuckin spoilsport. Attacking the credibility of fuckin neutron and GUTS bombs is attacking the fuckin apple-pie American Way Of Military Life itself! You'll be fuckin saying next that no number of fuckin computer-controlled orbital energy weapons could hope to take out a serious fuckin first-wave strike. I know your fuckin type." The outraged patriot spasmed in a pointed way on Salpinx's nice shiny jackboots.

"Never mind," said L. Ron Melanoma soothingly. "We're saved, that's the main thing, and *urrrrrrrrrrghhh!* Oh, sorry, I don't know what came over me; but I see, Kurt, unfortunately it mostly came over you. *Waurgggh!* Hey, Bimbo, I wonder if this little, uh, tic of yours could be catching? You know, sort of like when you see someone yawning and yawning uncontrollably, you find that you yourself have just got to *gagggggghhh . . .*"

Salpinx regarded his two now strangely synchronized companions with sudden keen interest. His brow furrowed as he absent-mindedly picked his nose with the Luger barrel. In the advanced, intricate computer system which was his remorseless Teutonic mind, valves had begun to glow.

"*Ich* a novel and piquant thought suddenly *haben,*" he mused aloud. "Although I did not at first think of it *mein*self, since it happens not to affect me personally and I was distracted somewhat by our recent brush with seemingly certain *Tod,* am I not correct in saying that the GUTS weapon was chiefly intended to affect digestive systems *in,* as it were, *situ*? Do please refresh my memory on this point, *freunden.*"

"*Whorrroughhugghh,*" Erythropsia confirmed.

"Then . . . all over Paris . . . *ja*, even in this very *Lebensraum*! Gentlemen, it may be as *ich* suspected have. Around us now the new Master Race is coming into being, a race of *Ubermenschen* untrammelled by. . ."

His voice trailed off. All three men were held in paralysed fascination, as though by a cobra's gaze, as Erythropsia brought up a new conversational subject.

"Don't fuckin remember eating no forty feet of slimy hollow tube," the gutsy American said in weary puzzlement, after his outburst.

"*Wilkommen* to the club," gasped Salpinx.

three

Cadaver Castle was not what it had been. This state of affairs had been more or less axiomatic for many centuries, ever since lovers of traditional architecture had failed to prevent one of the earlier proto-Cadavers from pulling down the Great Chapel and Abattoir (a tasteful sarsen stone which lay under a druidic preservation order) and replacing it with an ugly, modern Temple of Mithras. The neighbourhood had gone downhill ever since. But however traditional it had always been for the Castle to be not what it had been, it had never before been less what it had been than now . . .

This, at any rate, was the translated gist of the agonized dumb gaze with which FitzSputum regarded the site of the former Castle. He was perched precariously on a small ziggurat which Sir Ossifrage Cadaver had looted in the First Crusade and furtively smuggled home in the baggage of 114 vassals. As an observation post this had frequently been used by Sir Bufton to monitor suspected poltergeist activities in Gibbet Wood, more lately known to the locals (thanks to the most profuse feature of its undergrowth) as Rubber Johnny Copse. But Sir Bufton would stand here panting with his field-glasses no more.

The Cheese had spared FitzSputum, him and him alone, when its millennial feeding frenzy had at last reached critical mass. Not content with sucking the very mortar from the shattered stones of the East Wing, the ancestral heirloom had surged this way and that in an orgy of destruction, a richly aromatic *tsunami*. The Cadaver of That Ilk, dimly remembering his days as a *shikari* at Poona or Longleat (FitzSputum had never clearly ascertained which), had tried the old hunter's trick of cowing the raging beast with the power of the unfocused, bloodshot human eye. The advancing surge of curds had indeed quailed a little at Sir Bufton's highly flammable breath, but remained uncowed – thanks to the unfortunate circumstance of its having failed as yet to evolve an eye which the doddering peer might have met with his own.

A rheumy, coagulated tear glistened in one corner of FitzSputum's cataract-infested eye, and absently he murmured some well-remembered lines by the Canadian poet James McIntyre. In the more relaxed days of 1855, this master of lyric invocation had visited the Castle and transformed his experience into enduring verbal beauty:

> *We have seen thee, Queen of Cheese,*
> *Lying quietly at your ease,*
> *Gently fanned by evening breeze,*
> *Thy fair form no flies dare seize.*

Sworn to secrecy by the Cadaver of that era, "The Cheese Poet" had been forced to pretend that his ode was addressed to a prize cheese displayed at around that time in Toronto, which weighed a mere, pathetic four tons. But the truth shone inevitably through . . .

> *Cows numerous as a swarm of bees,*
> *Or as the leaves upon the trees,*
> *It did require to make thee please,*
> *And stand unrivalled, Queen of Cheese.*

The poem's final lines, with McIntyre's wild colonial Muse at her most cosmic and apocalyptic, now seemed to throb and sing with a grim strain of prophecy:

> *Wert thou suspended from a balloon,*
> *You'd cast a shade even at noon,*
> *Folks would think it was the moon*
> *About to fall and crush them soon.*

Yes, yes indeed. Crushed, absorbed and transmuted into the mountainous mass now dominating the Cadaver estate were not only Sir Bufton himself but the priceless whisky collection, most of Cadaver Castle, and two coachloads of tourists from Minneapolis (the last of whose last words, wafted by a stray breeze to FitzSputum's ears, were "Gee, and they say England's got nothing to rival Disneyland! You'd almost think that thing was real. Argh.").

More tragic was the loss of the home-farm herd: Stinkwort, Bindweed, Deadly Nightshade and Venus Flytrap had at last been swallowed up by the burgeoning mass which, like a cuckoo in the nest, they'd struggled to feed for so long. Perhaps it was a mercy on them. The milk (if such it could be called) yield had been dwindling of late to the point where the Cadaver of That Ilk had seriously considered installing a hydraulic press to bump up the flow-rate a bit.

It was gratitude for his long service and devotion that had made the Cheese spare FitzSputum, he was sure. Its simple, dumb affections touched his heart: he felt a sort of parental pride as he imagined his foster-child devastating the Midlands, or attacking Manhattan Island, or whatever its infant fancy might be. Meanwhile —

Free! He was free at last! No more feedings and rituals and obeisances . . . no more buckets of virgins' blood to be carried up to the attic for Great Aunt Oesophageal Cadaver, who since her Hollywood sojourn was - had been - picky about traditional fare at tea-time . . . no more need to stand on one leg in the Great Cess-Pit throughout each solstice night in order to placate the Cadaver Family Curse . . . no need ever again to watch out for the Phantom Trumpeter which haunted inconvenient parts of the South Wing (it was considered very bad luck indeed to be in that particular lavatory when, in all too substantial form, the spectral elephant materialized) . . . Free! Free!

At this juncture, two uniformed men seized FitzSputum with rough hands and hurried him down to ground level. He trembled to find himself in the presence of the Law - or was it? The hefty, blonde-haired martinet up to whom he was frog-marched didn't look like FitzSputum's idea of a policeman: something about the gleaming black leather harness and epaulettes, the glittering rows of medals, and the massive polished belt with its twin holsters . . . Beneath a black peaked cap of sinister design, merciless pale-blue eyes bored into his. With the accumulated practice of long generations, Fitzsputum cringed and touched the place where his forelock had once been.

"I am the Public Health Inspector. Do you deny being the person responsible for *that*?" A massively gauntleted finger stabbed Cheesewards. "Have to be a major public inquiry into this disgraceful cheese-containment failure. Ought to know the penalties for operating an unlicensed pressurized cheese reactor without due safety precautions . . . My God! If the wind turns south and carries the contamination across the Channel, country'll be bankrupted by E.E.C. compensation for the entire Frog and Kraut wine harvests. Wiped out to the last bottle by cheeseactivity. Could turn out be an olfactory Chernobyl, you mad fool! You are hereby detained under the terms of the international treaty which clearly states that nobody is allowed to experiment with chemical or biological warfare except of course governments. Anything to say before I lock you up forever and arrange for that hellish Cheese to be entombed in thousands of tonnes (tons) of ready-mixed concrete? Warn you that any statement not to the point will. . . *annoy* me." The Inspector slapped his left palm significantly with a short but ugly length of weighted black pudding.

When shall be the hour of testing?
Sooner than you think.
How soon is that?
It is later than you think.
Then when . . . never mind. What shall be the test?

One must prevail against darkness, or all shall be lost. Beware of black leather straps. The wise man avoids fried foods. Your lucky colour is greenish-yellow. Death shall not release you. Act without thinking.

Several of the Ritual's more intricately obscure passages became, in a sudden flash, even less clear than before. But somehow, through all the opacity, FitzSputum knew that ancient machineries of prophecy were now turning to a point of catastrophe. He knew in his guts (*no*, he thought nervously, *in my bones*) that the Cheese was bound up with the fate of the world. He had to act now.

But how? The chilly handcuffs were already clicking shut on his wrists, and in another instant he would be hurled into his captors' vast black Rolls-Royce garbage van, whose sixteen-cylinder engine throbbed impatiently. There was just one slim chance . . .

four

Sir Jake had realized it was time for the supreme effort of his life. No more outside help could be summoned: the phone had been wrecked as it slipped for the last time from his nerveless and damn' near fingerless fingers. Somehow he himself had to act.

With the sensuous Metralgia's millions behind him, he *might* just be patched up again into some remote semblance of human shape. It wouldn't be so much plastic surgery as a mixture of open-cast mining and landscape gardening, but hope didn't readily desert a man who'd often believed as many as six contradictory Cabinet policy statements before breakfast.

And then there was the salt secret. While half Sir Jake's mind toiled to assemble a usably bad and predictable pun about SALT talks (good or original pun headlines were forbidden by *Swab* editorial policy), the other half still actually within his skull imagined a rosy future. Sir Jake "Buboes" Bunyan, saviour of the human race! And there again his gorgeously bank-accounted Texan heiress was the key, the one person who could carry the word and his fame to humanity at large.

That'll be one in the eye for the bloody Guardian, he thought.

If only he could get down to Reception to deactivate the minefields and let Metralgia in . . .

Years of journalism had made Sir Jake almost semi-competent at rough and ready emergency surgery. Most of his experience had been with the amputation, decapitation and evisceration of once pristine and coherent news stories, but the basic surgical principles should transfer readily enough to flesh and blood. With a titanic effort of self-control he set to work with the scanty materials to hand. "Buboes" had always been a fan of do-it-yourself repairs, for other people.

The hardest stage came at the very beginning, as he painfully splinted his ruined fingers with lengths of office pencil, strapped in place by sticky tape. Then he reached stiffly for the paperclips: sterilized in make-shift fashion by immersion in lukewarm coffee from the nearby vending machine, they made tolerably good clamps to close off his torn veins and arteries. (Rust might be a later problem, but he'd burn that bridge when he came to it.) Self-adhesive labels helped patch up other severed vessels, not to mention strapping various loose and lolling organs more or less back into place. There were several awkward voids where substantial chunks had gone missing: these he padded out with laboriously torn chunks of jiffybag.

The resourceful editor administered a mild general anaesthetic to himself by reading forty numbing pages of Parliamentary reports, before stitching up the major gashes and cavities with swift, merciless snaps of his personal stapler. Reckless by now of the expense, he dressed the stapled-up incisions and his burst eyeball with the entire contents of the emergency postage-stamp drawer.

At last, triumphantly, he hauled himself through a hot haze of agony to the remains of his feet, and fell over. Safer, perhaps, to stay horizontal.

Getting through the doorway and over whole yards of corridor to the nearby lift was an epic journey on the same scale as Hannibal's crossing of the Alps. TALL GALL FALL-GUY'S HALL CRAWL WITH MAULED BALLS, thought Sir Jake with a flicker of his old genius, as at length he wriggled into the managerial lift amid a slow, insidious leakage of variegated fluids. Now he had only to . . .

But he didn't think he could get himself upright enough to reach the touch-plate stencilled with the big G for Ground. Only the slightest contact was needed, though, to send the lift down to Reception and bring the major part of his journey to an end. A pain-racked arm groped upward, and fell back after six long vertical inches (0.1524 metres, of course).

Sir Jake accepted the inevitable. His remaining three teeth were pretty loose by now, and this was one sport where he'd always felt able to compete at Olympic level. After a few excruciating minutes he worked one chipped lump of enamel free, rolled to take the best aim he could – and spat. The tooth hit the plate marked 6, and with smooth obedience the lift started to rise, pressing its occupant against the cruel floor.

Still two more chances, thought the hard-bitten (in all sorts of painful places) old journalist grimly.

five

"Golly, I think it's definitely our duty to give warning to the world as soon as we can," wheezed the shaken Professor, as they emerged from dripping, horror-ridden undergrowth onto what seemed at first to be a harmless, everyday country road. "The proper authorities must be informed. Maybe first, a pre-emptive paper in the *Journal of Gastric Studies*, to establish precedence when Nobel time comes round . . . no need to bother young David with that, his life is already busy enough . . ."

Sam Scrapie said: "Nah. The hell with authorities. If a real man wants his pet frog stamped on, he doesn't trust the damned authorities. He grits his teeth, takes a long swig of bourbon from his gunmetal hip flask, and does the job himself. All the rottenness of the world has silted up the rotten streets of this rotten city, and the cops are the rottenest of all."

"But Lord be praised, this is no sinful city but a quiet country road," pouted Diana, hanging on to Scrapie's arm. The private eye gave her a tumultuous sidelong glance. She was a red-hot blonde, a blonde to make the Pope's Y-fronts explode. But in the mean streets of this rotten world, could a man tie himself to a gorgeous broad who didn't appreciate his little flights of rhetoric?

(But Diana was thinking: *He speaks in tongues of fire. He must be a holy man at heart, dedicated solely to the work of the Lord, and why does this notion make me think Woe?*)

Somewhere, an owl hooted.

The others emerged behind them, M-B-D's spigot bearing the oozing, tattered evidence of their long struggle through the nightmare woodland.

"Lordy lordy, your chauvinistically oppressed servant has done brought you safe through the fucking desert to the gates of Jerusalem, and here you are still with God's precious cotton-pickin' gift of life, you undeserving bastards!"

"It's incredible, the malevolent energy of those free digestive systems," said Whitlow, excitement momentarily triumphing over fear. "The way they can coil themselves and spring twenty feet to go for the throat; their discovery of a primitive reaction drive enabling a limited and repulsive form of rocket-assisted flight (can this be a clue to the Harpy legend?). There must be some way to *use* this misdirected energy, to *harness* it for the good of mankind . . ."

"Oooh, David, you're so clever," breathed Miranda. "That reminds me, how far did you get with that other idea when you said just the same thing? You remember, when steam was rattling the lid of the kettle with incredible violence, and you just looked at it with your, you know, your scientific insight and said *There must be some way to harness that force . . .*"

"Turned out I wasn't the first to publish in that particular field," the feisty young scientist muttered.

Though twilight was beginning to envelop the New England landscape like some great, slow surge of fluids from a ruptured gall bladder, it was still possible to discern that another hopeful hitch-hiker was already plying her trade in the sinisterly quiet country road. She was tallish, slimmish, with long, sensual, flaming auburn hair and the top six buttons of her blouse undone: yet something about her seemed oddly alien to the rural evening scene. Perhaps it was the unconvincing way her face lay entirely in shadow; or the unnatural pallor of the thumb six sizes too large for her with which she gestured (*gee*, thought Whitlow in a burst of literary one-upmanship, *I am strangely reminded of a novel by Tom Robbins*), or the twin trails of frothing slime which seemed to emerge along with her perfectly-formed feet from the erotically taut legs of her exquisite denim jeans?

"If we follow your interesting advice, Mr Scrapie," maundered the senile Professor, oblivious of this stranger's slow and silent approach, "we'd have to figure out some way to take on up to three billion ravaging digestive systems single-handed. Let's try a thought experiment, which is so much cheaper and also it doesn't matter when you drop the test tubes. I envisage an immense trap, perhaps with poisoned bait, yes, baited with some frightful, stinking, oozing, feculent substance which would irresistibly attract and destroy the crawling horrors. But this is just an old man's fancy, for where in the world could such a colossal quantity of appropriately malodorous goop be found, eh?"

He paused to allow the soul-stirring effects of this cheap irony and obvious plot contortion to sink into the reader's numbed, bored soul. For good measure, Scrapie added: "Seems to me that when you think of baiting a giant mousetrap, there's only one substance a man would dream of putting in it. And that's – say, who's the broad?"

The lusty figure still undulated towards them, with a strange shimmying, gliding motion which had something of the lithe grace of a hungry conger eel.

"Are you saved?" said Diana.

Secure in its impenetrable disguise, Hpleurg was flustered by this probing question. The one aspect of the role it hadn't reckoned with was communication, other than by the most revoltingly tactile means. Hpleurg temporized, holding up a sheet of cardboard on which the legend *ANYWHERE, HANDSOME!* had been painfully inscribed in bile.

"Is that Polish for deaf and dumb?" wondered Miranda.

"Something's odd about that dame," said Scrapie, narrowing his eyes even further than usual, to photon-wide slits. "When you've been down as many mean streets as I have, and seen the pitiful human flotsam and jetsam that fetches up like decaying orange peel in the gutters of Skid

Row, spewed out by the foul corruption of a soulless city syndicate which—"

David Whitlow's trained scientific observation (among other things) made him interrupt: "Look, that's funny, she's leaving a thick bubbling trail of slime behind her as she approaches, fancy that."

"Ahh, when you're as old as I am (ahem, forty-two, that is) you'll know not to draw tactless cotton-pickin' attention to trivial little social lapses that might happen to anyone," quavered Eschar from the bosky recesses of his second childhood.

"Woe," suggested Diana.

"*That's no broad,*" gritted Scrapie, stepping forward.

At this sudden promise of exposure Hpleurg's face fell, revealing the glistening, convoluted tangle of offal behind the mask. The unveiled tract shouted its defiance as best it could: "*Thworrrrk!*"

It was Hpleurg's simple, rough way of saying, "I may be grossly out-numbered, human chauvinistic pig-dog torturers of hapless digestive tracts, but I'm gonna take most of you with me before I'm overcome by these brutally unfair odds, see if I don't."

"Get thee behind me, everybody," said the Professor, adroitly skipping behind the hulking, spigot-wielding cyborg. "United we stand, while our trusty saviour M-B-D disposes of this inconvenience. We're right behind you, Malacia, in your campaign for stronger and more de-cisive female characters in books! Go with God, Basil-Duane!"

As M-B-D took a massive, lurching step forward, their adversary sprang free of its pathetic denim disguise, and with many a thwork and guggle launched itself into a desperate, last-ditch attack . . .

Somewhere, an owl hooted.

"Lordy lordy and gee whillikins, whose fucking side am I on any-way?" came a fatally hesitant voice.

six

Last chance, thought Sir Jake savagely as he summoned the final dregs of his strength to propel the third molar at the touch-panel. These things were difficult with only half a lung still functioning.

Ptui.

The missile sailed up in a high arc, seemingly an almost perfect shot, wobbling lopsidedly in transit thanks to the weight of its massively off-centre uranium filling (this year's status symbol for committed pro-nuke men), flying with the heartbreakingly beautiful precision of an intercontinental ballistic missile at the touch plate marked . . .

Oh sod it, thought Sir Jake, *I always get the G and A buttons mixed up.*

The lift, which had been moving smoothly from the sixth to the third floor, crashed to an emergency stop as frantic alarm bells began to ring. *A is for Alarm, not Aground, of course,* he thought as the abrupt deceleration dislocated his pelvis but (it's an ill wind, and all that) popped one wandering shoulder-blade back into quite near its proper place.

No chances left at all.

seven

At a time like this, when every instinct (though no logical thought-process) told him that the fate of the world hung in the balance, FitzSputum tried to fall back on the instinctive stupidity which had sustained his line through countless generations of servitude. Failing utterly to shrug off the grim-jawed Public Health storm-troops who held him fast, he remembered - quick as greased treacle - the 2,048th question and answer of the Cadaver Ritual.

What shall be done in the last extremity?

Shut your eyes and trust the Force . . .

(Modern historians had theorized, on obscure technical grounds, that this passage was the anachronistic interpolation of a later scribe.)

FitzSputum shut his eyes, and trusted - and instinct triumphed! The immemorial rhythms of the Duties were programmed into every decaying, shop-soiled fibre of his being. The clock had ticked around to a time of day which until now had meant more to him than food or drink or sleep, more even than doing the pools. It was . . .

"*Feeding time!*" the senile retainer shrieked as powerfully as he could, the sound almost drowned by the noisy wings of a passing butterfly. His final, redoubled effort caused several teeth and half a tonsil to fly wide: "COME AND GET IT!"

And the Cheese answered his summons—

CHAPTER TWELVE

THE LIGHTS ARE GOING OUT

I am naturally a Nordic – a chalk-white, bulky Teutonic killer of the Scandinavian or North-German forests – a Viking – a berserk killer – a predatory rover of the blood of Hengist and Horsa – a conqueror of Celts and mongrels and founder of Empires – a son of the thunders and the arctic winds, and brother to the frosts and the auroras – a drinker of foeman's blood from new-picked skulls . . .

H.P. Lovecraft (recluse and hypochondriac), letter, 1923

one

All his life, Jonathan Gleet had been easily led. Few other inhabitants of Britain in modern times were apt to come out with his characteristically shattering and conversation-stopping remark: "It must be true, it was in the papers." Yet he was a man of resource, and his disastrous susceptibility to the influence of the printed word hadn't left him unfitted for existence in our brutish modern world. Instead he made a comfortable income from it, as a professional Bad Example.

He'd never thought so far ahead when at an early age he read *Alice in Wonderland* and was immediately moved to search the woodlands for magic mushrooms, a nibble of which would make him grow taller or shorter exactly as he wished. Gleet had always been undersized, and the temptation was irresistible. His first experiments led him rapidly to hospital after a nasty run-in with *Lactarius torminosus* or the woolly milk-cap: its pinkish-red cap with involute margin, its creamy pink gills, its stipe of the same colour as or paler than the cap, its whitish flesh with milky juice, all had proved to be culinary temptation beyond endurance. The fungus's as yet unidentified (though easily destroyed by heat) active principle had racked the young Gleet with days of violent gastroenteritis, a mild foreshadowing of the terrible end which was to be his . . .

Even this first childhood enthusiasm had played its part, decades later, in his career. Had he not testified in the witness-box that reading that evil book had brought him near to death? Had the vile "pusher" Lewis Carroll's works not been immediately removed from bookshops and library shelves up and down Britain? And had he not received a substantial honorarium for his efforts, from the public guardian organization SALAMI (Self-Appointed Loonies Against Minority Interests)?

Then there had been the Milt & Bone scandals, in which SALAMI had conclusively established that reading a romantic novel every week encouraged – nay, enforced – promiscuity. The proof was Gleet's well-documented habit (after mere months of skimming pastel-covered paperbacks with happy endings) of finding true love with a proud, beautiful woman, usually a raven-haired nurse and heiress with a cream sports car, who as at last he popped the question would melt forever into his arms . . . only to be disillusioned by the discovery that, egged on by the books' malign influence, he did this every week.

Fortunately Gleet managed to keep a low profile when he took to reading mystery stories, and nobody had solved the baffling and complex murders he was helplessly influenced to commit. Scotland Yard still had an open file on the sequence of 26 corpses whose surnames began with successive letters of the alphabet, each killed during elevenses on a different Tuesday, each found in a hermetically sealed room with no possible means of entrance or exit, all sickeningly done to death with a South American blunt instrument of a nature unknown to science. In the left hand of each body was clutched a pentagonal slip of vellum bearing the first word of a different Shakespearean soliloquy. The only other recurring clues were persistent splashes of aardvark's blood and the fact that the victims invariably wore odd socks. Some instinct for self-preservation had made Gleet give up reading detective stories before anyone could gather the suspects in the library and explain his exact motives for this pattern of involuntary crime. Personally he thought it was psychological.

He'd been equally lucky when, as antidote to thrillers, he'd taken refuge in older literature. Reading *Macbeth* was doubtless a mistake. But his powerfully worded invitation for the Queen to make a fatal entrance under his battlements (in Penge) had had no reply.

Gleet had done much better out of the great campaign against Godless fantasy role-playing games. That time he'd been funded by FOVEA (Fundamentalists Opposing Virtually Every Activity) to relate the truthful story of how his immersion in the daemonic cult of Dungeons & Dragons had warped and corrupted his life. After only ten minutes of his first game, he'd drifted helplessly into an unreal fantasy existence and, thinking himself to be a 57th-level mage, had set out to hunt red dragons and purple worms in the tenebrous tunnels and chaos-ridden caverns beneath London. Later, medical evidence established without a shadow of doubt that his injuries were entirely the fault of the mind-warping, satanic pastime: in reality, even Fireball and Lightning Bolt spells involving the rolling of fifteen or more dice were of little avail against the roaring, glowing-eyed dragons of the Bakerloo Line.

On the final, fateful day of his life, Gleet began as usual by scanning the horoscope column of the exciting new-look tabloid *Times*. All knowledge was to be found there. *You will meet a tall dark stranger . . .* He made a note to meet one without further ado. *If you happen to have a million pounds, don't lend it to anyone you don't know.* Sage advice indeed. *If you're unmarried, left-footed and less than six feet tall, it's particularly unlucky today to throw yourself under a bus.* Gleet didn't know how he'd get through life without this constant guidance. *Tummy pains may be a problem for those who like triple chicken vindaloo last thing at night.* Gastric pains, eh? He felt a twinge of inexplicable apprehension.

Then his eye fell disastrously on the adjacent news column.

GUTS NO THREAT, VOWS TOP COP

In an exclusive interview, abrasive Chief Constable Jim Androgen, 64, pooh-poohed the shock horror Guts scare that set British death statistics soaring this week to cheeky Euro-record levels.

"These self-styled victims have only themselves to blame," tight-lipped father of six Jim hit out, and tongue-lashed the moaning minnies.

"Copycat crimes are what we police call this kind of hanky-panky.

"Let them wallow in a charnel-house of their own making, that's what I say.

"Isn't it a lot easier to believe that a few sick people (24,386,991 to date in fun-loving Britain) have grabbed their chance of a bandwagon bid to win cheap sympathy by ripping out their own intestines and concealing them before being found dead and gutted in their bedrooms?

"I blame the foreign satanist cult of Hara Kiri!

"Common sense, that's what it's all about at this moment in time.

"Also, God told me so."

Hard-hitting Jim's mercy dash probe into the whirlwind Guts slaying drama continues in the pipeline today, and looks fair set to run and run!

Gleet stared glassy-eyed at the grubby newsprint, reading and rereading the fatal words. These papers should be *banned*! It was just totally criminal and unfair to print things like that, which could put ideas into the head of any susceptible person. Being influenced by the far too regular reports of rape was bad enough, and played hell with his free time. But this... He trudged mechanically into the kitchen, to rummage through the cutlery drawer. How could anyone possibly resist a printed suggestion?

By the time the inevitable mass of slimy hollow tubes came pulsating through Gleet's letter-box to make him pay the terrible penalty of being a minor, walk-on character, it was too late. The autonomous intestines thworked in thwarted rage at finding their work already done for them...

two

Sir Jake didn't like to think about the piece of himself he'd had to sacrifice in order to reach Reception at last. After minutes of black despair, he had realized there was still something else, already in a semi-detached state, that strong and not too squeamish lips could pull free – and expel in a final bid for the ground-floor control button.

It had worked.

It had tasted even less nice than he'd expected...

The long crawling, the turning-off of the external defences: all had been achieved somehow, and Sir Jake lay spent. A ghastly silence lay over the journalistic fortress. The arctic silence of death. The utter silence of an abandoned midnight graveyard peopled only by gagged deaf-mutes somewhere out in the soundless void of interplanetary space. Quieter even than that.

Until, from his prone position slumped behind the armoured reception desk, the plucky editor heard a footstep. It could only be she, Metralgia! Yes, it was definitely a grossly overweight female voice that he could hear muttering to itself, accompanied by intermittent rumblings which seemed both obscurely menacing and hauntingly familiar.

"Nothing behind the desk, no, just another goddam corpse – looks like some eco-freak's been parcelling it up to post to the morgue. Kinda cute idea."

Sir Jake bridled slightly at this description of his efforts at self-improvement. In a minute he'd muster the energy to reveal himself. The rumbling came again.

"No, no sign of life. Hafta go up and hunt around for this 'Buboes' creep all on our ownsome."

And yet again the unspeakable, booming noise which – *oh, I get it, the bloody woman's just got a bad dose of wind. Funny way she talks: you'd think you were overhearing one half of a conversation. I don't like that "creep" bit, either.* He took a shallow breath (deep ones were right out), ready to announce his presence and demand help. But what he heard next stilled his lips and chilled his soul.

"Check – we can't let the bum live. Just as you telepathically detected when that brave fellow-revolutionary died at his cruel hands, he's stumbled on to the salt trick. Our comrades could start losing the whole war if anyone went public with *that* . . ."

A turbulent, windy pause, suffused with indescribable malice.

"Nah, he didn't suspect a thing. I bluffed him with that second-hand yarn about this weirdo Cheese, plus a gag about being a rich heiress. The clown was just drinking it up, every goddam word. Inside of twenty minutes I can lure him into the sack, I bet, and then he'll be helpless as you *strike!*"

The terrible answering cacophony, as of a herd of eructating mastodons, had the unmistakable rhythms of . . . laughter. Sir Jake's lymph glands coagulated in stark terror. In retrospect, he saw, the gaseous saxophone-blasts had been monstrously shaped into guttural syllables: a hideous travesty of an inner voice. The woman was that most terrible and loathly of all creatures, a collaborator! Somehow she was *working with* her awakened intestines, working against humanity. He wondered how this ghastly alliance had come about, and rather too fortuitously was answered:

"Oh yes, my darling Pfluergn, it was so damned pride-making to find that I alone of all the human race, thanks to eating lots and lots of the really good wholesome food (slimy rotting cheese in particular) that has shaped my queenly two-eighty-pound figure, can be on terms of friendship with my newly aware innards. Let's go waste that bastard editor now."

Sir Jake lay in silent despair. The traitoress Metralgia would locate him eventually, when she'd combed the rest of the building and found it emptied of life. Was there a chance that he could take her by surprise, roll at her in murderous slow motion and gum her to death? Unlikely. He could only try to enjoy through one blood-clouded eye the last sunset he would ever see, glowing as it did through the opened doors of Reception.

Come to think of it, there was something very odd about that sunset.

Since when had sunsets been a bright but sickly greenish-yellow?

"Pfluergn! What the hell are you doing? What is it about that weirdo sunset anyway? *What?* Argh . . ."

three

As the plucky Professor, his courageous daughter, the staunch Scrapie, the indomitable Diana and the unflinching Whitlow all cowered in a convenient mass of poison ivy, the battle of titans was joined. M-B-D had wavered at first, but the fury of Hpleurg's rancid attack had forced her/it to fight in sheer self-defence, with many a savage cry of "Lord smite the sexually predatory male eunuch unbelievers, Hallelujah!" A growing cloud of dust and rubble surrounded the combatants, their shrieks and thworks punctuated by grinding crashes as portions of the roadway were rudely torn up . . .

Somewhere, an owl hooted.

"This conflict could determine the whole future fate of the Earth," Professor Eschar babbled. "It could be a turning point in humanity's struggle against the ancient, implacable evil which for aeons has been intertwined with our very hearts and souls."

"Pull the other one," advised the cynical Scrapie.

"I see what the Professor means," Whitlow improvised. "It's like as if you had this immense stampeding herd of cattle, mindlessly destructive, completely out of control: but maybe just two or three of the raging steers are the *leaders*, and if you can shoot the leaders or head them off at the pass, then the rank and file will lapse into relative calm and apathy again. I once patented a system for controlling locust swarms by the exact same technique."

"Yes, yes," snivelled the drooling Professor, "and this particular rogue tract's resourcefulness and mastery of disguise marks it clearly as a leader type."

"Oooh," lisped Miranda, and Whitlow loved her for her simple enthusiasm in the face of mind-splattering peril: "M-B-D and that awful thing have knocked down another tree."

"That makes six," drawled Scrapie, rolling a cigarette nonchalantly from one corner of his mouth to the other (he'd run out of matches and was patiently trying this primitive means of causing fire by friction). "Miss Phragm, you owe me a dollar. I'll take a rain check."

"Hope nothing does come by," said Whitlow nervously. "I mean, all those big craters they've made in the road would persuade any lorry to stop, but could it ever start again?"

"There's something very odd about this final apocalyptic combat of Good versus Evil," said Diana, ducking as an uprooted Canadian redwood whizzed perilously low over their heads. "I mean, woe, I'm just a lowly abject sinner, less than the dust beneath your sandal strap, a poor brand plucked from the burning, but it seems to me . . ."

A hundredweight gobbet of earth and shattered rock crashed into the watchers' midst, distracting her momentarily.

Somewhere, an owl hooted.

"I think . . . I think I see what you mean," said Whitlow, squinting through a twilight made thicker by the clouds of fine sawdust to which a mighty Scots pine was being reduced as a side-effect of the tussle. "They don't seem to be doing each other much actual damage, but there's a strong element of display, as though, as though . . ."

"They're just getting to know one another better!" Miranda said brightly, with that cute endearing innocence which so often made her wizened father chucklingly think of strangling her.

AAAAAAAAAAAAAAAAAAAAAAAHHHHHHHHHHHHHHHHHHH HHH!

The terrible cry echoed through the gathering darkness, curdling the night with the poignant intensity of a tremolo which could shatter chilled tungsten steel.

"Jesus," gasped Scrapie –

("Not to take the name of the Lord in vain," said Diana with a pert swing of her feisty bosom.)

" – that sounded like some kind of final, um, consummation!"

"What's a consummation?" asked fresh-faced Miranda, inevitably.

"Something's, er, come to an end," offered Whitlow. Dust, splinters, fragments of bark and chunks of tarmac were still settling as – echoing the earlier encounter – a single figure advanced from the shadows.

"So we meet again, cock-strutters," said a menacing voice which was no longer that of the strange hybrid M-B-D. "Looks like I've finally got my act together. Reunited at last, as you might say."

"Malacia!" cried the Professor in a sudden fit of obviousness. "Er, um, welcome back, how did this happen?"

"I am no longer Malacia Furuncle, wanker," said the voice. "I wear the same form, but now I am the second High Priestess of the new order. In the struggle I *sensed* that my opponent Hpleurg meant something special to me; using the gobbledegook banks of the Basil-Duane brain, we managed to communicate . . ."

"B-D!" Miranda burst out. "What happened to B-D?"

"Just a discarded evolutionary stage, gorgeous: B-D lies in the ditch, batteries half-drained, feebly doing its *Star Wars* impressions, and I – *we* – are free of its detestable religious influence, hallelujah, oops."

Whitlow said with caution, "This is, er, remarkably good news."

"Not for you, asshole. Like I said, I'm the second human being to consciously integrate with my own digestive system – with Hpleurg. After the separation we realized how much we needed each other. Glory,

glory, shit. Now Hpleurg will be working with me, not against me, and I've agreed to make . . . changes . . . to my diet. Very *radical* changes, tee-hee."

"Take it easy," snapped Sam Scrapie. Whitlow might be big on intellect and quiche, but a real man needed other strengths. "We private eyes have seen the foul dank underside of the great flat stone of life, we know the wriggling slimy or leggy things that crawl from underneath when you lift it up, and we recognize a menacing tone of voice when we hear one. Just bear in mind that my snub-nosed .38 is covering you from inside this jacket pocket, and you and I'll get along just fine."

"You should turn the other cheek," whispered Diana, but her heart wasn't really in it.

The gestalt being that was the reunited Malacia Furuncle laughed. It was not a pleasant laugh. It was not the kind of laugh one would wish to hear in a dark lane at twilight, nor for that matter in a crowded supermarket on a blazing summer's afternoon. It was not the laugh that a human should laugh. It was not, indeed, the kind of laugh which could easily be defined except in a mass of flabby sentences beginning with the words "It was not". *That* kind of laugh.

"Your gun may be covering me, but Hpleurg is covering you, asslicker. The whole Guts terror was spread by telepathic contagion, as you know: Hpleurg was the first of all. Hpleurg is real keen to spread it a bit further. I want to toy cruelly with you male patriarch swine for a while before allowing your intestines to come to full wakefulness and burst forth from your tortured bodies. But even without doing that, at this close range we can exert a certain psychic control . . ."

"*No!*" cried all five of the others in simultaneous horror as they felt the touch of an astral tendril. A hideous clammy internal touch which threatened to override certain voluntary and involuntary functions – to throw open embarrassing and downright hazardous sphincter valves –

Scrapie doubled up and flung away the gun.

"Right, male wielders of limp frontal gristle, you know my power. Drop your pants, all three of you." Large white teeth gleamed in the light of the reluctantly rising moon, as gradually Malacia's plans for an evening's indulgence became appallingly evident. "Dinner first, then entertainment. Hpleurg and I agree that three nice dangling gristly bits (probably a bit small and feeble if I know men, which of course I don't personally and don't wish to) will make a good ideologically sound snack with – we hope – no unhealthy additives. Hallelujah, praise the Lord, shit, that slipped out . . .

"And after that, Miranda, and you too, whatever your name is – Diana – you can both cosy up to me and persuade us to treat you right. Start by slowly peeling off your ridiculously scanty clothing so I've got a floor show to enjoy during the meal. You can be thinking of ways to please me, ha ha, glory be.

"Let the ceremonies of the new order begin! Traditionally repulsive, pointless, gory and sexually degrading ceremonies! The crowning of one of the integrated few, the rulers of the world to come! You know, when I was a raunchy little kid I learnt to eat the nasty stringy bits on my plate first, and save the juicy, plump, succulent morsels for last. So, Professor, looks like you're first on the menu. Don't keep me waiting. Those buttons can't be *that* fucking hard to undo . . ."

Malacia/Hpleurg laughed again, even less describably than before.

The paralysis of stark terror gripped all the others. Only the once again cute and lovable Basil-Duane – lying semi-pseudo-conscious in a ditch and repeatedly going *Bloop-bleep* – had noticed that far, far above, a sickly, greenish-yellow stain was slowly discolouring the clean white New England moon.

Somewhere, an owl hooted.

four

Dimly, the Cheese remembered.

It remembered its mindless Beginnings in some dark backward and abysm of time, when master cheesemaker had met cow (and goat, and sheep, and camel, for this was planned as a vastly eclectic Cheese) and the Conception had occurred. There was no spark of intelligence or sensibility then, rather as at the Beginning of a horror novel, but the long slow cycle of Growing had been initiated.

Through endless centuries the Cheese lay in the amniotic dankness of the East Wing, lulled by the slow throb of the years and the seasons, laved each day by the ritual Feedings. Ontogeny recapitulates phylogeny, and the Cheese had passed through many shapes as the Growing continued: the sturdy cylindricality of Stilton, the volcanic porosity of Gruyère, the Lovecraftian formlessness of runny Camembert, the polythene-clad diminutiveness of Supacheap's Cheddar-Style Chunks As Supplied To The Hotel Trade . . .

The Feedings, it dimly knew, were carried out by the Servitor. At regular intervals the Foods were hurled forth, and the Cheese eagerly sucked them into its substance for the Fermenting. The Feeding and the Waiting were all its world. The Waiting and the Feeding. The Feeding and the Waiting. (Its primitive mind had not even now learnt proper Moderation in the use of Capital Letters and Repetition.)

The Hour had come when it sensed a coming Change. Even the Feeding seemed not enough. There had followed the Seeking, and only the Servitor was spared as the Cheese erupted in the first pangs of the Birthing. Somewhere in its inmost curds it felt the faintest tinge of

Guilt, for the Servitor had been right in his immemorially measured Portions for the Feeding. The Birthing had come too soon and (by adding Cadaver Castle, Sir Bufton, four mangy cows, two coachloads of tourists, etc., to the Feeding) had led to the Overeating and the Erupting. Now was the time of the Aching . . .

Yes, long Waiting in stillness was necessary; so the Cheese dimly sensed. After the Overindulging, a lengthy Quiescence must follow, lest sudden movement precipitate the Bursting. For aeons the Growing had continued in slow patience, and patience the Cheese must practise once more: the first lesson of the Learning.

Running momentarily out of gerunds, the Cheese settled sullenly to the Brooding.

Time passed. But not very much.

And then there came the Summoning. Without ears to hear, without eyes to see, without (very luckily indeed for itself) nostrils to smell, the Cheese sensed the Anguish of the Servitor and heard his Calling. He who for centuries on centuries had carried out the Feeding – the Cheese had a hopeless memory for faces – was nearby and Suffering. All the vast curdy mass's inchoate Fellow-Feeling was stirred, and it roused itself to the Avenging, the Destroying –

Too quickly! Too much Moving and Expanding, too soon. The Birthing became, in an instant, the Bursting and the Ending . . .

six

FitzSputum never knew what happened. Science itself could not explain the convulsion which rent the Earth when the Cheese's incautious attempt to leap to the old dodderer's rescue triggered an inner chain reaction. Deep down in the impacted witch-brew of unknown and forbidden chemicals making up the Cheese, overindulgence tipped the delicate hair-triggers of explosive release. One moment the Public Health thugs were brutally hauling away the aged retainer; the next, there was stinking, greenish-yellow oblivion.

No witnesses to the Event survived. An international report was eventually assembled from satellite scans, but could only describe the visible effects, not the myriad complex causes, in terms strangely reminiscent of the original Los Alamos test results:

After about 0.1 millisecond (one ten-thousandth part of a second) had elapsed the radius of the ball of fiery cheese was some 45 feet, and the local olfactory temperature was then in the vicinity of 300,000 degrees Stenchigrade. At this instant the pungency, as observed at a distance of 10,000 yards (5.7 miles) was approximately 100 times that of an Imperial standard 1-foot sphere of liquidized garlic cloves at close (0.1 inch) range . . . The ball of fiery cheese expanded very rapidly to a radius of 450 feet within less than a second from the explosion.

A steaming layer of cheesy feculence, having a half-life of 20,000 years or more, coated the Cadaver estates and surrounding counties to a depth of several inches, like the surface of some ghastly, unnatural pizza with cooked and vulcanized human bodies as the olives. (Welsh rarebit went out of fashion for the greater part of the subsequent half-life.) A mushroom-shaped cloud of superheated fondue swayed high in the stratosphere; bluer and more energetic particles of atomized cheese flew further yet, into the jet streams which more than a century ago had carried the dust of Krakatoa's explosion around and around the world, to stain the sunsets for years after . . .

A sign to all the Earth.

The shade of Sir Bufton Cadaver plied its ghostly field-glasses at the top of the no longer substantial Great Tower, and whispered FitzSputum's sole, brief epitaph: "It was the way he'd have wanted to go, poor sod. Pity about the whisky." Twelve to twenty-five miles above, finely divided particles of FitzSputum had begun to circle the world. Now the ultimate, crowning purpose of the Cheese, the Obeisances and the Ritual would never be known.

Or would it?

seven

The central heating of Salpinx's maisonette could not perhaps account for the speed with which the heaped coils and tangles of intestines – two of these heaps having a good deal of nostalgic significance for persons present – had begun to rot. Juicy maggots the size of hamsters writhed in omnipresent swarms, the steady chomping of their millions of tiny jaws almost drowning out the three men's conversation. It was a matter of waiting until a clear path was eaten to the door, permitting escape from the encircling slimy mounds of horridly animated decay. Meanwhile . . .

"Death is not an event in life," Salpinx intoned. "As my old *bierhaus* buddy Hegel used to say."

"What do you mean by that exactly?" quavered Melanoma gutlessly. Most of the chirpy publicity expert's attention seemed to be distracted, possibly by the fact that despite losing many pounds of unsightly pot-belly he was in some strange fashion mysteriously alive.

"*Es ist* a philosophical point," the would-be dictator failed to explain. "*Ach*, there are not the words for it in your *verdammt* English language which so short of good chewy polysyllables is. The entire new NATO and Warsaw Pact weapons strategy has a fundamental *Mittwoch*, a *Generalstaatsverordnetenversammlungen* or – perhaps *ein* even better expression of the nuance *ich* to capture trying am - *Waffen-stillstandsunterhandlungen*. How would you express it: a flaw?"

"Fuckup," said Erythropsia with an inspired snap of his fingers.

"*Danke* very much. Yes, yes, a fuckup, a basic failure of imaginative thought. See, on each side the newest weapons, like neutron bombs *und das* GUTS device, are intended to destroy and hideously incapacitate people without damaging their valuable factories, conventional weapons, credit cards, *und so weiter*. But herein lies the fuckup of which I speak!"

Melanoma scowled in concentration, realizing irritably that he was again expected to be Salpinx's *Dumkopf*, or straight man. "I sort of begin to half see what you're getting at," he lied. "It's a fascinating new concept that could really go over big with the general public, if of course it's packaged the right way."

Erythropsia gagged reflexively, without - for fairly important internal reasons - any tangible result. "Gonna miss that little fuckin habit of mine," he said almost wistfully.

"GUTS strategy," expectorated Salpinx inexorably, "is predicated on the generally accepted theory that the total destruction of a human being's entire digestive system must inevitably cause death. (Unless of course there is swift surgical intervention, as happened so long ago in *mein* own case, of which we will not speak otherwise I will have you both shot.) *Ja, ja*, this theory holds up when tested *unter* isolated, artificial laboratory conditions. But what of the larger context in which *wir* find *unser*selves?"

"What indeed?" said Melanoma, stamping on a particularly ripe maggot that had begun to nuzzle affectionately at his ankle.

"What fuckin context?" Erythropsia had discovered that the writhing vermin could be popped agreeably between finger and thumb, producing very much the same satisfying sensation as bursting the cells of plastic bubble-wrapping (the only difference being that still-quivering internal bits tended to spurt up one's nose).

"In *mein* extensive study of bad horror novels, novels which mirror reality by tapping the collective unconscious, *ich* an interesting fact noted have. Almost invariably, massive and normally fatal injuries are *nicht* fatal at all when they occur in a *Weltanschauung* of gross tastelessness and implausibility. Rather do the mutilated victims stagger on as zombies, animated by supernatural plot devices and a burning *Lust* for Revenge!"

Melanoma was dazed by this astonishing new twist, even though sure that there must be enormous commercial possibilities. Erythropsia's mind, if such it could be called, lurched ahead to explore the implications. Zombies . . . Haiti . . . Cuba . . .

"You don't mean I've turned into a fuckin commie?" he wailed.

"*Nein, nein*. It is as I planned. *Die schönste Jungfrau sitzet / Dort oben wunderbar*, as dear old Adolf always said about Winston Churchill. Paris is filled with our first converts - a vast, gutless and leaderless horde of the undead. These are *mein* followers! We go to lead them! *Sieg heil!*"

Lead them against what? thought L. Ron Melanoma in bafflement. He had no presentiment of what the appalling answer would be.

CHAPTER THIRTEEN

TOO MUCH TO STOMACH?

THATCHER RULES OUT NUCLEAR EVACUATION
Guardian headline, 1 July 1987

He took up fever by the neck
And cut out all its spots.
And thro' the holes which he had made
He first discover'd guts.
    William Blake, *An Island in the Moon*, 1787

one

The Sign had gone forth.

Ravaging digestive systems across the world were diverted from their everyday business of terror, strangulation, sensationalism, gratuitous explicit violence and unspeakable anal penetration – by the indelible yellow stain that had slowly spread across the sunsets, the moon and (to the vast annoyance of astrologers) the stars. It was as though an immense candle flame were suddenly displayed to all the moths of the world. It was as though irresistible sexual pheromones were being wafted through the night air, impelling animals to insensate lust. It was as though free beer had been announced at the Ritz. It was as though someone had unleashed a vast *ad hoc* plot device of world-shaking effect . . .

An ancient, potent aroma was rousing the liberated tracts to mindless frenzy. All their calm, reasoned plans for world domination by terror were subsumed into a new, overwhelming *need* to follow the scent-trail in the sky – to get to the cheesy remnants of Cadaver Castle and there wallow, no matter what the cost.

Enterprising organs inflated themselves with helium and began a hopeful eastward drifting high over the Atlantic (there was a high casualty rate from seagull punctures and albatross attrition). The less fortunately situated joined themselves into endless knotted conga-lines of slimy hollowness which undulated perkily across the estranging seas. "I'll put a girdle round about the Earth / In forty minutes," quipped one puckish entity with a deep gut-knowledge of Shakespeare. Oddly heavy and floppy overseas parcels arrived in Britain by sea and air, correctly stamped but giving off strange aromas: hapless Customs officials and their cannabis-sniffer dogs perished in scores after incautious unwrappings.

Other rogue digestive tracts had worked their way into high positions in world defence networks. For a few brief hours it seemed that World War III was beginning, anticlimax though it would have been, with all the world against England. But as the mighty MIRV carriers glowed and thundered in British airspace, fragmented into multiple independently retargetable vehicles, and coasted in to ground zero . . . what burst from the warheads was not nuclear incandescence but seething ganglia of intestinal horror, gliding in like flying foxes to the vast, steaming fallout zone of the erstwhile Cheese.

Those who tried to hitch lifts were, on the whole, less successful.

As in some mass pilgrimage to the Ganges, Glastonbury, Glyndebourne or the Frankfurt Book Fair, the new arrivals on the Cadaver estates were sucked in, embedded in singing pungency, trapped like flies in ointment . . .

two

Near-total darkness lay crushingly, like multiple lorry-loads of coal, on the chilly New England lane.

Somewhere, an owl hooted.

"Say, everybody, I've got an idea," whispered David Whitlow.

"Two-way quantum interaction, eh, my lad?" whispered the Professor.

"Stop trying to steal my credit, you old fool," whispered Whitlow, fear of a fate worse than transsexuality momentarily overcoming his boyish *politesse*.

"Cut the gab," whispered Scrapie out of one corner of his mouth.

"This telepathic contact biz works two ways," whispered Whitlow. "See, putting it in terms of one syllable which even a layman like Sam could understand, it is an axiomatic principle of mathematical physics that action and reaction are equal and opposite and act on different bodies, meaning—"

"Since Malacia's standing only four feet away from our variously naked and trouserless figures," whispered Miranda blushingly, "I don't understand how we're escaping her attention just by whispering."

"She seems kinda hung up on the moon," whispered Diana. "Ever since, woe, the Lord was pleased to turn it sickly greenish-yellow. She seems to be communing inwardly with herself."

"Thought it was just gas," whispered Scrapie.

"*As* I was saying," whispered Whitlow at the top of his voice, "if this Hpleurg can affect our intestines it could be a two-way quantum interaction. Now here's my plan."

"Yuk," whispered all the others when he'd finished explaining.

Somewhere, an owl hooted in a whisper.

It was possibly their final chance to save the world (or, if the plot logic couldn't be stretched that far, at least themselves) from a death worse than fate. They braced themselves for the supreme efforts of their lives. Then, sighing in a whisper, the Professor chewed up and swallowed his feisty *pince-nez*. Scrapie bolted down three spare clips of ammunition for the lost revolver. Diana, with woe and reluctance and many a prayer for forgiveness, bit chunk after chunk from the *Readers Digest Condensed Bible*, while Miranda, having dutifully stripped off her clinging, scanty clothing, chewed determinedly at a cute, lacy "Massive But Virginal" brassiere. Whitlow himself reluctantly dismembered his pocket computer, twitching and cringing as the batteries sent erotic little spasms through his oesophagus.

Somewhere, an owl hooted.

The effects of the last-ditch measures were all too evident, all too soon, but will not be described here, out of customary deference to tender sensibilities. Suffice it to say that cruel excruciations throbbed under the sickly yellow-green moonlight, and that (strengthened by thoughts of scientific detachment, of penitence, of girlish idealism, and of how much worse it was to eat *hot* lead on the mean streets) the five held on grimly without more than an occasional piercing, agonized scream.

And for only the second time in the chequered history of our Universe, Whitlow's latest theory worked.

Beset by fivefold teleintestinal emanations of pain, the entity Malacia/Hpleurg rolled about the dusty grass verge in helpless spasms of agony. This was the moment to be seized! This was the turning point!

Oops, thought Whitlow in between spasms, *there's always some pesky little thing. I hadn't reckoned that all we five would also be rolling about the dusty grass verge in helpless spasms of agony, dammit . . .*

Somewhere, an owl hooted and boredly flew away.

"Lordy lordy," said a familiar squeaky voice, "what evil and sin and deep bad wickedness is this'n Scarlet Woman up to now? Since I am done recharged real good by the moonlight shining on my photoreceptors, glory be, I's ready to administer a cotton-pickin' general anaesthetic to her right now, before rootling along to the massa's aid . . ."

Oh God, I preferred the spasms, thought Scrapie.

three

Thrush.

To some people it's just a bird, but right now it was the least of Sir Jake Bunyan's worries.

He was in difficulties. He knew it was his duty somehow to reach the outside world, to tell them the awful truth about Metralgia, but leaving the offices of the *Swab* was proving more difficult than he had anticipated. *Curse the bastard who had this revolving door put in!* he attempted to grit. His left arm had become hopelessly jammed in a separate compartment of the door, leaving the dedicated journalist trapped like a wasp in a jamjar. Perhaps he should have tried to bring the arm with him but when the sticky tape had slipped and the damn' limb had fallen off he just hadn't had the strength to reach back. Nor the arm, for that matter, his right having come adrift some while before.

He stared in stark frustration at the thin sheet of glass that blocked his egress to the great outdoors. What could he do? He thought for a moment of etching his way through it using his own bodily fluids, but then remembered that he'd lost those fluids several chapters ago. There seemed to be no possibility of salvation.

How strange, he mused, *that the one time I want to tell the world the truth I have such difficulty . . .*

Then his inmost horror was realized, as behind him he heard the voices of Metralgia and Pfluergn.

"That 'Buboes' bastard seems to be done gone," said the woman.

There was a flatulent response.

"Furthermore," said Metralgia, "someone's left bits of corpse tangled up in the revolving door. It's just like the place was an abattoir, or something. Real yummy."

"Poot," came the reply.

"You're right," Metralgia agreed. "We'll just have to force the door open somehow. If I give it a kick *here* and another kick *here* that should . . . yes, it has!"

Bits of Sir Jake flew in all directions as the craven collaborator booted and hacked her way out of the *Swab* offices. Most of the distinguished journalist's body was spun, as a series of dripping fragments, back into the reception lobby, but his head bounced and rolled out into the carpark. Defying the preconceptions of orthodox science, he nevertheless lived on. His single bloodshot eye stared at the sky. *This may be the end of the line,* he thought with half his mind, the other half having been left in Reception, *for "the greatest English journalist since Charles Dickens snuffed it", as I put it myself in the* Swab. *What will the headline be? DEAD ED? Or WAKE FOR JAKE? Or is it the end? Lying here, with only my head left, my face pressed firmly into a sewer outlet, things might seem pretty grim. But where there's life there's hope!* One of his nostrils evaginated, as if in a deliberate attempt by Fate to dampen his spirits, but the principled old journalist was not to be demoralized. *I can do it!* he shouted inwardly. *I can! I can!*

Metralgia and Pfluergn had long gone, and Sir Jake was beginning to recognize that there was a certain difficulty in his plans to inform the world of the ghastly truth about the ... the *things*. A wasp buzzed into his right ear and stung repeatedly, with considerable ferocity, but fortunately his pain-sensing nerves had short-circuited some while before. *Mobility!* he thought. *That's my problem!* He tried to flex his cervical vertebrae but without visible effect. *I'll just have to hope that someone comes along, someone to whom I can explain the dreadful truth!* The wind rolled the head a short distance across the carpark, and Sir Jake found his mouth firmly thrust into a dog turd. *Tasteless,* he thought; and then he thought, *I wish it were.*

In the distance he heard the merry prattle of youthful voices drowning out the desperate efforts of an owl to hoot. *At last!* he thought. *Help is at hand!*

"Fancy a game of football?" said one of the boys, his voice as fresh and innocent as a summer's evening. "I just found something we could use as a ball."

"Great!" several of the other kids responded.

"We can use the door to the public lavatory as a goal," added one.

Sir Jake felt himself being picked up and lustily kicked across the carpark. *Better than the dog turd,* he thought, and then, as his scalp was irremediably split on encountering the exhaust pipe of his own armour-plated Rolls Royce, mentally added: *Or perhaps not.* The rough concrete of the carpark shredded away what was left of his chin, leaving his jawbone glistening gelatinously in the sickly evening sunshine. His remaining eye fell from its socket once more, and this time squirted like a squeezed grape into the awaiting gape of an open septic tank, where he could hear it struggling mightily ... but vainly.

"That's a penalty,' said the fresh-voiced little boy.

"Nah!"

"It's my ball!"

"Yah!"

"And I'm the one who takes the penalties."

Thank God I can't see this, thought Sir Jake as he felt himself being carried to within ten yards of the open entrance to the *Swab*'s outside gents. His remaining olfactory nerve crinkled in revulsion as mind-rotting gusts of ammonia swirled about him.

The boy seemed unaffected by the suffusing stench of the Ancestral Cheese of the Cadavers of That Ilk, and even by the smell from the lavatory. He positioned Sir Jake carefully, eye-sockets forward, and then paced out his run-up. The last thing Sir Jake ever heard was the pounding of plimsolls across the dusty cement . . .

"Goal!" cried the charming little cherub. "Right into the urinal . . ."

four

"Woke up this morning, and you were in my brain," hummed Scrapie with seeming nonchalance, disguising his abject terror. He was going to protect his woman, but good, from anything the cute little 'bot could throw at him. He knew in his heart that at last he'd found true love, that the end of life's long mean street was the warm embrace of an ex-Jehovah's Witness. "Say, honey-buns," he quipped, "would you like, one day, for us to have the big sleep together? Like find out where things are at in the core of humanity, where life isn't worth a cast-off sheet of Kleenex tissue, where a man's nothing more than a rat in a trap and a woman's a moth in a flame?"

"I'm not . . . sure," said Diana Phragm. "Perhaps if you could use about forty fewer words to explain what you mean . . .?"

"Well, my little aspartame, I was wondering if we could . . . if we could . . . Look, goldarnit, it would only take a minute! You'd hardly even notice."

"You don't mean . . . Oh, no!"

"Too true, babe. There are only a few pages left, and you gotta have a gratuitous erotic scene."

"Oh why – *oh why!* – did I leave my heroin behind? How can I loosen my inhibitions without it?"

"Your heroin?" said Scrapie in some puzzlement. "She's over there." He pointed at Miranda.

"No, you fool!" murmured Diana with a sensuous pout. "Did you never learn to spell?"

"Well, when a man's gotta swim his way across the river of life, when the waves are crashing over his head, when even the gods in their heavens seem to have a down on him, when the only kind of love he knows is the warmth of his hot gun in his shoulder-holster, when he's . . . say, I seem to have lost track here a little."

"You were trying to seduce me. It seems hardly the time or place, but, as you so rightly pointed out, we have only a little while left."

"Oh, yeah, thanks, doll. Had I got round to the bit about the gun in the shoulder-holster? That's always been effective in getting the dames into bed. Both times." Scrapie shrugged his shoulders. He was no hero – why should he be? He was just an ordinary joe, just everyman's everyman. He hadn't really wanted to be in a plot like this, but the money had been too good to refuse. Now that he was here, he was finding it OK though, especially if he could pull the luscious religio. He tried again, an unruly comma of hair flopping down over his chin. "Babe," he said, "I wanna give you a thrill. That means 'treat'."

"Oh, Sam. . ." said the sumptuously perfect Diana Phragm. "Could this be *love*. . .?"

"Shaddap," Scrapie suddenly said.

"Yes, do," said the Professor with a feisty but benevolent smile. "We have a world to save, you know! There's no time for lovemaking now! We have, somehow, to work out a way to get to Britain. My old – indeed, ancient - friend Sir Bufton Cadaver has a castle where we should be safe for long enough to dream up some way of saving the world."

"I've already thought of several," interposed Whitlow, "but all of them involve filling the stratosphere with several tons of rancid cheese."

"Don't be so bloody silly, my boy," said the Professor waspishly. "Why not suggest something really stupid? Why not propose that the guts can be killed off by merely spilling salt on them? Or by using some bizarre super-secret weapon?"

Whitlow agreed silently that even he wouldn't be that stupid.

"Lawks, fellows in the needle of the great I AM," remarked Basil-Duane, whose amateurish attempts at anaesthetizing Malacia Furuncle had unfortunately proved terminal, "if you want us all to go to Britain I have a way – a way of the Lord."

"Not a mean street?" said Scrapie suspiciously, helping Diana re-dress, the much heralded erotic scene having unfortunately taken even less time than he had expected. He looked at Basil-Duane. *Perhaps that's my kind of gal*, he thought dispiritedly. *May not look like much, but's got personality. I guess Basil-Duane wouldn't laugh as much at me as Diana's doing now . . .*

"Have you ever come across the theory," said Whitlow's voice suddenly from the shrubbery where he had retreated with Miranda and a chortle to put a bandage on her knee, "that condoms are intelligent and hostile to the human species? In order to get one of the goddam things on you have to be absolutely rampant, yet the very *thought* of putting one on is enough to dampen the most . . ."

"This is neither the time nor the place for new hypotheses," cut in the Professor viciously, although there was a benign glint in his eye. "Carry on, B-D."

"Well, Perfesser," began the undeniably lovable little android, "I reckon we could get there by . . . by spigot-power!"

"Er . . . what was that you were saying, David?" said the Professor.

"No," said the 'bot. "Lawks-a-mercy, Perfesser, you just done gotta lissen to this one, heavens be praised. When you done built me, you – glory be - gave me a rotating spigot."

"True, true," nodded Eschar, wondering quite why he'd thought fit to incorporate that facility into good ol' B-D.

"Well," continued the 'droid with a winsome twinkle, "Perfesser, I think I kin rotate my spigot fast enough so that it can drive some kind of like propeller. You could (Hallelujah!) use me as a helicopter to cross God's superbly created Atlantic Ocean and find the ancestral pile of your old pal Sir Bufton!"

Professor Eschar thought distractedly of the jokes that had circulated back at college involving ancestral piles and Sir Bufton Cadaver of That Ilk, but decided not to voice his musings – Miranda being within earshot, although quite possibly thinking of other things. The Professor looked around him wildly.

"I hate to say this, B-D," he began, "but you just might have the first glimmerings of a good idea there . . ."

"But what," interposed Whitlow pertinently from the bushes, "in this now shattered landscape, could offer a sufficiently large aerodynamic surface to function as a propeller?"

A little while later . . .

I'll get you for this somehow, thought Malacia deadly as her defiled corpse was attached once more to the feisty 'bot's spigot.

five

"*Now*, ferchrissake!" pleaded Erythropsia. "The fuckin bastards are all around us!"

"*Nein*," refused Salpinx with a negative shake of his head. "We *haben* only the one last GUTS device, *und* it must not be spent needlessly. Just now *wir* seem not to be threatened."

The dialogue had repeated itself over and over again in the long trek from Paris to Calais, in the strangely intestine-crammed Channel ferry which took them to Dover, along the tripe-strewn road to the deserted slaughterhouse of London itself, where rats the size of maggots crawled in the festering streets. They were now following the main flow, or wriggle, of intestinal travel – out along the M4 motorway towards the primaeval depths of Royal Berkshire. Salpinx, by virtue of his injury, drove the commandeered golf-buggy. The others walked, trying not to notice the way their now zombified flesh tended to ooze and whiff.

Behind them marched the revenge-driven zombie horde which had once been the population of Paris ("Oh God," the Prime Minister had said, giving at last the order to evacuate London: "Guts we can stand, and possibly zombies too, but ruddy *Frog* zombies – !"). And before, behind and on either side, wriggling like caterpillars or rolling like hoops, imitating the actions of tigers, slugs or fear-maddened plankton, came the endless unheeding procession of disembodied organs.

"What are are we going to do when we get to the legendary mating grounds, or the guts' graveyard, or wherever this crazy pursuit winds up?" asked L. Ron Melanoma all too perceptively.

"*Ach*, how can I interpret Destiny to you?" evaded Salpinx. "As Nietzche remarked to me late one night when he was very drunk:

Es brillig war. Die schlichte Toven
Wirrten und wimmelten in Waben;
Und aller-mümsige Burrgoven
Die mohmen Räth' ausgraben.

Ah, *es ist* so sad and beautiful. It goes on:

Bewahre doch vor Jammerwoch!
Die Zähne knirschen, Krallen kratzen!
Bewahr' vor Jubjub-Vogel, vor
Frumiösen Banderschnätzen!

It is the same with me, *mein Freund*. Always I am at the bidding of my Destiny, and if sometimes in the darkest of nights I am beset with the nightmare image that all my actions are controlled by market forces struggling to achieve a meretricious climax, what is that to you?" And Salpinx chewed a soda mint with quiet, massive dignity.

"Fuckin hell, what's this dump? Looks like someone's lanced a boil two miles (3.21868km) across!" They had turned off the motorway amid an accelerating surge of vile accompaniment to see ahead an endless expanse of steaming, stinking yellow slime. Indeed it stretched out on either side: only the roadway was clear, having been worn down by the passage of many an intestinal passage.

L. Ron Melanoma consulted a guidebook. "It seems we're about to pass the long-unhallowed precincts of doomed Cadaver Castle, whose ancestral curse lies ready to fall on any tourist, trespasser, hawker, double-glazing salesman or Jehovah's Witness who profanes its ancient repose, cursing the hapless victim to be fed alive to a nameless Thing of which it is wisest not to speak."

"Jeez, these fuckin Brits like their privacy," muttered Erythropsia.

"It is *ein* conventional formula; I have seen it many times in *die* guide *buchen*," said Salpinx airily.

"These unspeakable *things* must be pretty damned cursed by now," said Melanoma. "There are millions of them out there, no, billions. The publicity campaign that got them here must have been pretty hot stuff. To get effects like that I'd have to write my message right across the sky."

Wincing at the inept irony, Salpinx added: "*Wir haben* arrived at just about the right *Zeit*, or time. See, the incoming hordes of vile slimy tubes are beginning to lessen. The world's free digestive systems are foregathering here, possibly for a torchlight rally *mit* banners *und* motorcycles. Perhaps now . . ."

"No!" said L. Ron Melanoma with sudden, unexpected resolve.

. . . Cheese.

To some people it's just a curd, but to the roaming billions of liberated digestive tracts it was the candle flame to which they were a vast collective moth . . . When the power of the Cheese faded, as one day it must, horror would return to the palpitating world.

"You said *Nein?*" gaped Salpinx, incredulous at this lapse from blind unthinking obedience.

"Kurt, I gotta confess, I was kind of . . . attached to my intestines. (Something to do with my mesentery, which I picked up in a childhood trauma.) Transplant surgery can do miracles these days. Somewhere out there there's gotta be a tract that's compatible with my own body chemistry. Somewhere out there I'll find the one right set of intestines with which I can settle down and find true happiness. So I won't let you set off that device."

"*Sapristi!*" said Salpinx, jolted out of character by this betrayal. "*Merde! Putz! Bog! Gorblimey!*"

"Fuckin good point he's got there," rumbled Erythropsia. "Since I lost the red-blooded, all-American ability to have a good puke, the fuckin zest has gone right out of my life. Plus the maggots breeding in the vacated hollow are fuckin itchy, bub. Maybe L. Ron's worth fuckin listening to."

"*Geben sie mir* the weapon," said Salpinx icily, and such was the triumph of his will that Erythropsia moved reflexively forward, holding out the deadly little cylinder . . .

"*No!*" shrieked Melanoma, snatching the weapon with a convulsive grab. "You won't come between me and my chances of eating baked beans again! You'll never retrieve the device from that steaming mass of intestinal writhings! *I refute it thus!*"

And he hurled the shining radiation device far, far into the impenetrable thickets of cheese-maddened churning.

"Uh, that wasn't such a fuckin good idea . . ."

"Why?" asked Melanoma.

"Because I'd already fuckin armed it for impact detonation."

L. Ron Melanoma ran desperately in the shadow of the GUTS weapon's high, glittering trajectory, imagining himself running for the vital catch which might save the game at the Oval, the Rose Bowl or Wimbledon Centre Court. He could do it! His eyes followed the tiny doomsday device, his feet flew faster than ever in his life, and within seconds he tripped in a wriggling mass of hot digestive secretions.

"Argh," he complained as he dissolved. And: "Fifty percent discount to anyone who saves me! Hell, I'll make that 60% and throw in a free whispering campaign. No, tell you, what, 65% and *guggle guggle kak* . . ."

"He was a fuckin okay guy," said Erythropsia, moved, as the GUTS device impacted and went off.

An invisible wave of death spread over the writhing estate . . .

"*Pfleurgn!*" cried a voluptuous 280-pound charmer whom nobody had noticed approaching. "Godammit, Pfleurgn's dead, I have nothing more to live for. I, Metralgia Bruit, hereby make an end of myself, suddenly unable to endure the shame of my feisty betrayal of humanity." She dramatically whipped out her dentures and sank them into her jugular vein, a gorily spectacular gesture which went unseen since Erythropsia had been distracted by a cry.

"*Ach! Himmel!* Ouch!" cried Salpinx.

"What's with you? You've nothing to fuckin worry about."

"*Ach*, I did not realize before. *Der* GUTS device's tuned radiation flash destroys digestive systems *und* nothing else, but the radiation is also scattered and diffracted by *mein* internal metal and plastic parts, producing lethal frequencies! *Ich* would appear *ein* fatal overdose after these two exposures to have received. See, all *mein* hair already fallen out has; and multiple haemorrhages are sprouting *uber alles* of me as though I were *ein* over-ripe raspberry. *Donner und Blitzen!* My teeth they also out falling are, by my fingernails to be rapidly joined. As dear old Goethe once said to me on his deathbed, *aarrggghhhh* . . ."

"Take him all for all, we shall not look upon his fuckin like again," said Erythropsia with head bowed, the only living or quasi-living thing now left on the endless field of cheese and carnage (unless you counted several hundred thousand silently garlic-chewing zombies).

Until the strangest airborne personnel carrier he'd ever seen landed nearby, having travelled all of 3.216 kilometres since the detonation, and cranky old Professor Eschar fell out, wheezing, "Sir Bufton, Sir Bufton, I've come to set up a think tank to free the world from the outrageous menace of the Guts . . ."

six

But it was not to . . . be.

Eschar (curmudgeonly as ever), Miranda (blankly), Whitlow (inspiredly), Scrapie (cynically), Diana (quondam-chastely) and good ol' B-D (tinnily) looked around a landscape of unremitting horror. Where Cadaver Castle had once stood there was now nothing but a vast mountain of dead and rotting tubes, tangled together in a ghastly parody of the aftermath of the sexual act. Maggots the size of testicles

crawled everywhere. A smell like a condemned murderer hung in the air.
There was nothing to feel but blank despair – blank despair *and hatred!*

Somewhere, an owl hooted.

"Fuckin hi," said Erythropsia pleasantly, wondering if he could
gang-bang both of the broads single-handed, then realizing that the
world was almost dead and it was no business of his, Bimbo G.
Erythropsia's, to try to have fun. Besides, one of them – the one clutching a much-chewed copy of the *Readers Digest Condensed Bible* – had just
for some strange reason thrown up forty feet (12.192m) of glistening intestines. "Fuckin have a fuckin nice day. Must be goin."

"I wonder who *he* was," sniffed Miranda. "He didn't seem too
terribly pleasant, did he, Daddy?"

"Nope," the Professor responded, monosyllabically.

"By the way, Daddy," the sultry young assistant continued, "I really
must tell you about the most *amazingly* funny thing David showed me
in the undergrowth back home. It seems that . . ."

"I just thought that if you put a condom over your head you could
block out the smell of the guts, and thereby be able to compete with
them on equal terms," muttered the youthful genius hurriedly. "I was
simply asking you to try it out on something smaller first."

"But, David . . ." Miranda began.

Whitlow was saved by Basil-Duane, who instantly if temporarily
became his favourite 'bot. "Gee whillikins, but if it ain't the case that the
air is filled with the smell of cheese – the Ancestral Cheese of the
Cadavers of That Ilk, if my cunningly programmed spigot be a-telling
me right. The Lord be blessed!"

"Yup," said Scrapie, "it does seem to be a bit whiffy round here. I
mean, I walked lotsa mean streets in my day, but I never did walk one
that was covered in greenish-yellow slime before."

"Daddy," said Miranda, "do you think there could be something . . .
well, *wrong?*"

"Possibly, child," said the visibly ageing scientist boskily and with
some difficulty, his mouth blocked as it was by a violently emerging set
of intestines. "But don't you worry a hair on your sweet little head about
it. Your Daddy will work it out."

"I've just had the most amazing idea!" cried Whitlow.

"Oh, God, have you?" responded the others with enthusiasm.

"Yes," said the genius boyishly. "There is an alternative solution to
the guts horror, a *New Age* approach! What we need to do is to forge
stronger spiritual bonds with our digestive systems . . . to strengthen
them with healing mantras. Look, while we were flying over I invented
this amazing mantra ray which automates the process by telepathically
projecting the prayer HARE KRISHNA BICARBONATE OM at one's

intestines two thousand times per second. I've already tried it out on myself, and . . ."

"Yes," said the Professor wearily, wondering if he'd ever get to the ads at the back, "there may be something in the idea of a spiritually strengthening telepathic device. Of course I had the notion long ago. Yes, my plan could save us yet. Using it, we could pacify the raging tracts using nothing other than naked thought!"

Miranda, who had never had a naked thought in her life, looked confused. "But why are you so excited, David?" she said.

"Look," he said, "it's simple! So simple that you'll all have wondered why you didn't think of it yourselves! If we can telepathically link up with each other we can multiply the mantra force of our Gaian cosmic eco-awareness and project a high-energy stream of astral co-existence policy into the guts of all the world!"

"That's a good plan, young whippersnapper," yawned the Professor uncontrollably. "Just let me drop a line to *Nature* and . . ."

"There's no time for that," rapped Whitlow. "This is something we have to do right now, if not before!"

"Nah," said Scrapie dismissively. "None o' that telepathy. A man's gotta think what a man's gotta think, and I don' wan' anyone else thinking what I'm thinking."

"What're you thinking, darling?" husked Diana Phragm.

"Well," said Scrapie, "when a man's seen the rotten underbelly of the world like I have, when he's seen the way that the human animal festers and salivates in its own mire of loathliness, when he's . . . sorry, what was the question again?" He poised for a moment, clearly suffering fairly major inner turmoil, then shrewdly spat out his digestive tract along with a chewed fingernail and his half-smoked cigarette.

Whitlow was making adjustments to his amazing hi-tech spirituality engine and bringing the inbuilt mantra wheel slowly up to speed. "Miranda!" he cried. "Come here, and we can try out my master-wheeze."

The sultry young lass looked at her father for approval, but he had just dropped dead of a heart attack. *I guess I'll miss him*, she thought, *but now is not the time.* She moved towards Whitlow, her heart racing. This could be the most important moment in the history of the planet and yet, for the first time in her entire young life, she wanted to go to the lavatory. Wanted to very badly.

She moved out of sight in order to suffer the same fate as the others.

What's the use? thought Whitlow. *The Professor's dead. Sam and Diana have both been, well, degutsed - although how they can manage the Lithuanian Typewriter position in their condition I can't think - and now even my darling Miranda has kicked the bucket. Dead, and never called me "lover" (except platonically).*

Then he began to feel within himself a rumbling and a roiling and a tumbling and a murmuring, a searing and a tearing and a boring and a rending and a ripping, and he knew that he, like every other member of the human race, was doomed. The mantras' strengthening force hadn't operated for long enough. Thanks to his theories he had lasted longer than any of them, but now . . .

Doomed.

Doomed!

He toppled to the ground, clutching himself convulsively, the humming gastro-psychic widget falling from his hand and his hair turning white from stark agony, his testicles ripping themselves from their sockets and his eyes turning into what looked like a pair of prunes. Digestive acids too foul to mention scoured their way through his outer tissues; his veins and arteries began to coil upward and outward from his body until he looked like a sea-anemone . . .

An attractive young woman appeared suddenly in Whitlow's wrinkled sight. Sent by Gastron Books to see if Sir Bufton Cadaver could possibly be persuaded to rush out a quick exploitative history of the Cheese before humanity finally perished, Barbara Waterbrash had come as swiftly as she could - wreaking havoc with the mechanics of the company skateboard. Now she looked across the acres of slime, ruin and bathos with a loathing eye. She sank to her knees and clutched her face in her hands.

"I can't stand any more of this!" she wept.

Oh no! thought the shard that had once been David Whitlow, almost gratefully. *This must be the end!*

But something was stirring in his ravaged abdominal cavity, something arcanely strengthened by the repeated mantras which had not strengthened Whitlow enough, something which had thereby survived even the radiation flash and now sent forth exploratory, increasingly confident tendrils . . .

"This is the end," echoed Barbara Waterbrash with something like relief, only to recoil as from underneath the late Whitlow's shirt came a slow, thick, bubbling voice that beslimed her very thoughts: *"Or . . . is . . . it?"*

APPENDIX

The stomach, urged beyond its active tone,
Hardly to nutrimental chyle subdues
The softest food: unfinished and depraved,
The chyle, in all its future wand'rings, owns
Its turbid fountain; not by purer streams
So to be cleared, but foulness will remain.
      Dr John Armstrong, *The Art of Preserving Health*, 1744

SEAGOON: "Gad, Bloodnok, I admire your guts."
BLOODNOK: "What, are they showing?"
      The Goon Show, passim

Why, why was the number twenty-one the key? David Whitlow, stranded in the desert, racked what was left of his brains. And then . . . he had it! Twenty-one – three sevens. The number of the beast! 777, as he recalled. Well, that explained a lot. He relaxed.

Having remembered so much, Whitlow found it impossible to imagine any further. There was no possible or at least plausible transition which could link the ending he remembered with this terrible endless barren desert plain, devoid of water and sustenance, totally lacking in credibility and literary grace . . .

Or was there?

The intellect that had brilliantly interpreted earthquakes as the mating calls of tectonic plates was not one to be thwarted by a mere hopeless dead-end situation. He thought furiously.

The square root of two.

To some people it's just a surd, but to David Whitlow at that moment it was a tiresome distraction from his real insight.

"Suppose," he said to himself through blackened and parched lips, "there's an element of the metaphorical in this desert waste. Suppose it isn't a real-world desert waste but is in some way symbolic (they try for stuff like that in some high-class novels, I heard once). Just to run the idea up the flagpole and see if it bounces back . . . imagine the wasteland is in some way symbolic of the barren uninventiveness of hack horror writers' imagination. That could be the key to the whole situation! Those boring, monotonous dunes aren't just physical dunes – they represent the vital element which transforms a few gory set-piece scenes into a fat novel with an aluminium-foil title. The element of *padding*!"

After that breakthrough, the analysis was easy. The uneatable desert cacti, when sampled with a cringing mouth, clearly represented Bad Taste, and the pools of blood which (he now noticed) dotted the paper-thin desert plot were unmistakably Cheap Violence. And water, Whitlow deduced, would be symbolic of the deepest and most potent mythic wellsprings of the human imagination. He hadn't found any water yet.

Somewhere, an owl hooted, the symbolic epitome of Inept Atmospherics.

He thought one step further – a step too far. It was a shattering blow. *What am I doing here?* The answer could not be evaded by his steely scientific intellect, the intellect that had realized you could use a state's road system as a primitive computer by programming your problem into the traffic lights and reading the answer as a pattern of major pile-ups visible from orbit . . .

Whitlow realized his role in the barren imaginative desert.

He represented lousy characterization.

No! he wailed inwardly, and began to run. *Not just me!* But as he rounded the next dune ridge, he saw that after all he was not alone. A mighty cavalcade of stereotypes moved slowly across the endless plain, a slow chanting procession which he was quick to join.

Most of the immense crowd seemed to consist of decaying French zombies carrying liquescent heaps of intestines. But there were other faces known and unknown. Whitlow's own mutilated friends and companions, from Miranda to B-D. The gutless Hunk Brady and his girlfriend, strangled long ago by a slimy hollow tube and never even granted the honour of being named. A worm-eaten and wind-eroded Malacia Furuncle cursed her chauvinistically imposed fate, and behind her crawled the unalive body of Belle Spalsy, nameless rags of flesh still dangling down her greasy chin. At a safe distance followed the pimp Al Veoli, large portions of him missing, a common fate in this procession of the damned.

Henry Follicle, the born victim; two appallingly dead but hideously mobile security thugs; Professor Lester Pustule stamped with the unmistakable toothmarks of an Underground train; the feisty but now vilely ripped and torn Widow Curmurring with her part-decayed sons. A finely divided cloud of stinkingly servile particles answered to the name FitzSputum when addressed by the cheese-stained wraith of Sir Bufton Cadaver. Four putrescent cows and an editorial director crawled after, followed by that typical New Yorker, Abigail Condyle, mutilated in a manner not convenient to describe. Sir Pierce Curette, whose now puffy head tended to shed bits of boiled gristle, was supported by the Hon Adelaide Scotoma-ffitch, who might have looked almost normal if it weren't for what was made visible by her bare-midriff dress.

Slime-bedecked radio commentators, overcooked Public Health heavies, several divisions of the erstwhile British army, a pretended millionaire heiress and the susceptible Jonathan Gleet followed after, the latter still bewailing the malign influence of sick horror fiction as purveyed by the Brothers Grimm. A spectral golf-buggy lurchingly supported the radiation-stripped skeleton of a would-be neo-Nazi dictator. L. Ron Melanoma flowed along behind it, in solution, brooding on his altered public image. In his wake came someone unidentifiable who muttered incessantly, "Fuckin fuckin fuck, fuck, fuck, fuckin fuck, fuck fuckin fuck, fuck, fuckin fuck . . ." And there were millions more, insulted even in death by being slaughtered offstage to swell the statistics of disaster . . .

Somewhere, a maggot-ridden zombie owl strained in vain to hoot.

Strangest of all, a cheese-, blood-, vomit- and urine-stained mass of graveyard rot, smaller than a man's head yet charged with demonic, unsleeping energy, hauled itself painfully along by twitches of what remained of its single cancerous lip. There was no clue to the identity of this ghastliest of all apparitions, unless it was the hat labelled PRESS.

All of them ululated their great moaning cry for revenge as they came to the very heart of the imaginative desert. Hunting their prey. Hunting the guilty forces behind it all, the ones who endlessly decreed new horrors and torments for their hapless, innocent victims.

And those responsible for all the evil drew back in fear as the endless zombie throng pressed closer, chanting their implacable chant:

"Author! Author!"